A DROP

in the

OCEAN

A DROP
in the
OCEAN

A Novel

JENNI OGDEN

swp

SHE WRITES PRESS

Published 2016
Printed in the United States of America
ISBN: 978-1-63152-026-6
e-ISBN 978-1-63152-027-3
Australian ISBN: 9781925281613
Library of Congress Control Number: 2015948660

Book design by Stacey Aaronson

For information, address:
She Writes Press
1563 Solano Ave #546
Berkeley, CA 94707

She Writes Press is a division of SparkPoint Studio, LLC.

The characters in this book are fictitious and any resemblance to real persons, living or dead, is purely coincidental. Turtle Island is also fictitious, although similar in many ways to Heron Island on the Great Barrier Reef. Cyclone Hamish was a real event.

For my family—in the widest sense

May the road rise to meet you
May the wind be always at your back
May the warm rays of sun fall upon your home
And may the hand of a friend always be near.

May green be the grass you walk on,
May blue be the skies above you,
May pure be the joys that surround you,
May true be the hearts that love you.

—Traditional Irish Blessing

CONTENTS

READING GROUP QUESTIONS
and
TOPICS FOR DISCUSSION

O N E

──────────

On my forty-ninth birthday my shining career came to an inauspicious end. It took with it the jobs of four promising young scientists and catapulted my loyal research technician into premature retirement, an unjust reward for countless years of dedicated scut work.

That April 6th began in precisely the same manner as all my birthdays over the previous fifteen years—Eggs Benedict with salmon, a slice of homemade wholemeal bread spread thickly with marmalade, and not one but two espressos at an Italian café in downtown Boston. On my arrival at eight o'clock sharp, the elderly Italian owner took my long down-filled coat and ushered me, as he had for more years than I care to remember, to the small table by the window where I could look out on the busy street, today frosted with a late-season snow that had fallen overnight and would soon be gone. He always greeted me with the same words: "Good morning, Dr. Fergusson. A fine day for a birthday. Will you be having the usual?" as if he saw me every morning, or at least every week, and not just once a year.

Perhaps the unusually deep blue cloudless sky, almost suggesting a summer day, should have warned me that something was not quite as it should be. But superstitious behavior is not a strength of mine, and after my indulgent breakfast I walked to my laboratory in one of the outbuildings of the medical school, taking pleasure in the crisp winter air and stopping to collect my mail—in this e-mail era, usually consisting only of advertising pamphlets from academic publishing houses—before entering the lab.

Rachel looked up from her desk with her hesitant smile and gave me a beautifully wrapped parcel—a good novel, as always, the thirtieth she had given me. One for every birthday and one for every Christmas. I have kept them all. "Happy birthday Anna," she murmured, not wanting to advertise my private business to the others in the lab. Two of my four young research assistants were already at work, hunched over their computers. The other two would be out in the field interviewing the families who were the subjects of our research program. Huntington's families, we called them.

The research I had been doing for the past twenty-four years—first for my PhD, then as a research assistant, and finally as the leader of the team—focused on various aspects of Huntington's disease, a terrible, genetically transmitted disorder that targets half the children of every parent who has the illness. Often the children are born before the parents realize they carry the gene and long before they begin to show the strange contorted movements, mood fluctuations, and gradual decline into dementia that are the hallmarks of the disease. Thus our Huntington's families often harbored two or three or even four Huntington's sufferers spanning different generations.

Thankfully I was spared having to deal with them; I have never been good with people, and especially not sick people. I didn't discover this unfortunate fact until my internship year after I graduated from medical school. But as they say, when a door closes, a window opens, and I became a medical researcher instead. Of course it took a bit longer, as I had to complete a PhD, but that was bliss once I realized that my forté was peering down a microscope at brain tissue.

So there I was on my forty-ninth birthday, looking at the envelope I held in my hand and realizing with a quickening of my heart that it was from the medical granting body that had financed my research program for fifteen years. Every three years I had to write another grant application summarizing the previous three years of research and laying out the next three years. Every three years I breathed a sigh of relief when they rolled the grant over and sometimes even added a new salary or stipend for another researcher or PhD student. I had become almost—but not quite—blasé about it. The letter had never arrived on my birthday before; I had not been expecting it until the end of the month. So I opened it with a sort of muted optimism. After all, it was my birthday.

"Dear Dr. Fergusson," I read, already feeling lightheaded as my eyes scanned the next lines, *"The Scientific Committee has now considered all the reviewers' comments on the grant applications in the 2008 round, and I regret to inform you that your application has not been successful. We had a particularly strong field this time, and as you will see by the enclosed reviewers' reports, there were a number of problems with your proposed program. Of most significance is the concern that your research is lagging behind other programs in the same area."*

I stared glassy-eyed at the words, hoping that I was about to wake up from a bad dream with my Eggs Benedict still to come.

"The Committee is aware of your excellent output over a long period and the substantial discoveries you have made in the Huntington's disease research field, but unfortunately, in these

difficult financial times, we must put our resources behind new programs that have moved on from more basic research and are able to take advantage of the latest technologies in neuroscience and particularly genetic engineering."

My head was getting hot at this point; latest technologies and genetic engineering my arse. Easy for them to dismiss years of painstaking "basic research," as they called it, so they could back the new sexy breed of researcher. No way could they accomplish anything useful without boring old basic research in the first place.

"A final report is due on the 31st July, a month after the termination of your present grant. Please include a complete list of the publications that have come out of your program over the past fifteen years. A list of all the equipment you currently have that has been financed by your grant is also required. Our administrator will contact you in due course to discuss the dispersal of this equipment. The University will liaise with you over the closure of your laboratory.

We appreciate your long association with us, and wish you and the researchers in your laboratory well in your future endeavors."

The other tradition I kept on my birthday was dinner at an elegant restaurant with my friend Francesca. I could safely say she was my only friend, as my long relationship with Rachel was purely work-related, except for the novels twice a year. I was tempted to cancel the dinner and stay in my small apartment and sulk, but something deep inside wanted to connect with a human who cared about me and didn't think of me as a washed-up old spinster with no more to discover. Fran and I had been friends since our first year at medical school, when we found ourselves on the same lab bench in the chemistry lab, simply because both our surnames began with 'Fe.'

Fran Fenton and I were unlikely soul mates. She was American, extroverted, gently rounded, and 'five-foot-two, eyes of blue,' with short, spiky blond hair. I was British, introverted, thin, and five-foot-eight, eyes of slate, with straight dark hair halfway down my back, usually constrained into a single plait, but on this occasion permitted to hang loose. Fran was also, in stark contrast to me, married, with three boisterous teenagers. She worked three days a week as a general practitioner in the health center attached to the university where my lab was, and we did our best to have lunch together at least once a fortnight. I once went to her house for Christmas dinner but it wasn't a success; her husband, an English professor, found me difficult, and her teenagers clearly saw me as a charity case. But the birthday dinner was always a special occasion for Fran as well as me, I think.

When she read the letter she was satisfyingly appalled, and said "*swines*" so violently that there was a sudden hush at the tables around us. When the quiet murmur in the room had resumed, she reached over and put her small, pretty hand over mine. I felt the roughness of the skin on her palm and blinked hard as I realized what a special person she was, never seeming rushed in spite of the massive amount of stuff she did— including slaving over a houseful of kids. Her eyes were watering as well as she said softly, "It's so unfair. How could they abandon you like this in the middle of your research? What will happen to all your Huntington's families?" Sweet Fran, always thinking of the plight of others worse off by a country mile than people like us, whereas all I'd been thinking about was myself and how I'd let down my little team.

I blinked hard again and turned my palm up and grasped her hand. I'd been aware how close to tears I'd been all day, but of course I hadn't allowed myself to succumb; not my style at all. In fact my brave little team all remained tearless as I gave them the news at our regular weekly meeting, which just happened to be today. Rachel had disappeared into the bathroom for a long time as soon as the meeting was over, and when she finally reappeared looked distinctly red-nosed. That's when she told me that she would take this opportunity to retire and go and live with her elderly sister in Portland. Dear Rachel, loyal to the end.

Fortunately, the last PhD student we had in the lab had submitted her thesis a couple of months ago. I'd promised my four shell-shocked researchers that I would personally contact every lab that did research similar to ours and put in a good word for them. They had become quite attached to their Huntington's families, which is not a recommended practice for a research scientist, but was a characteristic that I'd learned was essential for effective field workers. Releasing four Huntington's researchers on to the market at once was practically a flood, but they were young and good at what they did and would surely get new positions in due course.

Fran was asking me about other grants, and I wrenched myself away from my gloomy reverie. Taking my hand back, I grabbed my wine glass and emptied it. "Not a chance, I'm afraid," I told her. "The fact is, I'm finished. God knows how I lasted as long as I did."

"Anna, stop it. It's not like you to be so negative about your research. You've done wonderful things. You can't give up because you've lost your funding. Researchers lose grants all the time; they just have to get another one."

"Trouble is, the reviewers' reports were damning. And

they're right. I was lucky to have the funding rolled over last time. They were probably giving me one last chance to do something new, but I blew it. I simply carried on in the same old way because that's all I know. I'm a fraud. I've always known it deep down, and now I've been sprung." As all this was spewing out of my mouth I could feel myself getting lighter and lighter. I felt hysterical laughter burbling up through my chest, and I poured myself another glass of wine and took a gulp, all the while watching Fran's face as her expression changed from concern to shock. Then a snort exploded out of me, along with a mouthful of wine, and I put my glass down quickly and grabbed the blue table napkin, mopping the dribbles from my chin and dabbing at the red splotches on the white tablecloth.

Fran's sweet face split into a grin and she giggled. "You're drunk. Wicked woman. It's not funny."

"It's definitely not funny, but I'm bloody well not drunk. This is all I've had to drink today, and half that's on the tablecloth." I wiped my eyes. "Let's finish this bottle and get another one." We grinned at each other and then sobered up.

"So what now?" asked Fran.

I looked at her, my mind blank. My pulse was pounding through my whole body. I forced myself to focus. "I suppose I *will* have to apply for more grants, but you know how long that takes. I don't think I've got much hope of getting anything substantial."

Fran screwed up her face. I could almost see her neurons flashing as she searched for a miracle.

I tried to ignore the churning in my gut. "I'll be okay for a while. The good old Medical School Dean said I could have a cubbyhole and a computer for the rest of the year so that I could finish all the papers I've still to write." I swirled the wine around in my glass, and watched the ruby liquid as it came dangerously near to the rim. "Given that boring old basic research is no longer considered worthy, I wonder why I should bother, really."

"Is he going to pay you?"

"Huh, no hope of that. Although he did say that I might be able to give a few guest lectures, so I suppose I'll get a few meager dollars for those."

"Why don't you go back to clinical practice? You know so much about Huntington's disease. You'd be a wonderful doctor for them and other neurological patients."

"Fran, what are you thinking? You of all people know that I'm hopeless at the bedside thing and anything that involves actual patient contact. That's why I became a researcher."

"But that was twenty-five years ago. You've grown up and changed since then. You might like it now if you gave yourself a chance."

"I haven't changed, that's the problem. I don't even like socializing with other research staff. You're the only person in the entire universe who I feel comfortable really talking to."

"Well you have to do something. What are you going to live on?"

"That's one of the advantages of being a workaholic with no kids. I've got heaps of money stashed away in the bank. Now at last I'll be able to spend it. Perhaps I'll fly off to some exotic, tropical paradise and become a recluse."

"Very amusing. But you could travel. At least for a few months. Go to Europe. It would give you time to refresh your ideas, and then you could write a new grant that would blow those small-minded pen-pushers out of the water." Fran sounded excited by all these possibilities opening out in front of me.

I could feel my brain shutting down, and shook my head

to wake it up. "Perhaps I *could* take a trip." I pushed my lips into a grin. "Go and see my mother and her lover in their hideaway. Now there's a nice tropical island."

"Doesn't she live in Shetland? That's a great idea. You should visit her."

Fran didn't always get my sense of humor.

"Fran, it's practically in the Arctic Circle. I do not want to go there. And right now my mother and her gigolo are the last people I want or need to see." I rolled my eyes.

"Don't be unkind. Your mother has a right to happiness, and I think her life sounds very exciting. I thought she was married?"

"She is. And good on her. But she and I are better off living a long way apart." I yawned. "I can't think about all this any more tonight. And it's way past your bedtime; you have to work tomorrow."

Fran frowned. "I wish you didn't have to go through all this. It's horrible. But I know something will come up that's better. It always does."

BUT NOT FOR THE NEXT FOUR MONTHS. I CLOSED UP—OR down—the lab, took the team out for a subdued redundancy dinner, and moved into the cubbyhole, where I put my head down and wrote the final report on fifteen years of work. Then I wrote a grant application and sent it off to an obscure private funding body that gave out small grants from a legacy left by some wealthy old woman who died a lonely death from Parkinson's disease. I had little hope it would be successful, as all I could come up with as a research project was further analysis of the neurological material we had collected over the past few years—hardly cutting-edge research. At least waiting to hear would give me a few months of pathetic hope, rather like buying a ticket in a lottery.

That done, I dutifully went into the university every day and tried to write a paper on a series of experiments that we had completed and analyzed just before the grant was terminated. But my heart wasn't in it, and I could sit for eight hours with no more than a bad paragraph to show for it.

Boston was hot and I felt stifled. Fran and her family were away on their regular summer break at the Professor's parents' cabin on a lake somewhere, and the medical school was as dead as a dodo. I used to begrudge any time spent talking trivia to the researchers in my lab, but now that I didn't have it, I missed it. Even my once-pleasant apartment had become a prison, clamping me inside its walls the minute I got home in the evenings. I was no stranger to loneliness, but over the past few years I'd polished my strategies to deal with it. I would remind myself that the flip side of loneliness could be worse— a houseful of demanding kids, a husband who expected dinner on the table, a weighty mortgage, irritating in-laws—it became almost a game to see what new horrors I could come up with. *You, Anna Fergusson*, I'd tell myself sternly, *are free of all that.* "I'm a liberated woman," I once shouted, before glancing furtively around in case my madwoman behavior had conjured up a sneering audience. If self-talk didn't work, or even when it did, more often than not I'd slump down in front of the TV and watch three episodes straight of *Morse*, or some other BBC detective series, and one night I stayed awake for the entire 238 minutes of *Gone with the Wind*.

When Fran finally returned from her lake at the beginning of August, I was on the phone to her before she had time to unpack her bags. Understanding as always, she put her other duties aside and the very next day met me at our usual lunch place. She looked fantastic: brown and healthy and young. I felt like a slug. It wasn't until we were getting up to leave, me to go back to my cubbyhole and Fran to the supermarket, that she remembered.

"Gosh, I almost forgot. Callum was mucking about on the Internet while we were at the lake and came across this advertisement. He made some joke about it being the perfect job for him when he left school, and I remembered how you said after you lost your grant that you should go and live on a tropical island." Fran scrabbled in her bag and hauled out a scrunched up sheet of paper.

"Fran, for heaven's sake, you know that was a joke. What is it?" I took the paper she had unscrunched and read the small advertisement surrounded by ads for adventure tourism in Australia.

For rent to a single or couple who want to escape to a tropical paradise. Basic cabin on tiny coral island on Australia's Great Barrier Reef. AUD$250 a week; must agree to stay one year and look after small private campsite (five tents maximum). Starting date October 2008. For more information e-mail lazylad at yahoo.com.au.

I looked at Fran in amazement. "You printed this out for me? I think the sun must have got to you. Lazylad is looking for some young bimbo. And he wants to be paid to look after his campsite. What cheek."

"That's what I thought at first, but Callum pointed out that thousands of people would give their eyeteeth for an opportunity like this if the cabin were free. But that's the beauty of it; you can afford it. And wasn't your father Australian? You mightn't even need a visa."

"Fran, you're a dear, but can you see me on an island on the other side of the world, singing jolly campfire songs with spaced-out boaties?"

"Have you got a better idea? Or are you just going to continue to fade away in your cubbyhole?"

"No, I'm out of there as soon as I finish this damn paper I'm writing, and then I thought I might try my hand at writing a book." *So there*, I felt like adding.

Fran's face lit up. "A book? That's fantastic. What sort of a book? A novel?"

I started to laugh. "What happened to you up there at the lake? This is me, Anna. I haven't suddenly morphed into a normal person. I'm still the same old ivory tower nerd, clueless about people. No, I thought I might be able to write some sort of account of my experiences getting research grants and running a lab. All the highs and lows. Perhaps I'll discover where I went wrong." I could hear the gloom in my voice as the words came out of my mouth.

"But that's a great idea. And you'll need somewhere to write it." I could see the mischief in her eyes as she grinned at me.

"I know what you're thinking, and no, I do not want to live on a desert island at the end of the world."

"Oh well, worth a try. It wouldn't hurt to check it out though, would it?"

TWO DAYS LATER I COMPOSED A CAREFUL E-MAIL TO Lazylad, not expecting a reply. Surely the cabin had been snapped up by now if it were such a dream opportunity. I got used to holding my breath as I turned my e-mail on each morning, scrolling rapidly through all the usual stuff looking for Lazylad, telling myself I didn't care. But the idea of going to Australia had got stuck in my head.

I had all but given up and stopped daydreaming about writing a book on a deck looking through the palms across an azure blue ocean, when there it was—a reply from Lazylad, who I later found out was actually called Jeff.

Thanks for e-mail. Been away sorry for delay in reply. Cabin still available if you want it. Photos attached. Island called Turtle Island (after the sea turtles here) and is a coral cay just above Tropic of Capricorn about eight hectares in area with a large reef surrounding it. A few eccentric people own houses here and that's about it apart from my small campsite. Only transport is fishing boat or charter. Cabin basic but comfortable, everything included. Solar hot water (roof water) and solar power for lights and computer, gas fridge and stove, no telephone. Satellite broadband from some locals' houses you can use occasionally in return for a few beers. One of the local fishermen brings supplies over about once a fortnight in his boat and locals can hitch a ride for a small fee or more beers. Fantastic snorkeling and diving, birds, turtles, etc. Weather always perfect (almost). If you are interested e-mail me your phone number and I'll call you when next on mainland to chat. Looking after campsite is a doddle. First come, first served (no bookings), take their money, and make sure the old guy on the island does his job of emptying the toilet and the rubbish bins. It would be good to get someone here before I leave for UK on 18th October so I can show you the ropes.

When I scrolled down so I could see the photos my hand was trembling. The first one showed a rectangular wooden building with what appeared to be an open front with a wide deck. A big wooden table and a few white plastic chairs, along with a heap of what looked like diving stuff—a wetsuit and flippers and a tank—sat on the deck. In the dimness of the inside I could make out a bed on one side of a partition and what looked like a kitchen on the other. The cabin was surrounded on three sides by trees with large leaves, and in front of the cabin was a sweep of white sand. The sand had something black on it, and when I zoomed in I could see it was a cluster of three large black birds just sitting there. The second photo showed a narrow strip of white sand, fringed by trees with feathery-looking leaves, and then the truly azure blue sea and sky. The last photo was like something on a travel brochure: a tiny, oval, flat island with green vegetation crowning the center and white sand around the edge, surrounded by blue. In the blue I could see dark patterns, the coral. I grabbed my pendant and brought it to my mouth. The last time I had seen coral sea had been when I was twelve years old, and I had thought then that I never wanted to see it again.

T W O

I stood hanging on to the railing that ran round the bow of the fishing boat and looked at the white-and-green spot on the horizon. "Heavens, it's tiny," I said, obviously louder than I had intended.

"Don't tell me you didn't know?" I turned to see the weather-beaten face of fisherman Jack, who was kindly delivering me to my new home. Presumably his son was driving the boat while he took time off to chat.

"Well yes, I knew, but it somehow looks a lot smaller than I'd imagined. I suppose it's the isolation of it in that great expanse of sea, rather than it being so small."

"Think of it as the whole reef." He leaned over the side and nodded his head like a pointer. "Look, we're already over it; you can see the coral below now. The island is just the bit sticking out at high tide. So it's really a massive area." He grinned at me.

"Right. That's very comforting." I looked back to the island, which was getting marginally bigger. Not another island to be seen. Not even another boat. And then a dark speck appeared in the blue, weaving back and forth and increasing in size until I could make out a small dinghy. "What on earth is that boat doing?" I asked, pointing. "It looks as if it has lost control."

"Some would agree with you there. It's the turtle rodeo. I'll cut the engine when we get a bit closer in and you can watch for a bit. It's a sight not to be missed."

"What do you mean, a turtle rodeo? Surely people aren't allowed to ride turtles." I was shocked.

Jack chuckled. "Now there's a good idea. You hang on there and I'll get up to the wheelhouse and bring her closer."

We turned towards the smaller boat and our engine went quiet. I could hear the screeching of the dinghy's outboard motor as it sped first one way, and then, in a mighty spray of water, turned back and then around again in dizzying zigzags. I could make out three figures, one standing dangerously near the bow. Suddenly the boat screeched to a stop, and the black figure at the front dove into the water as the engine was silenced. I held my breath as the figure disappeared below the surface. Minutes seemed to go by before the diver's head came out of the water right by the dinghy. He seemed to be carrying something—it looked like a large body. We were still too far away for me to see.

I remembered my binoculars and scrabbled for them in my backpack. It wasn't a body—well, not a human one—but a massive turtle that the man—I supposed it was a man—had clasped in front of him. I could see the big head and the front flippers flapping desperately as the people in the boat struggled to get ropes around them. The man in the water was grasping the shell, which was much wider than him. The others in the boat were leaning over the sides trying to grab the flippers, and then I saw them tying the poor thing to the side of the boat. They seemed to be measuring its shell. This went on for some minutes while the dinghy pitched and swayed—it was quite choppy—and then they untied the unfortunate creature and it sank below the surface, and I hope got well away. The diver was clambering back into the dinghy, and one of the others waved at us. Jack was standing beside me again, waving back at them. They started their outboard and made a beeline for us. Their dinghy did a sort of side-skid like a teenager in a hot rod as they reached us and pulled up short, their motor grumbling to a low *putt-putt.*

"Tom, gidday," Jack yelled. "Just telling this young lady about your rodeo. She thought she'd like to go for a ride on a turtle while she's here."

Cheeky sod. I wonder which he thinks is more amusing, the 'young' or the 'lady'?

"Hi Jack, any time, tell her. Does she want to come for a ride now?" the diver was shouting back, his black wetsuit glistening in the sun, his hair springing from his head in wet spikes. I tried to appear nonchalant as I stood there gripping the rail, my heart pounding as I looked down at the dinghy. I could see them all grinning at me, and I was glad I could hide behind the enormous pair of D&G sunglasses Fran had given me as a going-away present.

Jack's arm shot out and landed around my shoulders, pulling me towards him. I could feel myself tensing as his hot breath exploded on my cheek. "This is Anna Fergusson. She's going to be looking after Jeff's campground for a year." His free hand gestured sweepingly towards the dinghy. "And this daring fellow is our resident turtle whisperer."

The man in the wet suit dipped his head and raised his hand in a desultory wave. "These are my two research assistants, Bill and Ben," he said, still grinning.

Am I meant to return their banter?

"Hullo," I said creatively.

All three of them nodded at me and I tried to make my face look pleasant.

"So, do you want to come on board?" asked the diver. "We've about finished the rodeo for the day—one more turtle, perhaps—so we'll be back at the wharf by the time Jack's got your gear to your place. Blow the smoke out of your lungs." "Thank you," I said, knowing how stiff I sounded. "But I don't think I'm dressed for it." I felt ridiculous in my long black pants and blue shirt, even with the top buttons open and the sleeves rolled up. "No worries, another time maybe." His grin flashed again and his eyes crinkled in his young brown face. I smiled back at him without thinking. It was impossible not to. I realized I had taken off my sunglasses and our eyes were connecting. Then their motor roared and they sped away as I hurriedly replaced my glasses, hoping jolly Jack hadn't noticed the heat in my face.

THE SMELL HIT ME FIRST AS I STEPPED OFF THE SMALL wharf and onto the brilliant white sand. A hot, dry, musty smell. Not unpleasant but definitely not lavender. Then the sound of birds, hundreds of them. I looked over to the green rim of trees bordering the twenty meters or so of sand; black-and-white birds were flying in and out, busy as bees. The heat rose up from the sand, and I was glad I had put a pair of shorts in my bag. I nearly hadn't, as my legs hadn't been exposed to the elements for at least twenty years. The shorts were another present from Fran.

Jack's son had disappeared into the interior of the island as soon as we tied up, and Jack had already dumped my one suitcase and computer bag onto the sand. He was now carrying off armloads of banana boxes stacked three high, his biceps distorting a labyrinth of tattoos. Numerous food boxes, seven of them mine, food and supplies that had to last for two weeks minimum until Jack came back from the mainland with the next food haul. An old tractor with a trailer behind it was now chugging through the gap in the trees and down to the wharf, driven by Jack's son. I stood and watched as they rapidly loaded all the boxes, my luggage, large gas bottles, enormous tins with DIESEL written on the outside, and various other things onto the trailer. I made a weak attempt to help but was obviously in the way.

"Come on, I'll walk you to your cabin. Nick will drop your bags and food off in a bit." Jack walked towards the gap in the trees and I followed him, increasing my stride to keep up. He was a broad man, and must have been well over six feet. My feet felt hot in my well-worn hiking boots. I nearly tripped over a group of the busy birds that seemed to be chattering to one another on the sand. They were so pretty. A neat, soft black body with a perky white cap. Big black feet and a black beak completed them perfectly. Jack looked back as I stopped.

"They're white-capped noddy terns. Not so many here yet, but there'll be hundreds of thousands in a few weeks, and all these trees"—he waved a hand at the large-leaved trees we were walking through—"will be loaded with their nests."

"They're beautiful. There seem to be an awful lot here already."

"Wait 'til you see their babies. They must be the prettiest little birds alive."

We continued walking.

"The other bird we have here in the thousands is the wedge-tailed shearwater. Ghost shearwaters, we call them, because of the howling noise they make. Once they're nesting it's almost impossible to move without stepping on a bird or collapsing one of their nesting tunnels. Even sleeping is difficult with the racket they kick up."

I felt a strange sensation in my belly and chest, a sort of bubbling. Excitement, that's what I was feeling. Pure excitement.

My cabin was even smaller than I had envisioned. "Minimalist living" would be putting it mildly, but that was fine by me. I was a minimalist from way back. Jack stopped long enough to demonstrate the vagaries of the enormous and scarily ancient-looking gas fridge/freezer and the even older gas stove. Next came the shower, an ingenious contraption that involved filling a bucket with water from the taps over the large sink, hauling it up to the ceiling of the shower cubicle on a rope pulley, and then, by pulling on another rope, tipping it over so that it emptied its load into a funnel that filtered down to a large shower nozzle. The water that spurted from the taps was disgusting—full of black bits and smelling slightly off. Jack grinned when he saw my expression and suggested that I boil it before drinking it. The only fresh water on the island came from rainwater tanks fed by roof water thick with the droppings of thousands of birds, especially foul following a downpour after a long dry period. I silently thanked Jeff—alias Lazylad—for his wise counsel when he helped me buy my food supplies on the mainland, especially his insistence that I fill two banana boxes with plastic bottles of drinking water.

The power came courtesy of two solar panels on the roof, stored in batteries under the cabin and converted from 12 volts to 240 volts by a humming piece of equipment in a cupboard. It hadn't even occurred to me that power might be a problem, so I felt a jolt of simultaneous horror and relief. Perhaps I could have coped without my iPod, but I would have had to turn right around and go back if I couldn't use my Kindle and computer. I had brought a universal plug adaptor with me, of course—part of my overseas conference travel kit.

Jack disappeared, and Nick arrived on his tractor, dumped my bags and boxes on the deck, and with a "See ya round, mate," roared off. I returned to the kitchen end of the cabin and opened the few cupboards and checked out the mismatched crockery, glasses and cutlery. A blackened kettle sat on the stove, and an equally blackened fry pan and a couple of battered saucepans hung from large hooks suspended from the low ceiling. I looked at the few photos stuck on the walls with tacks. One of them was a picture of Jeff and another man, both dressed only in shorts, standing in the shallow water, an enormous turtle between them. When I first decided to take the cabin, Jeff had been going to meet me there and show me the ropes, but then he decided to meet me on the mainland and introduce me to Jack, who did the regular supplies run once a fortnight. Jeff would be in Sydney now, and soon on his way to the UK and a trial run living with his girlfriend for a year. He'd told me all this while we shopped and then had fish 'n chips in a local café. I looked again at the faded photo and peered at the other man in it for a few seconds before realizing it was the turtle whisperer. He looked different without his wetsuit. Both men had that Australian look, rugged and brown. The turtle whisperer—Tom, I think Jack called him— had quite a lot of dark-blondish hair. I'd got the impression that it was black when I saw him earlier, because it was wet I suppose. He was grinning his infectious grin, and his dark eyes were almost hidden in the crinkles of his smile. Both men had nice faces, open and friendly. Tom's was sort of lopsided, but perhaps that added to his attractiveness. How old would he be? Jeff had let slip that he was thirty-five—the right age to settle down, as he put it—so perhaps Tom was about the same age. I'd meant to ask Jack why he called him the turtle whisperer, but hadn't in the end. I suppose it's another

Australian joke because of this turtle rodeo thing he does—the exact opposite of a turtle whisperer, if you ask me.

I finally got around to emptying my case into the small wardrobe and tallboy. I thought about putting my shorts on, but decided on my light safari pants and a T-shirt instead. The shorts would have to wait until I'd shaved my legs; the poor things hadn't seen a razor since my student days. I went brown quite easily as a kid, so fingers crossed I still would, and the Australian sun wouldn't burn me to a cinder.

After burying my black trousers and blue shirt at the back of the wardrobe and swapping my boots for sandals, I felt much better. I unpacked the food boxes and squashed the packs of rapidly defrosting meat into the freezer box, and the other refrigerator stuff into the fridge part. I managed to find space in the few cupboards and on the open shelves above the sink for the rest of my food, and hoped it wouldn't soon be infested by god knows what creepy crawlies. I made a mental note to beg, borrow, or steal some plastic containers from somewhere. I had a few scary moments lighting the gas hob, but finally managed to boil some of the bird-shit water and make a cup of tea. It had a very peculiar taste but I was cautious about using my precious bottled water except for drinking it cold.

I took my cup of musty tea and a plate of biscuits and cheese out on to my deck—I was already thinking of it as mine —and sat in one of the plastic chairs. It was still and hot and all around me were scuffles and birds calling, and through a gap in the trees was the white sand and then the blue sea, now with bits of coral sticking up in it as the tide went out. I sat there not believing it was me, and that I was there for a year with nothing to do but write my memoir—not that anyone else would give a damn if I did or didn't, and right then nor did I.

What on earth would I do for a year? Surely the campsite I was yet to see wouldn't take much of my time? Luckily my Kindle was stuffed with at least sixty books and my iPod loaded with my favorite music. And I'd better at least make some attempt at the memoir just to keep my brain ticking over.

After a while I got up, reluctantly, and followed a sandy path around the side of the cabin and through some trees for about two hundred meters. Jack had told me the campsite was back there. And there it was, quite a large sandy, grassy area with trees all around but with a gap showing the beach and sea. A wooden building near the edge turned out to house a toilet that looked fairly unsavory when I looked down it, but didn't seem to smell. Thankfully I didn't have to deal with it. A man called Basil, whom I was yet to meet, apparently did the honors. On the outside wall of the toilet was a shower like mine. A little way from that was a large open shelter with a concrete floor and a wooden picnic table in the middle. A gas barbecue and a couple of gas bottles took up one side. A guttering around the roof of the shelter led into a pipe connected to a water tank on stilts, and at the base of that was a concrete tub with one tap. A notice stuck to the tank said that the water was undrinkable without boiling and to use sparingly.

All in all a very pleasant spot, but obviously not on the main backpacker trail, as there was not a single tent to be seen. Keeping an eye on this should be an easy job. I wandered out onto the beach, where even more coral was now exposed, and looked both ways. I thought I must be in the middle of the long part of the oval island. Looking to my right, back towards my cabin, I could see the wharf where we had landed, with Jack's boat and a few others bobbing alongside it. Jack had explained that there was an artificial deep water channel there that the original occupants of the island—that is, the European occupants—had made with the help of a few sticks of dynamite. In the other direction the beach stretched for a few hundred meters before disappearing around the corner.

The light had become softer and the blue of the sky had taken on a sort of transparent luminescence. I glanced at my watch and was surprised to see that it was five o'clock. I'd already been here four hours. Basil could wait 'til the morning. *Basil Brush.* I grinned as an image of the unknown Basil, complete with bushy red hair and tail, flashed in my head. Perhaps all Australians have these sweet, old-fashioned, simple names. Bill and Ben the flowerpot men, Jack and the beanstalk, Tom, Tom the piper's son . . . *Christ, I'll never remember who is who. I wonder when I'm going to meet Waltzing Matilda? That's if there are any females here. Not that I'm likely to have anything in common with them.*

THREE

Basil showed up around nine o'clock. I'd been up for hours after a hot and sleepless night tossing and turning on the hard mattress, trying to block out the phenomenal noise of thousands of shearwaters as they made their ghostly howls at each other. Jeff had warned me about this, but it had to be experienced to be believed. At times, as I dozed, it almost sounded like an orchestra, but then a small gaggle of the birds sitting right on my deck would start up— *whoooo* up the scale and then *hoooo* down the other side, followed by their mates' slightly higher *whoooo-hoooo*, and so on around the entire gaggle, firmly banishing the orchestral illusion. At one point I stumbled out on to the moonlit deck to chase them away, but apart from doing a short sideways shuffle, they ignored me, and continued to *whoooo-hoooo*. Fortunately for them they were decidedly lovable, and quite impossible to kick—large and soft and dark gray, with a bumbling gait when on land and when landing. Every few minutes there would be a loud swish as another bird hurtled out of the sky, skidding along the ground when it hit dirt. Then it would waddle slowly off to its nest—a hole in the sand, under a tree root, under the cabin, or sometimes right in the middle of the sandy path.

When, at six o'clock, I finally gave up on sleep and made myself a cup of tea, the noise stopped—of course—and, going outside, I saw the last bird waddling rapidly along the track before taking off like a drunken jet plane and spreading its great wings, soaring up over the low trees and out to sea. There, it was in its element—one of the greatest fliers in all the bird kingdom. The sacrifices a parent will make for its babies—not that I would know, but it awes me anyway.

Basil seemed like a nice chap, in his sixties I would guess, and a true-blue Aussie like everyone I'd met so far. Bald as a baseball. He didn't say a lot, and what he did say I had a bit of trouble understanding as he didn't open his mouth very wide, but his eyes had a blue twinkle and his grin was friendly. He indicated that he'd empty my rubbish bin as well as the ones in the campground, and he would clean the toilets once a week. He gave me a large book and a small metal box with a lock; the book to record campers' names and payments—$5 per adult per night and $2 for kids; and the box to keep the loot in. He turned the small key and opened the box to display a pile of notes and coins—change, he said, in case a camper didn't have the right amount. Most of them would be university students who would come on their summer holidays from mid-November to the end of February, and would stay for two weeks, between Jack's boat trips.

"What do I do with the money?" I asked.

"When it gets too much to fit in the box, stick it in a plastic bag and give it to Jack. He'll deposit it in Jeff's bank account back on the mainland. He'll take cash checks as well, if you've been paid that way, and he can cash your own checks too, if you need any money."

"He's the island banker as well as the transporter, by the sound of it," I said.

"I suppose so. Someone's got to do it. Give him your grocery list and a blank check as well when you want more
supplies. You have to be organized, though, because you won't
get them until he comes back two weeks later." He looked at
me doubtfully, as if he thought I wouldn't cope with this.

"Thanks. Jeff explained about the grocery thing. I'll soon
get the hang of it, I think." I grinned to show him I wasn't
being sarcastic. "What about phoning out? Is that possible?"

"Yeah. I have an old computer and satellite broadband—
it's pretty slow—and so does Tom Scarlett."

"Tom the turtle whisperer?"

Basil guffawed, his mouth opening at last, exposing a
crooked row of nicotine-stained teeth. "That's him, the turtle
whisperer. But his place is on the other side of the island. My
place is closer, the next house just up the track a bit. If you
need to e-mail anyone or phone out on Skype, or in an emer-
gency, just drop by."

"Thank you. But I'll try not to impose. To tell you the truth,
I'm rather looking forward to a life free of e-mail and the
Internet."

IT DIDN'T TAKE LONG TO SETTLE INTO A SORT OF ROUTINE.
At first I did find myself worrying about being out of contact
and a couple of times had to stop myself from asking Basil if I
could use his computer to access my e-mail. But by the end of
the first week, I couldn't give a damn about it. By now I could
just about sleep through the ghostly night chorus, and I often
rose early and spent an hour walking on the beach before
coming back and eating a bowl of muesli and luxuriating in a
cup of real coffee, brewed using crystal clear bottled water.
The aroma as my little espresso machine farted happily over

the gas flame was the aroma of happiness. If I was still hungry I made toast under the efficient gas grill, inevitably burning a slice or two in spite of standing over it. I ate breakfast on my deck, with my Kindle in hand, and it was pure bliss. It took great strength of mind to close the Kindle after an hour or so of sloth and replace it with my laptop. Then I settled down to writing my "memoir," as I thought of it. This was usually painfully slow, but on rare days the words fairly flew out of me. I found that my early-morning beach walks were the perfect time to reminisce about my past life—my life, that is, as a researcher. My "memoir" was to be about that. I decided to begin at the beginning—that is, when I landed my first job as a junior researcher in the Huntington's lab not long after completing my PhD. Then I would write about my rise to senior researcher and becoming the head of the lab in the space of just six years. It bordered on exhilarating, remembering those heady times when I was full of passion for my research, with ideas tumbling over themselves. Writing a cutting-edge research grant was a breeze back then—well it seems so now, looking back—although I also recalled bouts of despair and even depression, not to mention night upon night burning the midnight oil.

I'd stop my memoir writing for a sandwich or piece of fruit when I was hungry, and allow myself another hour of reading, sometimes lying on the bed trying to catch any tiny breeze from the wide-open sliding doors that stretched across the entire front of the cabin. Of course, more often than not, my eyes refused to stay open and I woke hours later feeling hot and sticky and annoyed with myself. But a walk on the beach as the evening began its tropical journey through every shade of yellow, orange, red, and pink soon revived me, and I would sometimes veer off the beach onto one of the meandering tracks through the center of the island, marveling at the thousands of birds chattering and calling as they flew about their business, and breathing in the balmy air with its musty, birdy smell. Dark fell quickly and early, and if I forgot to take my torch I would find myself stumbling over tree roots as I made for the lighter sky reflecting off the sea and, once on the beach, found my way back to the familiar track leading to my cabin. By the time I'd negotiated the intricacies of the shower, concocted something for dinner, and eaten it, sitting as always on the deck—a complete absence of flies, mosquitoes, and other biting insects being one of the glories of being on a tiny coral cay on the outer edge of the Great Barrier Reef—I was well and truly ready for bed. The solar-powered lights were hardly bright enough to read by anyway.

In that first week I often went all day without speaking to a single soul. Occasionally when I was walking I would see someone on the beach and nod a greeting, but apart from that the only human I saw was Basil, who wandered past on the track about once every two days. He'd grin and raise his battered hat with its shady Aussie brim, but often he wouldn't actually utter a greeting. But I didn't feel in the least lonely. No campers appeared wanting to put up their tents—I supposed they were most likely to arrive when Jack's boat returned —so I was truly in a honeymoon period.

Ten days after my arrival I set off for my hour-long morning walk around the circumference of the little island a little later than usual, heading in the direction away from the wharf. On the home stretch, just as I was coming to the wharf, I saw the turtle boat leaving. I watched it head out over the reef flats and then walked farther along the beach so I wouldn't be so noticeable. I must have sat on the sand with my binoculars glued to my eyes for two hours, ghoulishly fascinated by the dinghy's crazy zigzagging and the diving cowboy catapulting himself into the sea before the dinghy had skidded to a halt, bringing turtle after frustrated turtle up to the side. Jack had explained that the turtles were mating, the male on top, allowing the diver to grab the poor thing and measure it.

By the time the boat turned to come in, I could see a small group of people down at the wharf, two of them clearly children by their small size. Probably too small to be in school yet. I did know there was no school on the island, and that the few houses were mostly holiday homes, occupied only in the school holidays. I considered wandering back to the wharf to introduce myself but then felt stupidly shy. I was hopeless with children, and I couldn't imagine what I would say to the turtle whisperer.

Back at my cabin, I looked at the faded photo on the cabin wall again. I could almost hear Fran's admonishment—"He won't bite, you know. Just go and say hi. You'll have to talk to him sooner or later on an island as small as that." But it was another two days before I purposely decided to take a casual late-afternoon stroll along one of the tracks that ran across the center of the island to the other side, passing within about fifty meters of the small house nestled in the trees that I had noticed before on my walks. I had seen no other buildings on that side of the island so I figured it must be the turtle whisperer's home. My legs were already becoming quite tanned, and they were now as smooth as a baby's bum, but even so I pulled on my light long pants; I wasn't quite ready to expose myself to that extent. As if the turtle whisperer would even notice the skinny legs of a middle-aged spinster.

My heart sped up as I neared the turnoff to the house, and I walked right past it and onto the beach a little farther on. I stood for ages gazing at the reef, bits of coral sticking out as the tide receded, and the turquoise sea farther out. I told myself that he probably wasn't there anyway, and turned back along the track. This time I took the side path to his house and as I reached it I could hear him whistling. He sounded as if he were around the back, so I tiptoed past the front of the house with its wide deck, rehearsing what I'd say when I saw him. *I was just walking past and heard you whistling so thought I'd call in and say hi.* Then I was around the side of the house and he was only a couple of meters in front of me, oblivious to my presence and still whistling. He was standing under an outdoor shower attached to the wall, and was stark naked. He had his back to me and was vigorously soaping his body, his towel hanging between us on a large hook high on the wall. I began to tiptoe quietly backwards, praying he'd keep whistling, but before I'd taken three steps he reached up, switched the shower off, and turned around.

"Sorry, sorry," I mumbled, my entire body flaming as I almost fell over in my hurry to back around the corner.

The turtle whisperer grinned and reached up and grabbed his towel, wrapping it around his waist in one smooth movement. "Gidday," he said. "Don't run away. Anna, isn't it? It's nice to see you again. I was wondering what had happened to you."

I stopped and managed to look at his face. "I'm so sorry. I heard you whistling and it never occurred to me you would be . . . it wouldn't be convenient."

"Well, you weren't to know I'd be starkers. Don't be embarrassed. Look, give me five to get something better on than this towel, and we can have a drink."

I must have looked strange or horrified because his face lost its smile and he added, "I hope I haven't offended you?

Perhaps you don't drink? That's okay. We can have a cup of tea or coffee if you'd rather."

"No, no, I do drink," I said. "Well, socially only. I'm not a big drinker but I like a wine, or a beer is good too if you have no wine." I burbled on but he was smiling again now.

He walked past me around the corner of the house, and I followed.

"Have a seat and I'll be back in the flick of a turtle's tail."

I sat on the edge of his deck with my back to the wide-open French doors. I didn't want to risk seeing him drop his towel. I heard him moving about inside and then he reappeared, dressed in shorts and a T-shirt, his hair still damp and roughened from a brisk toweling. "Red wine okay for you?" he asked.

I nodded, and he bent down and put the bottle and two wine glasses on the deck, then disappeared inside, returning with a packet of biscuits and a wooden board complete with two types of cheese—a wedge of blue and a hunk of tasty— and a bunch of purple grapes.

"Gosh, this looks very civilized," I said, accepting a glass of wine.

"It does, doesn't it," he agreed, grinning again. "I like my little luxuries; got to have something to stop myself turning into a wild man."

"How long have you been here?" I sipped the wine. It was good: rich and round and Australian.

"Six years, off and on. Before that I spent about three months a year here while I was doing my PhD research. Fell in love with the place and decided to stay a while."

"Your PhD was on turtles?"

"Yep. Addictive creatures."

"Do you work on them all year round, or only when they're mating?"

"The full-on field work is now—October, when they're courting, and we study mainly the males—then November to March, when the females are laying, and through to about May we study the babies when they're hatching. But there's plenty to do the rest of the year, analyzing data and writing papers and thinking up new research projects, as well as less frantic field work on the health of the reef more generally, and the distribution of the turtles, what they're feeding on and so on."

"How fascinating. It sounds the perfect job," I said, realizing that I was envious. I also noticed that my stomach had stopped churning and my heart had stopped thumping. Perhaps it was the wine, but I felt relaxed sitting there talking to this unusual young man.

"I think so," he was saying. "If you're interested, you should come out one night when the females start nesting. It's pretty special."

"I'd love to. I've seen documentaries on it, but never the real thing. When does it start?"

"Any day now. At first just one or two females will come up, but by late December and through January we can have any number from fifty to one hundred a night laying." He poured me some more wine and then refilled his own glass.

"What do you do? Count the eggs?"

"Sometimes. We wait until they've dug their nest and started laying, and then we read their tag if they already have one, or if not, we tag and measure them. That way we can keep a record of how often they nest in a season, where they lay, and any damage they have."

"Doesn't that disturb them?" I asked.

"Not usually. They're easily upset before they begin dropping their eggs, but once they're at that point nothing can stop it. A physiological imperative. A bit like orgasm, or I suppose birth, although I can't relate to that experience so easily."

I felt myself flushing and bent to smear some more blue cheese on a cracker. The light was going. I should leave before it became too dark to find my way. I stuffed the biscuit into my mouth and tried to eat it fast without making too much noise.

"What about you?" he was saying. "Are you here for long?"

I swallowed the last of my biscuit and gulped down the last of my wine. "I'm here for a year, looking after Jeff's campsite and doing some writing." I wanted to take that revelation back the second my words hit the air.

"What are you writing?" he asked.

"I'm a researcher too. Well, I *was* a researcher. I lost my grant and thought I'd have some time off to rethink what I want to do. When this opportunity came up it seemed far enough away from what I'd been doing to be very attractive. So far I haven't had a single camper, so it's not exactly a big job."

"What is your research area? Are you writing papers?" He sounded genuinely interested, and I looked over at him, his face blurred in the dusk.

"Not interesting like your research. It's medical laboratory research. And to be honest, I'm not sure what I'm writing; it's a sort of memoir on my work. Pretty silly, really."

"No writing is silly. It'll happen. Just give yourself some slack. This is a pretty magic place to write. Just let it work on you in its own good time." I could sense the warmth in his tone and I was glad it was nearly dark. I felt quite shaky. Clearly too much wine.

"Thanks for the wine and cheese. And the company. It was

lovely," I said, getting up. "I'd better make tracks before it's completely black."

"Will you find your way okay? Do you want a torch?"

"I'll be fine. I might go back along the beach. If the moon is up it will be easy to see." I tried to sound lighthearted. Thank heaven he hadn't offered to walk me home.

"It should be rising right now on your side of the island, and it's almost full. Thanks for calling in. I'll let you know when the girls start laying."

I made my way along the path to the main track, sneaking a look back towards his house. The light came on inside and I heard his whistle and a clatter of glassware.

FOUR

I had begun to talk to myself, out aloud. I also talked back to the radio. If this continued I'd be a raving lunatic by the time I left this island. Since I got there ten days earlier I'd spoken to only two flesh-and-blood people—Jack and Nick excluded—and in total time, I couldn't have spent more than three hours in their company.

In Boston, I relished my weekends of isolation after being duty-bound to communicate with the others in my lab all week. When I arrived on the island I was anticipating with rampant pleasure being on my lonesome for twelve whole months. Now I'm desperate for the sound of a human voice other than my own, or a disembodied radio substitute.

Basil was a man of few words and I couldn't see myself spending hours with him. And Tom the turtle whisperer was hardly going to be hanging around, waiting for another excuse to slurp wine with me. He couldn't be much older than thirty-five.

An image of his body inserted itself between my thoughts again. I rolled my eyes, ignoring the fact that there was no one there to notice my exasperation. Naked men do not, in theory, do anything for me. I did, after all, train as a doctor and even worked as one for a brief period. On the other hand, the last time I'd seen a naked man in the flesh had been more than twenty years ago, and my memories of that occasion were, thankfully, dim. So perhaps I could be forgiven for replaying the image of a wet, brown, healthy male body, especially as I was too embarrassed to make the most of the vision at the time. I could feel myself blushing at the very thought. And his casualness with the whole thing. He was probably used to walking about in front of women stark naked. A matter of course for the younger generation.

But he had seemed genuine about my going out with him when the turtles were laying. I noticed he didn't ask me if I'd like to accompany him and his friends on the turtle rodeo. Thank goodness. I might have said yes and then I'd have had to find an excuse not to go.

Concentrate on the memoir, woman. Boring, boring, boring. Who was I kidding? No one was going to want to read this. A pedestrian account of a dried up, middle-aged academic's broken dreams. Not even that, really—just tedious descriptions of working in a lab. But I had to do something for the rest of the year. For people not keen on going in the sea, there was a limited selection of activities to choose from. Bird watching, walking.

I snapped shut my laptop, grabbed my binoculars and hat, and set out in the direction of the wharf. Time to find some other people to converse with. They must be out there some-where. *Where do Tom's research assistants live? What about those kids I saw; they must have parents. Stop moping woman, and get a life.*

TO MY SURPRISE I DID MANAGE TO STRIKE UP A conversation with the mother of the two children I had seen.

Violet was her name, and she seemed very friendly. Five-year-old Chloe and two-year-old Danny were the sort of kids I like, lots of fun, and Violet intended to homeschool them until they had to go to secondary school. Lucky, lucky kids. Bill, one of the two men who assisted Tom with the rodeo, was her husband. She invited me over for lunch on Sunday so I could meet some of the other islanders.

As for Tom, I saw him in the distance once, on his boat leaving for another rodeo. I stayed well away from the wharf for the rest of the afternoon so I wouldn't have to talk to him when he returned. I'd had some success in banishing his body from my thoughts, but what if he was at this lunch on Sunday? At least he was unlikely to be naked.

On Saturday there was the excitement of the supplies boat arriving. On Jeff's instructions I had given Jack a grocery list and a blank check when he brought me over to the island, so I got three more boxes of food and drinkable water, and a letter from Fran. In return I gave Jack my next grocery list and a letter for Fran, and another for my mother, on the other side of the world in the Shetlands. Strange to think Mum and I were both living on remote islands—not a prediction either of us would have made five years earlier. Fran's letter made me both homesick—they had already had their first snowfall—and happy that I was here in the tropics and not there for the long winter ahead. It brought home how much I missed not having Fran to talk to, although in truth we never talked more than fortnightly when I was in Boston. I couldn't quite see Violet becoming a soul mate, nice though she was.

I'd just finished reading Fran's letter when four people—two guys, two gals—showed up at the cabin, large packs on their backs and each carrying a food box. My first campers. I think I disguised the fact that I was a newbie and didn't have much clue about what my role was other than to show them the campsite and tell them how much it would cost. I asked them how long they were planning on staying and they said they didn't know, but two weeks at least given they were dependent on the supplies boat to get away. They seemed happy enough, and I left them to it.

At midday on Sunday, I trotted off to Violet's lunch, carrying a bottle of wine and feeling like an adolescent going to her first teenage party. Whatever would these Aussies make of me? I could hardly be more of a fish out of water.

I was the first to arrive, and Bill was in the process of cleaning his barbecue. He looked about forty, and he told me that he and Violet had been on the island for three years, ever since he'd been made redundant from his job in Sydney. Apart from helping Tom out when he needed it, he and Violet managed a group of four holiday cabins for an absentee owner, and also ran a low-key café in the holiday season. They loved it and intended to stay until the kids had to go to secondary school.

Over the next hour four other guests appeared, including Basil, Ben—the third rodeo man—his partner, Diane, and Pat Anderson, a gray-haired woman who looked as if she might be in her early sixties. Ben and Diane were from England, in their twenties, and working their way around Australia. They had been there since June and planned to stay until April of the next year. Diane was helping Violet with the cabins and Ben was helping Tom. Their real love was scuba diving, and that's what they talked about most of the time. Pat was a retired teacher. After her husband died a few years earlier she'd decided to live on the island, in their holiday house, permanently. She told me she swam and snorkeled every day, and invited me to join her. I explained I had a writing project that took most of my time and that I wasn't a swimmer. If you can float, she informed me, you can snorkel, and if you are going to live here, snorkeling is a no-brainer. I smiled and changed the topic to books, another of her passions.

By this time we all had plates piled high with the most delicious seafood I had ever eaten, some of it caught by Bill and some brought along by the other guests. I discovered that there were areas nearby where fishing was permitted, and Bill and Ben both offered to drop me off a fish from time to time. It seemed that the entire permanent island population was there now except for Tom. I could feel myself relaxing and enjoying the balmy air, and the laid-back conversation. I pushed away the little niggle of disappointment. Perhaps he was off island? Perhaps he went back to the mainland with Jack for some reason? I finally managed to bring his absence up in a conversation with Ben about the turtle rodeo.

"Tom seems like he'd be a good person to work with," I remarked. "Isn't he into social occasions like this?"

"He's a bit of a loner, but he'd usually be here, especially if it's just the locals. He's not so keen on the tourists. But he's off on one of the other islands for the next week checking for nesting turtles; they've just started coming up."

"Oh," I said. "I didn't realize the turtles laid on other islands. Are they far away?"

"Depends. There are a few small cays within about two hours from here that Tom goes to regularly."

"How does he get there? In Jack's boat?"

"No. He goes in the tinnie we use for the rodeo," Ben replied.

"Tinnie? What's that?"

Ben laughed. "That's what the Aussies call a dinghy."

"Isn't that a long way to go in such a small boat?" I asked.

"Not for Tom. He knows what he's doing. It can be dangerous if the weather gets up, especially in cyclone season, but that's a few months off yet. Don't worry, he'll be safe as houses."

"Goodness, I'm not concerned. I was just curious, that's all." I laughed gaily, and Ben grinned.

"Ah yes, he's an intriguing fellow, our Tom. A man of mystery."

OVER THE NEXT WEEK I BEGAN TO FEEL AS IF I BELONGED. I wandered every track on the island, spent a couple of evenings talking with the campers and sharing some beers with them, and stopped by Basil's house for a cup of tea one morning. He offered to let me check my e-mail, so I did, but found that I could delete all but about six messages without even reading them. Of the six I did read, five were related to leftover university business. The sixth e-mail was from Rachel, telling me she was enjoying her retirement but missed the lab sometimes. Fran knew not to e-mail me here. I logged off with a sigh of relief and a firm decision not to bother with e-mail again. It was too much of a reflection of my sad social life.

One moonlit night, right before high tide—when I had been told that the nesting turtles came up—I walked the beach, and was disappointed when I didn't see a turtle. I did meet Bill, who was also checking for turtles, and he told me that it was still too early in the nesting season for there to be many. For some reason they started nesting a week or so earlier on some of the uninhabited cays where Tom had gone.

On Thursday morning, Violet, Diane, and Pat appeared with a plate of scones and a banana cake, and said they had come for their gossip group. I was quite overcome. I can't ima-

gine such generous sharing of friendship happening so easily
in Boston, or for that matter in England. My new friends told
me they rotated around each other's houses every Thursday
morning, and I was the first American they had ever had in
the group. I explained that I was in fact British by birth and
upbringing—and I thought by accent—but they said they
would overlook this. They stayed for two hours and the
conversation never faltered. They talked about books, food,
star signs, education, politics, and their families, and drew me
into every topic without me noticing. My memoir writing
fascinated them, and when I tried to explain, rather unsuccess-
fully, what the point of it was, they enthusiastically interrupted
with their own ideas. They didn't know what they were talking
about, of course, because they didn't know me and my limi-
tations, but later I wondered if I could write a sort of parallel
personal memoir about my life. The problem is—and of
course I couldn't admit this to them—I didn't have a personal
life. That had stopped around the time I completed my PhD.

Nevertheless, it wouldn't hurt to try. I could write up bits
and pieces about my past life, just to see if I could write more
creatively. As a kid, I loved to write. So on Saturday, after I
had eaten the fish Ben had dropped off earlier, I opened a new
Word document and headed it *My Life*. I thought I'd begin by
writing about my friendships at school as a sort of comparison
with these easy relationships my new Australian friends shared.
Had I always been so bereft of friends? Surely not. By
midnight I had had enough of feeling miserable, angry,
annoyed, irritated, frustrated, lonely, and sad about the words
that spilled out of me once I got going. I went to bed and slept
fitfully, waking every hour, hot and vaguely disturbed by something I had been dreaming about but which was now gone. I
got up and opened my laptop and reread what I'd written:

I remember my first friend at school when I was five. She was pretty and called Julia. We stayed friends until I was taken away from that school when I was eight. I must have had other friends back then, but can't remember anyone in particular. Other than Julia, my best friend was my father. He was always fun, and on the weekends, when he was home, he'd take me somewhere new in London. We'd go on buses and the underground and he'd treat me just like a real person. Looking back, I'm not sure if he behaved like a kid or if I behaved like an adult—perhaps it was somewhere in between—but the important part was that we loved doing things together and being together. Sometimes Mum came with us, and that was okay, although she never quite got it—our silliness. But she tried to enjoy herself. Even when I was little I think I could sense her embarrassment when Dad tried to kiss her in public. "Stop acting the goat," she would tell him, pulling away.

Dad was a freelance journalist, and that's why he spent a lot of time away from home. We lived in a small- ish townhouse with an even smaller garden in Chelsea, but it was a nice house and a nice area. When Dad was home he walked me to school every morning and Mum picked me up and walked me home every afternoon. I wanted a little sister like Julia had, but when I asked Mum why she didn't have another baby she went quiet and turned away. Dad jumped in and swung me up in the air and told me that I was all they wanted; our life was perfect without more kids. I didn't ask again but I often wished I wasn't the only one. Even a brother would have been better than nothing.

When I was eight everything changed. Back then I didn't realize that the happiest days of my life were already over. Dad moved out. He and Mum told me one Saturday night after Dad and I had spent the afternoon at the Science Museum. It was cold and wet, so that was about all there was to do. Mum was trying not to cry and Dad was sad. I screamed at them and stamped my foot and ran out of the kitchen and locked myself in my bedroom. Next morning, when I finally came out, Dad had gone. Mum and I had to move to a tiny flat over a greengrocer's shop in a horrible street in a horrible, scary part of London. The street smelled and was always filthy. I had to go to a different school where nobody liked me. They all had their little groups of friends and they weren't letting me in. Not that I wanted to be friends with any of them. They were rude and scruffy and laughed at my voice and my clothes. They called me toffy-face. I told Dad when he came to take me out for the day, and he said it was because they didn't know any better. They thought I was posh, and that made them uncomfortable. He told me to just keep being friendly and in a while they would see I wasn't really any different from them. But he was wrong and they never liked me.

I went out on the deck and looked up at the starry sky. Through the trees I could see the lagoon, as still as a swimming pool. The moon was rising late tonight, and I watched as it peeked above the horizon, then soared into the heavens, perfectly round. Back in the cabin, I made a cup of tea and sat down at my computer again. Better that than lying in my hot bunk feeling sorry for myself.

Once a week in the summer term our whole class would get the bus to the public swimming baths and have swimming lessons. Dad had already taught me to swim because that was one of his favorite things. He loved scuba diving and he always said he'd take me away when I was older to a tropical beach where I could learn to snorkel and see the amazing world beneath the ocean. So I was quite excited about going to the swimming baths and thought that the other kids might like me better when they saw I could swim.

How wrong I was. First we all had to swim across the pool one at a time so the swimming instructor could see what level we were at. Most of the kids couldn't swim at all and just walked or floated holding on to a board. I did freestyle and then the instructor asked me if I could do other strokes so I went across the pool again doing breaststroke, then again doing backstroke. After that, the instructor said we could all play together in the shallow end for ten minutes before we had a lesson, and he went off to the other end of the baths for a smoke with our teacher. As soon as he had gone, two of the biggest boys jumped on me and pushed me under and held me there. I was sure I was going to drown. When they let me up I was coughing and spluttering and crying and I could hear all the kids laughing, and they pushed me under again. But I came straight up because the teacher had heard them and was shouting at them from the side. The instructor hauled me out and I scraped my knee on the side. Then the teacher told me to go and get dressed, and when I came out I had to sit and watch while the other kids had their lesson.

That night I couldn't go to sleep and I was crying and Mum came in and asked me what was wrong. When I told her she gave me a quick hug but then said I just had to toughen up now that I was nearly nine. She said that if I acted like I was scared they would just bully me more. So I decided there and then never to cry in front of anyone ever again. And I never have. But I never made a single friend at that school.

When I was eleven, I passed the eleven-plus exam and went to grammar school. That was better because the girls there were more like me, and I got on all right with a couple of them. I didn't very often do much with them outside school hours, though, partly because I had to get the bus home and it was an hour's drive. Mum said I could invite someone home for tea and to stay overnight, but I never did. I think I was a bit ashamed of our flat and the smelly street. Once I went to a party at one of the girls' homes and stayed the night—it was a pajama party —and her house was about three times the size of the house we used to live in.

Mum didn't seem to have any friends either. She worked in a bookshop a couple of streets over from our flat and all she did apart from that was read. So Dad was still my best friend. I saw him about once a month, when he was in London, and he would take me out for the day on a Saturday or Sunday. But best of all was in my summer school holidays when Dad and I would go away together for a whole month. When I was nine he took me to Greece, where we sailed around the islands on a boat with friends of his. He had a girlfriend who was nice to

me but she didn't last. When I was ten we went to Egypt,
just the two of us, and stayed in an apartment on the Red
Sea. That's where I first went snorkeling. It was beyond
words and made up for all the bad things I had ever
experienced. When I was eleven we went to the Bahamas
and stayed in different places where Dad and his new
girlfriend could scuba dive and I could snorkel. That's
where I had my first scuba diving lesson. The next year it
was Belize. Dad had the same girlfriend this time. We
went to a little island and as soon as we got there Dad
said he'd go and check out the diving first and we could
all go together the next day after we'd had a good sleep.
But we didn't and I've never been in the ocean since.

When I finished banging away it was a bit after four in the
morning. I closed *My Life*, pulled on my shorts and a T-shirt,
and went down to the beach. The moon was now high in the
sky and the sea well over the reef. It was unbearably beautiful.
I sat on the sand and a few tears squeezed out of my eyes. I
wiped them away and licked one off the side of my hand. The
salty taste made me smile, and more tears welled up and slid
down my cheeks. I hadn't cried, even when alone, since I was
in my twenties, and it felt wonderful in a strange sort of way.
Then I saw a dark shape pop out of the sea, only a short
stone's throw from where I was sitting. I could see her bright
eye in the moonlight and then her head disappeared and I
stayed still and quiet. Up her head popped again, and this time
her great shell followed. I hardly dared breathe as she hauled
herself on to the sand and then lolloped on her great flippers
up the gentle incline of the beach. Every four or five lollops
she would stop, her eyelids closing over her big eyes, and then

she would start again. I felt exhausted just watching her. Exhausted but exhilarated at the same time.

As she passed me I could have reached out and touched her, she was so close. A little farther on after another long rest she made it to where the trees began. After a few experimental flips of her long front flippers in the dry sand, she began digging, using her flippers to shoot the sand away from her, gradually making a saucer in the sand, and then a pit. When it was so deep she'd almost disappeared, she began to use her right back flipper as an elongated scoop, delicately inserting it into the deepest part of the pit and extracting the damp sand that lay below the drier sand on the surface. I had crept up to her by this time and was kneeling just behind her and to the side. Every so often I would get sprayed with sand, but I didn't move. In the moonlight I could see into the deep hole she was fashioning, narrow at the top and ballooning out deep down in the damp sand. How long this took, I couldn't say exactly, but at least thirty minutes.

At last she was happy with her nest, and she squatted and inserted what looked like her tail into it. And then in the moonlight I saw a translucent, white, perfectly round egg ooze out of the end of her tail and plop down into the depths of the hole. It was bigger than a golf ball. Then came another and another, and I started counting. When she had dropped in eighty-two eggs, she blinked a few times and I could see tears in the corner of her eyes. She closed them for a few minutes before retracting her cloaca—I had figured out it wasn't just a tail—and, using her back flippers again, began to fill in the nest.

FIVE

————————

"Magic, isn't it." I heard his quiet voice and knew immediately whose it was.

"How long have you been there?" I whispered, turning around to see him sitting in the sand behind me.

"About half an hour," he whispered back.

"Why didn't you say anything earlier?"

"Nothing to say." I could see his smile in the soft dawn.

"Shouldn't you be tagging or measuring her or something?" I ducked as a spray of sand hit me in the chest.

"She already has a tag, and I didn't want to break the spell for you. See that metal tag on her left front flipper? I'll check her number when she's on her way back to the sea."

We sat in silence, watching her. The wide pit filled up rapidly and when she was satisfied that it had been obliterated, she slowly rotated her great body, flipping sand and leaves about until there was no evidence there had ever been a hole. She rested for a few minutes, then swished her front flippers back and rowed herself down the gently sloping beach to the sea. Behind her she left wide tractor marks, picked out by dimpled shadows in the glowing sand. When she was about ten meters from the edge of sea, Tom scooted down and grabbed her front flipper, shining his torch on the tag. She increased her pace, almost lifting up on her flippers, and he let her go and picked up the clipboard he had dropped on the sand, writing her tag number on the sheet. He stood and watched her slide into the tiny waves swishing onto the beach, and then she was submerged, first the top of her shell and then just her head sticking out as she swam over the reef and out to sea.

"That's her first laying this season," Tom said as he walked back towards me. "You're honored. Eve is one of the first turtles ever tagged on this island."

"So you won't see her again now until next summer?"

"Oh yes, she'll likely come up to nest a number more times yet over the next three months, but then we won't see her again for two or three years."

"How amazing it is. All that effort. I'm so glad I saw her," I whispered, although the need for whispering had obviously passed. "Do you have names for all your turtles?"

Tom dropped down onto the sand and wrapped his arms around his bent knees. "No, only Eve. The others are just tag numbers. Scientists aren't meant to get close and personal with their subjects; it might bias their research." His grin flashed in the luminescent light.

"Yes, it's rather the same in my line of research. Best to keep it impersonal," I said. Tom didn't comment, and we sat for a while in what felt like a comfortable silence. Then Tom shifted, and looked as if he were about to get up.

"Was Eve the only turtle nesting tonight?" I asked.

"Two others, a bit earlier. Eve was cutting it fine. They come up to lay on the high tide but need to leave enough time to get back before the tide goes out again and it becomes too shallow for them to swim back to the deep water. It's early days yet, and by December on some nights there might be eighty or more turtles coming up."

"Ben was telling me you had been to one of the other islands looking for nesting turtles."

"Yes. Two coral cays close to here. I visit them fairly regularly. One of them seems to attract more loggerheads than here for some reason. I found six nesting on one cay last night."

"Eve is a green turtle?"

"She is. Greens are by far the most common turtle here, then loggerheads. Just occasionally we get a hawksbill nesting; they're much more common farther north, around Cairns."

"Are the coral islands you go to inhabited? By people, I mean," I asked.

"No. That's their beauty. They're pristine."

"Not even a hut to sleep in?"

"No, not even that. At this time of the year, a sleeping mat is all I need. The main downside is being used as a landing site for shearwaters. But I don't get much time for sleep usually, once the turtle nesting season is in full swing."

"It must be amazing, sleeping there under the stars, the only human in the middle of all that ocean."

"Everyone should sleep on a beach under the stars at least once in their lives," Tom said.

I felt the jagged edge of pain slice through my chest and tighten my throat, and I turned my head away from Tom's gaze.

"You should try it one night before there are too many turtles coming up." Tom's voice was quiet.

I swallowed, and waited as the pain receded. "I'd like that," I finally managed to croak. "Once, when I was a kid, I slept on the beach with my father."

Tom was silent.

"We were going to do it again, but my father died, and I've never been anywhere since where it would have been possible." My fingers felt for my dolphin pendant.

"Until now," Tom said.

We sat for a while, not speaking, as the sun rose out of the sea and the light lost its early magic. The tide was rapidly retreating, exposing bits of coral.

Tom yawned and then laughed. "That's my day job over. If I want to get in some shut-eye before lunch I'd better be on my way." He got up, and made a funny sort of wave-salute in my direction. "I'm glad you met Eve. If you want to give us a hand later when the nesting is in full swing, let me know."

"Oh yes, please," I said. "I would like that."

Tom nodded, smiled his lovely smile, and walked away.

BACK IN MY CABIN I TREATED MYSELF TO A FEED OF pancakes, made in the English way as my mother used to make them for me when I was a child, not artificial and puffy like the American ones. In the small fry pan I fried three rashers of bacon while I mixed a batter of flour, egg, milk, water, melted butter, and a pinch of salt, beaten to the consistency of runny cream. I took the large fry pan, melted a lump of butter in it, and poured in just enough batter to film the bottom. When bubbles began to form and pop, I flipped the pancake over with the help of my only spatula and browned the other side. Two minutes and then it was ready to be flipped onto a plate, slathered with lemon juice and sugar, and rolled into a long sausage. While I consumed the first pancake with one of the crisp bacon rashers, my next pancake was cooking. After three large pancakes, I could hardly move, so I lay on my bed and fell fast asleep.

Apart from a walk on the beach late that afternoon, I didn't do much else, but after a solitary meal that evening— just a slice of cold ham and a green salad after my breakfast extravagance—I sat at my computer, trying to decide whether I should continue with my account of my research career or write more of *My Life*. Truth to tell, I had been thinking about my father all day, and I suppose it was inevitable that I would feel an urgency to write it down.

It was in the Bahamas that I slept under the stars with my father. It was our third summer holiday after he and Mum broke up, and we—Dad and his girlfriend, Louise, and me—were staying in a holiday apartment right on the beach. One night, Dad said he had a surprise for me, and we drove quite a way to a secluded little bay along the beach, away from the houses and apartments. Louise didn't come; she said this was to be a special father-daughter treat. We had brought a large tarpaulin, pillows, and our sleeping bags. I was beside myself, I was so excited.

We spread the tarpaulin out on the sand, not far above high tide mark, and snuggled into our sleeping bags, although it was warm enough not to need them. Dad had brought a plastic box of supper—cold chicken, bread, cheese, cake, and mangoes. We ate the lot, and then after sneaking into the trees higher up the beach for a pee, we lay in our sleeping bags looking up at the starry sky. Dad pointed out Orion and lots of the other constellations, although I think he made some of them up. We talked about everything: school, my favorite books, what I wanted to do when I left school—that was easy, I wanted to be a journalist like him, and travel the world—and the scuba diving adventures we'd have on our holiday. He told me about all the adventures he had had that year, seeking out stories.

When I woke up it was just getting light, and the sea was pink. I felt as if I'd died and gone to heaven. When Dad woke up, we changed into our swimsuits and went for a swim and then a run along the beach. After that we went back to the apartment and went out to a café for breakfast with Louise. We had pancakes, of course. All the next year, whenever I felt gloomy or sad, I'd think about that night under the stars, and count the months, then weeks, then finally days until our next summer holiday, this time to Belize. Dad and I had made a solemn pact to sleep under the stars again.

I stopped writing then. Enough was enough. I wandered down the beach but the sea was way out. The turtles wouldn't start coming in until around two in the morning, on the incoming tide. I walked along the beach until I came to the spot I'd stopped that morning, when I talked to Tom. I could just make out the disturbed sand where Eve had covered up her nest, and I sat on it thinking about the eighty-two eggs beneath me and the millions of eggs that had been laid by turtles over millions of years on isolated beaches like this. How Dad would have loved it.

SIX NEW CAMPERS ARRIVED ON JACK'S BOAT ON Saturday. It was mid-November, and the end-of-year university exams were over. Jack had given them two letters for me, and my boxes of food arrived on Nick's trailer. One of the letters was a long one from Mum, and I put it aside to read later. The other was from the secretary in my old university department. I had asked her to open my mail and send on any she thought

I would want. She had enclosed a letter from a small funding body I had applied to before I left. The letter politely declined my application for a pitiful amount of research money. The other enclosure was a reprint of a recently published research article I had had accepted almost a year ago. I could hardly understand the title it was so full of jargon. About the only term that made any sense was "Huntington's disease." A slither of nostalgia—or guilt, perhaps—froze my snigger as I scanned the list of co-authors—all my research assistants and my last doctoral student. *I wonder what they're doing now?*

The campers were loaded up with the usual scuba equipment. Four of them had never been to Turtle Island before, and I found myself telling them all about the birds and turtles as if I had lived there for years. I'd been finding out more from Basil and Pat. By now there were more than one hundred thousand birds nesting on this tiny island. The most numerous by far were the wedge-tailed shearwaters, with their ghostly night cries, and the charming noddy terns busily putting the finishing touches to their scruffy nests, which balanced precariously on every branch of the sticky Pisonia trees—sometimes thirty nests in a single small tree. Reef herons also nested there, and quaint little buff-banded rails fussed about on the sandy ground, bobbing their heads. Tiny silvereyes darted through the trees and I had learned to identify the common migratory birds—ruddy turnstones and eastern golden plovers—who returned from the Northern Hemisphere every September, and flew north again every March.

Pat was a mine of information about the birds, and we were on our way to becoming firm friends. We had begun to meet up for morning walks. Pat would stop every few minutes to watch birds through her binoculars, and although I wasn't devoted enough to follow suit, I was content to stand quietly until she was ready to move a little farther. Sometimes our walks took up to two hours at this pace, and by the time we got back to the wharf we were both ravenous. Often we would go to one or other of our places and brew up some coffee to enjoy with bowls of muesli and slices of toast. If Pat had spotted an unusual bird she would get out her bird books and study them intently, pointing out the color patterns that distinguished her discovery from other similar-looking birds. We'd talk about other things as well: her life before she retired, and mine before I lost my grant. One morning, as we were sitting on her deck relishing our second cup of coffee, she asked me again why I didn't swim or snorkel, and this time I told her.

"When I was a kid I was a good swimmer, and I even tried scuba diving a few times. My father was an experienced diver and spent every summer somewhere in the tropics where he could explore new reefs. He took me on snorkeling trips to Egypt and the Bahamas, and when I was twelve we went to Belize."

I pulled myself out of my chair and walked to the edge of the deck. The sea sparkled through the trees. Pat didn't speak. I swallowed, and felt the unfamiliar prick of tears at the back of my eyes. I could feel the hot sun of Belize on my hatless head, and the smell of sea and birds. "It was early afternoon when we got to this little island where Dad had booked a cabin for two weeks. Louise—his girlfriend—was with us. We'd had a long trip, and Dad thought we should take it easy that afternoon and have our first snorkel the next day. But there was a local there who had a dinghy and was going out for a fish, so Dad decided he'd go for a quick dive just to check it out. Two hours later they weren't back and it was beginning to get dark. Then the dinghy came back and the man was by himself. He couldn't speak much English and he was in a state.

Louise was shouting and screaming and then other people from the resort were there.

"I kept expecting Dad to swim up to the beach, but he didn't, of course. It wasn't until much later, when the local police came over and we found someone who could speak reasonable English, that we managed to piece it together. Apparently Dad hadn't come back an hour after he'd left the boat for a dive. The boatman had been fishing and after another half hour he'd gone in himself—he just had snorkeling gear—and couldn't find Dad, so in the end he came back. They took a motorboat with big lights out to look around but it was hopeless. It was dark by then. At dawn next day they started a proper search but didn't find him. They never found him. All anyone could come up with was that he must have got caught somehow and used his air up before he could free himself. It wouldn't take long for the sharks to find him."

"My god," I heard Pat say. Then I felt her hands on my shoulders and I turned around and buried my face in her neck as she held me.

S I X

Pat was standing on my deck festooned with snorkels and masks and flippers. It was a new day, and to my surprise I had slept well. No nightmares, no night sweats. Perhaps I'd wept every last drop of water out of my body yesterday.

"I thought we'd begin in the shallow part of the lagoon," Pat said. "The tide is perfect for beginners—about a meter over the top of the reef. In just a few flips you can be over sand and standing up without harming the coral."

"I'm not sure. I think perhaps I need a day or two resting, to get over yesterday."

"Trust me, this will be better than days of rest."

"I haven't got a swimsuit." The banal words came out of my mouth and I waited for Pat to laugh.

"I have heaps of swim suits, and bikinis too. I never throw them out. Some sort of fantasy about miraculously waking one day to find that my body is thirty years old again—or even fifty would be good. But some of them would fit you; we're about the same height, and you're as slim as a reed." She thrust the snorkeling stuff at me. "Come on. We'll go to my place first and you can select one."

Not a hint of a smile. I didn't think Pat had a sarcastic bone in her body. I was already following her as she turned and strode down the track. She glanced back over her shoulder. "I've got spare wetsuits too—a short one will be perfect. You don't need it in the lagoon but it will make you feel safer."

The flippers banged against my leg, and the sun glinted off the mask, the snorkel dangling from its strap. *How hard can it be?* My mouth was dry, and I concentrated on keeping up.

KITTED OUT LIKE A DEEP SEA DIVER, I STOOD AT THE edge of the lagoon and let the warm sea lap my feet. The beach was deserted. *Thank goodness.* I squinted over the blue to the white fringe farther out, where the sea was breaking over the edge of the reef. I closed my eyes but the picture in my head of the reef edge dropping away into the deep blackness wouldn't budge.

"All we're going to do today is play around in the shallow water. The corals and little fish in the lagoon are enough to keep us content for hours." Pat splashed water over her face and spat in her mask. She already had her flippers on.

I sat on the sand and wriggled my feet into my flippers, wincing as the muscles in my right foot cramped, contorting my toes. Standing up awkwardly, I weighted my foot until the cramp lost its grip, then I turned around and began to back into the water—one step, two steps. Now for the mask. I wet my face and the mask with seawater, and spat on the glass. My mouth was still dry and the small bubble of saliva I managed to produce was barely enough to smear over the glass. I swilled it out and eased the mask over my face. It was a tight fit. Good, I didn't want any chance of a leak.

"You haven't forgotten," Pat said. "Snorkeling's like riding a bike; once you learn you never forget." She stuck her snorkel in her mouth, twisted around, and floated off, her flippers barely moving.

I could see the white sand under my feet. A little group of slender white fish swam by. About twenty meters farther out were the dark shapes of the coral. Pat was out there, lying motionless, facedown, in the still water. I saw her mask flash as she looked up and then with two flips stood at the edge of the coral, the water coming up to her breasts. "It's only this deep," she called out, her voice clear in the still air.

I looked around, thankful that there was not another soul in sight. I stuck the snorkel mouthpiece between my teeth and took a few experimental breaths. Kneeling down, I gingerly laid my face on the water, keeping my eyes wide open. The mask had steamed up a bit but I wasn't about to fix it. All I could see was the white sand. Then I let go and I was floating, the short wetsuit giving me buoyancy. I told myself to breathe. Some brightly colored fish flashed below me, and I moved my flippers. *Don't splash. Move your legs smoothly from your hips.* I heard Dad's voice and I was ten years old again.

A funny little brown-splotched fish looked up at me from a hole in the sand and then disappeared backwards into its lair. I raised my head and saw Pat waving. A few more flips and there were her legs. I stood up, gasping.

"Okay?"

I nodded, grinning around my snorkel mouthpiece.

"Follow me. We'll stay within a few meters of the sand."

Then she was ahead of me, flippering along. I heard my own flippers splashing as I went after her. She stopped and I stopped, looking down. We were over a ring of corals—red, orange, white, and fluorescent blue—and immediately below me was a large anemone with two clownfish backing in and out of the poisonous tentacles, warning me off. A shoal of black-and-white-striped fish floated by, and their name floated through my head from all those years ago—*moorish idols.*

Nipping at the corals were myriads of other small fish: silver, blue, striped, yellow, orange, red. I focused on a white-and-yellow fish and tried to remember the pattern of black stripes crisscrossing its side so I could look it up later. *One of those impossible butterfly fish.* Dad's voice again.

I looked sideways under the water surface at Pat. She was pointing farther out. She flippered off and I followed, my eyes glued to the kaleidoscope beneath me. Water slopped about in the bottom of my mask, and spying a small patch of sand I stood up and pulled the lower rim of the mask away from my face, letting the water escape. I breathed in again and clamped the mask back on my face before sinking back into the water to follow Pat. She was circling a large round coral—*a bommie*—the name came back to me. She pointed down and I realized we were in much deeper water. I felt myself breathing faster and forced myself to slow it down. Around the bommie crowded much bigger fish—green, orange, and pink parrotfish busily rasping at the surface of the coral, the funny little scratchy noise they made with their beaks magnified under the water.

An oblong green fish outlined in brilliant blue with a bright yellow mouth and yellow tips to the fins streaming behind it swam below us. I pointed at it, and Pat stuck her head out of the water and I heard her say, "Angel fish." Then she beckoned me farther and we glided over more gardens, over some beautiful brain corals—I had no trouble remembering what those were called—and then we were over a patch of sand covered in waving sea grass, and there it was below us. A turtle. It must have sensed us above it, because it floated gently off the sand where it was grazing and flippered calmly away. We flapped after it, but even though it seemed to be moving slowly, it soon lost us.

✄

AFTER LUNCH AT PAT'S HOUSE—I COULD HARDLY EAT I was still so buzzy—I went home and spent hours poring over a large, well-thumbed book on the fishes of the Great Barrier Reef, one of the books in the small collection on the shelf under the bedside table in my cabin. The book was annotated with dates and places, presumably referring to Jeff's sightings of the fish. The dates went back fifteen years.

Snorkeling in the lagoon at high tide became a daily ritual, sometimes with Pat but more often alone. Her idea of snorkeling was out over the reef edge. I wasn't quite ready for that. In truth I wasn't sure I ever would be, but I didn't care. The treasures in the lagoon filled me with joy, day after day. What with my nightly wander around the island looking for laying turtles—more and more were coming up every night, and I lived in hope that Tom would make good on his promise to let me to join his tagging team—I barely had time to write my memoir, although I did manage to read a few of the novels that crowded my Kindle.

The campground was getting busy as well, and I enjoyed my twice-daily stroll around the tents to make sure the campers were behaving themselves. They were almost entirely university students—skinny, tanned girls with long, salt-infused hair, wearing very little, and muscular young men, hair in stiff spikes and often wearing wetsuits half on. Diving tanks leaned against the low wall of the barbecue shelter, and beach towels festooned the top. The bin for recycling beer cans seemed always full in spite of Basil's now-daily visits to empty it and the rubbish bins. Most of the tents were small two-person affairs, with the occasional larger tent where everyone congregated in the evening for a shared meal cooked on the big barbecue. They were a friendly bunch, and I sometimes accepted their casual offer to join them for a beer. Their conversation was of diving and fish, giant manta rays and moray eels, and mind-blowing sightings of a pod of killer whales, hunting in a pack. I had little to offer—my toddles about the lagoon embarrassed me—but at least I was able to contribute a few bits of information about the turtles.

The girls were friendly and seemed unaware that I was old enough to be their mother as they swapped trivia while they threw salads together and turned sausages on the barbecue. All of them snorkeled and some were scuba divers, but they gravitated towards their own gender for light relief from dive-speak. I had a hard time sorting out who was with whom, and while there were a few set couples there, the overall impression was one of mix and match. Very different from my day, and probably a lot more fun.

One of the girls, Kirsty, was pregnant, and I was amazed that she was there at all. She had her own little tent and was on a working holiday, helping out Violet in the café and cleaning the holiday cabins over the summer. One afternoon she wandered past my cabin when I was reading on the deck, and I offered her a cold drink. We chatted about this and that, and I discovered she had no partner, was only nineteen, and had decided to take this job because she figured it would be her last chance for a bit of freedom. She intended to keep the baby, which wasn't due until April. Her job finished in mid-March, when the summer season petered out. I cautiously expressed my concerns about the lack of health facilities on the island should she need them, but she brushed them off, saying that she'd be back on the mainland by her due date. The confidence of youth.

I asked her if the father would have any contact with the

child once it was born, and she grimaced and rolled her eyes.

"I'm sorry," I managed to say. "I hope he's going to support you financially, at least."

"Nope. He doesn't want to know."

"It's his legal obligation, surely?"

"Only if I can prove he's the father, and that'll break up his marriage and stuff up his kids, so I've decided to count my blessings. The main one is that I never have to see the bastard again."

FINALLY. ONE NIGHT I SAW TOM ON THE BEACH AND plucked up the courage to ask him if I could help.

"Sure, that would be good," he said, just like that.

Why didn't I ask him sooner?

I spent the rest of the turtle watch with him as he explained how to record the tag number if the turtle was already tagged, measure the carapace—the proper name for the shell—and note any damage to it or the flippers, and mark it on the turtle outline on the data sheet. About half the turtles were untagged, and fitting the nasty metal tags into the pinchers and maneuvering them over the edge of the turtle's front left flipper without disturbing her laying was surprisingly easy, but squeezing the pinchers shut so that the sharp points of the tag pierced the flipper and locked together took quite a lot of strength and both hands, and I thought it must hurt her. I winced every time, feeling it biting through.

My third turtle had completed her egg laying and had almost finished filling in her pit when we came upon her high up on the beach under the trees. She had no tag and Tom told me to tag her quickly and try and measure her before she began her journey back to the sea. She ignored me until I managed to get the tag over her flailing flipper—by then I was covered in sand from her efforts—but as I squeezed the pinchers shut, she turned, reared up on all four flippers, and almost ran down the sand to the sea with me running—almost dragged—along beside her. All at once the beach was littered with dead branches with sharp bits. As she reached the water's edge and with a loud sigh slithered into her own world, I at last managed to pull the pinchers from her flipper, hopefully leaving the tag firmly attached. I ended up on my butt in the shallows as she glided out over the reef flats. And there I sat, catching my breath, until Tom appeared beside me, laughing his head off.

"Good one, Anna. Did you get the tag number down?"

"Oh, shit."

"Well, I suppose you remember it?"

"Very funny. Sorry. What will happen now? You'll have no record of her next time she comes up."

"Luckily for you, I wrote it down on the form when I gave you the tag."

I was on my feet by now, my shorts clinging to my scratched legs and dripping onto the sand. "I'll tag you if you don't wipe that satisfied grin off your face." I thrust the pinchers at him and he caught my wrist, still grinning his Cheshire grin.

"The lady has balls after all," he said. "Welcome to the team."

The next night, and every night after that, I did my turtle patrol alone. Kitted out with a head torch and my very own wide leather paraphernalia belt, and clutching my clipboard with the data forms, I took on the stretch of beach from the wharf to just past the campground, while Bill, Ben and Tom did the rest of the beach. Sometimes I was joined by a couple of the campers, and as the owners of the few holiday houses on the island arrived, kids would silently appear to watch the show. I didn't mind the company as long as I got some time alone. When the last turtle on my stretch had returned to the sea with the outgoing tide, I went back to my cabin. Sometimes it was still dark and sometimes it was dawn, but it always took a while to fall asleep in the unbearably hot room, the pillow over my head to muffle the *whooo-hooos* of thousands of ghost shearwaters.

When I woke, I'd be famished, and more often than not had a massive breakfast. In the afternoon I would walk across the island to Tom's place to hand in my completed data forms and get more tags if I needed them. Sometimes he was there and sometimes he wasn't. But when he was I usually stayed a while. We talked mainly about turtles—Tom's knowledge of the research literature was impressive—but apart from discovering that Tom was thirty-nine, came from Sydney, where his parents still lived, and had a younger married sister with two kids who lived in Melbourne, I found out nothing about him. He was about as forthcoming about his past life as I was.

CHRISTMAS LOOMED, AND IT WAS GETTING HOTTER BY the day. Official temperatures hovered around 32 degrees, but it was a bloody sight hotter in the sun, and nights were steamy and sticky. With a sea almost as warm as the air, I no longer bothered with Pat's wetsuit when I went snorkeling. I was becoming an expert at identifying the small fish in the lagoon, although the cryptic patterns of the different varieties of black-striped yellow butterfly fish continued to defeat my visuospatial memory powers.

The Pisonia trees with their sticky buds were loaded with

twiggy nests full of seriously cute baby noddy terns, all squawking endlessly for more food. The trees could be deadly if the adult bird misjudged its landing spot and became ensnared by the sticky buds. One day I rescued a stuck-up bird flailing about on the ground, and it was a slow and painstaking process pulling the jellybean-sized seeds off its feathers, one by one. But I was rewarded when the bird, finally seed-free, balanced on its webbed feet, shook out its ruffled feathers, and flew unsteadily up into a tree. When a baby fell out of its crowded nest there was nothing to be done; as far as I could see, the parents never came for it.

Underfoot the shearwaters waddled about, not so many during the day, but thousands returning from sea each evening. I'd sit on the beach with my glass of wine, sometimes alone, sometimes with Tom or Pat, and great flocks of birds would darken the pink evening sky as they silently soared and wheeled in ever lower circles, the kings of the air. Then they would plummet clumsily to the ground, running along the sand for a meter or two before skidding to a stop near their burrow. After greeting their mates, stuck there on incubation duty, they would hang around in groups discussing their day, ignoring the people walking past.

On the reef flats there were many waders, including the lanky and elegant herons, some white and others blue-gray. Once, when we were sitting quietly on the beach, Tom pointed to a dot far out over the reef, and as it came closer I could see it was a large bird of prey. It landed high in the feathery branches of a Casuarina tree, no more than ten meters from us—a white-breasted sea eagle, with a five-foot wingspan and deeply hooked bill.

Violet and Bill had one of their barbecues on Christmas Eve, and this time I had no second thoughts about joining the party. Everyone brought some food as well as alcohol, and by midnight we were all fairly happy. High tide was at one in the morning, and Tom, Ben, and I staggered off to do the turtle count. It was five before my last turtle returned to the sea, just making it before the coral was too exposed for her to swim safely back to the deep. I counted twenty-eight laying turtles on my patch during that watch, and eighteen of them had to be tagged. It was a struggle in my slightly woozy state, but as the dawn broke, I collapsed on the sand, fizzing with the pure joy of it. I raised an imaginary glass to my long-gone research assistants, hopefully now happily working for a better boss than I. "Here's to you," I sang into the cooling salt breeze. "I finally understand what it's all about."

SEVEN

"Are you going to take something American on New Year's?" Pat asked.

"Pardon?"

"For the party. I thought you might bring an American specialty."

"What party?

"On New Year's Eve."

"I haven't been invited. Is it at Bill and Violet's?" I didn't know if I felt embarrassed or pissed off. I was sitting at Pat's table scoffing her wonderful pikelets, still warm from the pan and slathered in butter and raspberry jam. I'd been telling her they were called flapjacks in America, although no flapjack I'd ever eaten could hold a candle to these.

"It's at Tom's place. Everyone goes. You don't need an invitation."

"He never mentioned it. I didn't think parties were his sort of thing."

"Ha. That's what he wants us to believe." Pat's chuckle was almost wicked. "The first year he came here we had a party on the beach, and it started to rain. So we fled to Tom's place—we were around that side of the island and it was nearest. He was there all on his lonesome, so we took over. It was the best party we'd ever had, and lasted until dawn. After that it became a tradition. Tom always protests but we always ignore him."

"That's terrible. Poor Tom. I'd hate it too, having it forced on me like that."

"Watch it, my girl, or we'll swap to your place."

"Don't you dare. We'd have all the campers gate-crashing as well."

"So? They usually end up at Tom's as well. It's a free-for-all. But we do take pity on the poor guy and everyone brings a plate."

"'Ladies a plate please.' I haven't heard that expression since I was a kid."

"I thought it was an Aussie expression. I guess it originated in England. Anyway, that's what I meant. You could wow everyone with something quintessentially American."

"My cooking would do nothing for America's reputation. Anyway, pumpkins aren't too common around here."

"Surely pumpkin pie isn't the only American dish you can make?"

"You're right. I can't even make that. Anyway, I'm British."

"Hmmm. Well, you'd better come up with something."

"I think I'll give it a miss. I'm not much good at that sort of party, and Tom never even mentioned it."

"He would assume you knew about it, that's all. It's not an option. Everyone goes. And for heaven's sake, you're one of the turtle research team now. What's more, it's the only night of the turtle tagging season when Tom gives his taggers a night off."

PAT PICKED ME UP AT SEVEN ON NEW YEAR'S EVE, SHE with her carrot cake and me with my Thai green chicken curry. A quintessential American dish. Tom's place was already overflowing when we got there; I didn't think there were that many people on the island. How the campers knew about the party was a mystery, given I nearly missed it altogether. But they were there en masse.

We deposited our food in the kitchen, where Violet and Diane were bustling about heating stuff up. We eagerly offered to help but they shooed us away and we went outside, where a long trestle table was set up, already laden with food and booze. Basil was wielding a large ladle in a large punch bowl, and filled us a glass each of something that tasted deliciously fruity and tropical but was certainly mostly alcohol given the rapid onset of lightheadedness after a swig or two. Loud modern music was blaring from speakers set up on the deck, and I recognized some of my campers dancing in the way youth dance these days. Most of the partygoers were standing or sitting in groups on the deck and grassy sand that surrounded Tom's house. I looked around for Tom, and spotted him talking to some people I didn't know.

"Come on. Let's say hi to our host," Pat said, pushing me in front of her.

I felt stupidly shy and out of place. Tom grinned at us, and introduced me to the couple with him. I forgot their names instantly, but managed to retain the information that they had arrived that day to stay in their holiday house for three weeks.

The night wore on and I followed Pat around, talked to Basil, and continued to feel like the proverbial fish out of water. By ten o'clock the food had mostly disappeared and everyone was dancing. The moon hadn't risen yet and the stars were, as one of the campers said to me, awesome. I managed to avoid dancing by sitting in the corner of the deck until Bill came over, hauled me to my feet, and dragged me out onto the grass. I jiggled around to the music but it was almost impossible to keep in time to. Everyone else seemed to know the words to every song and I felt as old as Methuselah. It was more of a group dance than a couple thing, and once Bill had done his duty and gotten me in there, he melted into the crowd and I was left jiggling about randomly. I caught glimpses of Tom, who, rather to my surprise, was acting as crazily as the rest of them. Here was me thinking he was a quiet, solitary type. Then he was in front of me, grinning and yelling something over the din.

"Enjoying yourself?" I think he said.

"Yes, great," I shouted back, waving my hands in the air and jiggling up and down.

He bent over and shouted in my ear, "Do you like this group?"

"What group? Do you mean the music?"

He nodded, still grinning.

"A bit too modern for me."

"Shall I put on some decent music?" he yelled.

"Yes, please. What's decent?"

"Wait and see." He shimmied away and disappeared inside the house. The song came to a loud end and the dancers stopped, some drifting off to get another drink. Abandoned, I saw Pat in a knot of people and started towards her.

The Rolling Stones cut through the night, and the dancers still hanging around became instantly innervated again.

"More like it?" Tom was beside me, already movin' and groovin'.

"A bit before my time, but it will do," I mouthed back. After that I concentrated on matching his moves and looking like I was as overtaken by the music as everyone else. Soon not even Basil was left on the sidelines.

※

"GET THE MUSIC OFF AND TURN ON THE RADIO," someone called out. "It's almost midnight." The hyped-up voice of the talkback radio host from Brisbane took over, counting down the seconds to the end of 2008 and the beginning of a new year.

"Ten, nine, eight, seven, six, five, four, three, two, one," we all chanted. "Happy New Year."

All around me people were kissing and hugging. I looked desperately for Pat amongst the dark shapes, and then I felt Tom's hands turning me towards him and he bent and kissed me. I had a fleeting sense of his lips, soft on mine, and then I was almost bowled over as a woman threw herself at him. Recovering my balance, I backed off, and to my relief immediately came upon Pat. I hugged her tightly and we were swirled into the circle of hand-holding merrymakers singing "Auld Lang Syne." Across the circle I could see Tom clutching the hand of the female who'd so effectively halted any chance I'd had of kissing him back. She appeared to be dressed in her underwear—tight, tiny white shorts that cut her vertically in two, and a brief top that exposed most of her perky boobs and flat brown stomach. Her legs, of course, were gorgeous. She was laughing up at Tom, all eyes and a boy's haircut that only models can get away with. *Where the hell has she sprung from?* I'd never set eyes on her before.

We'd got to the second verse of "Auld Lang Syne," where everyone crosses their arms and plods into the middle of the circle. This brought Tom and me together briefly, and he gave me an exaggerated wink. Model girl looked through me. I was horribly aware of my khaki safari pants and classic white shirt —the perfect party attire for a forty-nine-year-old neuroscientist.

"Who is that?" I asked Pat when we were safely ensconced with Basil, drinking a quiet toast to 2009.

"She's the daughter of Sadie and Frank—over there." She pointed to the couple Tom had introduced me to when I first arrived. "They have a holiday house here. Polly has been coming to the island since before she was born. She's grown up a bit."

"She seems to have a thing for Tom. Isn't she a bit young?"

"Probably. But she isn't as young as you think. She must be close to thirty. In normal life she is a staid lawyer."

"I don't believe it. Lawyer, perhaps. Staid, never."

"She's actually very nice. Tom's more like a brother than a boyfriend I think."

"Whatever. Where's Violet, and Diane? I must wish them a happy New Year. I bet they're in the kitchen."

I THOUGHT ABOUT MAKING TRACKS FOR HOME FROM time to time after that, but no one else was leaving. Violet had somehow managed to get her children to sleep on Tom's bed, and other older kids were running in and out of the dancers and back and forth from the beach. Goodness knows what the nesting turtles thought. Would they be able to hear all this racket? Perhaps their hearing wasn't too sharp.

I was feeling pretty relaxed, having had more than my share of Basil's fruit punch and a glass or two of wine. I danced some more, this time with Diane and Ben, and caught occasional glimpses of Tom, sometimes dancing, and sometimes in one of the huddles of people drinking and smoking on the grass. *Grass on the grass.* I noticed the staid Polly was usually close by his side. The sweet smell took me back to my student days; I'd never used it then either. Control was my middle name.

It was two o'clock when Violet and Bill picked up their sleepy children and wove their way over to us. Pat decided to go home as well, and I started off with them, but decided to sit a while on the moonlit beach. I walked along the sand until I could barely hear the music. I was full of feelings. Homesickness for snowy Boston. Missing my lunches with Fran. Missing Dad—how he would love it here. Awe at the beauty of this island. Joy for the undersea bounty I could now float above. Worry about what I'd do when all this was at an end. Happiness that I'd become friends with Pat, and Violet and Diane.

A turtle emerged from the sea and began her timeless journey up the sand.

Love for these beautiful animals. Feelings for Tom. Feelings I failed to—dared not—put a name to, even in my private thoughts. I wiped a ridiculous tear from my cheek. Relief that I could cry, perhaps? No doubt made easier by alcohol.

"I wondered where you'd got to. Thought you'd crept away without saying goo' night." Tom's familiar voice seemed a part of the dream. He lowered himself down and stretched out on the sand. The mother turtle was on her way back to the sea, her eggs safely laid and her nest camouflaged.

"I didn't think you'd notice my absence. You seemed to be well occupied."

He chuckled. "Polly, you mean. She's okay. Just missing her boyfriend."

"She's very sexy."

"Good golly, Miss Molly. I do believe you're jealous." He sounded bloody gleeful.

"Don't be daft. I was simply concerned that you might be had up for cradle snatching and the turtle program would go down the gurgler."

He sat up and pulled a plastic bag out of his pocket. I watched him as he rolled a joint. He and I were poles apart. Good to be reminded. He flicked a lighter and sucked in a deep breath. Then he handed it to me.

"Have a puff. Think of it as medicinal."

"I don't thanks. I like to be in control."

"That I know. But guess what, a few puffs won't take that away from you, and I won't tell a soul if it does."

I looked at him, expecting to see amusement in his eyes. But what I saw there was softness. My hand went out and I took the joint and put it between my lips. I coughed a little; it had been more than twenty-five years since I had given up smoking—tobacco that is, never marijuana.

After a few puffs I handed it back. I lay down and looked at the stars. The joint floated back to me. I was eager for it now. I turned on my side and smiled at Tom lying there looking at me.

"That's a pretty pendant." He moved my hand from it and tugged it gently and our lips met. I pulled away, a small frisson of shock at my behavior shivering through me. He kissed me again and I tasted the smoke in his warm breath. I rolled its sweetness around and then felt his tongue in my mouth. It was what I wanted. Where I wanted to be.

EIGHT

On New Year's Day I woke groggy and headachy and generally a mess. How on earth would I face Tom? I needed new data sheets before my turtle watch, so I forced myself along the track to his place, rehearsing what I would say to defuse the situation. He was leaving on his own patrol when I reached his house, and before I had a chance to speak he grinned at me, gave me a chaste peck on my cheek, and carried on as usual. I suppose last night was just jolly New Year japes to him. For me, not quite so simple.

By nightfall the turtles were everywhere. So many were laying that I couldn't keep up, and saw, too late, at least two returning to the sea before I'd had a chance to see if they were already tagged or to measure them. By now there were so many buried nests that quite often a turtle would dig up eggs from some poor mother's earlier efforts.

About an hour into my patrol Polly appeared, all rigged out in her own tagging belt and headlamp. She had shorts on but they were not as skin-tight as her party outfit.

"Tom asked me to come and help you out," she said as I struggled to tag a turtle already on her way back to the sea.

"Thanks, but I can manage." I could hear how unwelcoming I sounded.

"It doesn't look like it. I've been doing a tagging stint for five years now, so I know the drill. It's like this all around the island tonight; our turtle mums have decided to come up in their droves."

She sounded friendly. Perhaps I'd misjudged her—and it was hardly my call to make if Tom had told her to help.

"Sorry. You're right. Why don't you start where the beach rock begins and work back towards me; so far I have only got from the wharf to here."

"Will do," she said, and off she went.

Hours later, when the last turtle had cleared the beach, we met up and counted data sheets. She had tagged and measured eighteen turtles, and I'd managed twenty with my hour's start. She took my data forms to deliver to Tom's house before going back to her own place. I felt usurped, but at the same time relieved. After that, each evening she collected replacement forms and tags for both of us, so I had no reason to see Tom. For the next three weeks we did my patch together, and I came to like her quite a lot. She loved it as much as me—in fact, one night she told me I was doing what she wished she had the guts to do: chuck in her lawyer job and live here. I missed her when she left for her other life in Sydney. But I felt positively gleeful that I got to stay. My past life in Boston seemed almost a dream, and a bad one at that.

I never did discover whether there was anything going on between Polly and Tom. I didn't think so, but what would I know?

BABY TURTLES WERE ERUPTING EVERYWHERE. THE FIRST time I saw it, I was sitting quietly by myself on the beach near my cabin, having a pre-dinner gin and tonic. Out of the corner of my eye I caught a movement in the unblemished, innocent sand. First a little head, then two small flippers, and then the whole body popped out. It reminded me of a baby being born. Which is what it was, of course. Another emerged and then another and all at once the sand had turned into a miniature volcano spewing out baby turtles, all perfectly formed and exact copies of their parents. They scuttled down the gentle slope towards the lightness of the sea, tumbling over each other and sometimes turning head over tail and landing with all flippers flailing in the air in their hurry to get away. They were like little clockwork toys. Each one about five centimeters long from head to tail.

Every night after that more and more nests expelled their young. Sometimes I'd be sitting on my deck with the light shining in the cabin behind me, and I'd spy a gaggle of clock-work turtle babies scuttling towards me. Their instinct told them to move towards the light, usually the sea, and on a moonless night the cabin lights confused them. Grabbing my shower bucket, I'd scoop as many up as possible and take them down to the edge of the sea and watch them swim off, either to be eaten by something before they got to the reef edge, or, if they managed to escape that fate, never to be seen again until they were dinner plate size.

Nesting turtles still came up nightly, laying extra eggs in the ancient hope of replacing all the babies that would be lost. All around me, life was exciting. And for once I was part of it. When Polly departed, Tom and I took up where we left off— that is, before our marijuana-fueled lapse into inappro-priateness. It was as if that had never happened.

Soon we made a plan for me to go with Tom on one of his trips to Lost Cay, a tiny coral island about an hour's boat ride from Turtle Island, to do a turtle count. We would camp on the beach for two nights. I was nervous about the boat trip;

Tom said it was usually pretty rough careering over the reef in a small dinghy. But he'd also made it clear that I didn't need to feel nervous about being alone with him on a deserted tropical island. That didn't stop me dreaming though.

TWO HOURS AFTER MY STIR-FRIED CHICKEN DINNER, I thought I was going to die. Drenched in cold sweat, I crawled into the bathroom and lay on the floor with my forehead on the concrete slab in the shower cubicle. I had no chance of getting outside to the toilet. When the vomit exploded out of me, covering everything in sight, I was barely able to lift my head out of it. The rest of the night I lay on my bed, swathed in towels with a bucket at the ready, and waited for the next wave of stomach cramps to send me crawling outside to the toilet. But I didn't vomit again. I wondered if Tom would realize I wasn't doing my turtle patrol, but it seemed unlikely, as I had already collected new data sheets and tags before the stir-fried chicken—the last chicken I'd be eating in a long while. I must have touched my mouth with my fingers before washing them after cutting the bird up. Bad mistake.

I was meant to meet Tom at the wharf at nine o'clock, and by eight I knew that wasn't going to happen. Although I was over the worst, I felt weak and my stomach and head were still aching. The thought of bouncing over the briny in a small boat was not pretty. Fortunately, just before nine Kirsty came past, whistling as usual, on her way to help out Violet with the cabin cleaning. I called her over and she took about a second to realize I was sick; apparently I was as white as bird shit. She said she would tell Tom to go without me and promised to make him understand that I didn't want him coming to check on me; I felt far too miserable.

I was boiling some of my precious bottled water for a cup of peppermint tea when he appeared. I was still dressed in the T-shirt and knickers I had pulled on after I'd covered my pajamas with vomit. The T-shirt just covered my knickers, which were plain and beige. I was acutely aware of how I looked, with my hair a wild mess and my face pallid and drawn. Tom had never seen me in anything shorter than my longish shorts. I grabbed a towel that was hanging over the back of a chair and wrapped it around my waist, drawing attention to my mortification.

"How are you feeling?" Tom asked.

I looked at him. He appeared concerned and unaware of my ridiculous behavior. "A bit better. Why are you here? Why haven't you left?"

"No problem. We can put it off a day or two, until you feel better."

"I didn't want you to change your plans. I might not be better for days."

"Let's wait and see. If it's just a tummy bug you'll be right as rain in twenty-four hours. We'll plan to go the day after tomorrow. You can get two good nights' sleep without having to do a turtle patrol."

I felt the panic rising, and my heart began to pound as I remembered how much courage it had taken to walk up the gangplank onto Jack's big fishing boat. What had I been thinking, agreeing to go on that tiny dinghy with him? What if it turned over?

"Can I get you anything?" Tom was saying.

"No. Thanks. I'll just have a sleep I think. When I've had this tea."

"Good idea. You do look a bit under the weather. What do you think it was?"

"A violent reaction to some chicken I ate last night I suspect."

"Yuck. Poor you. Should you be drinking that tea?"

"I think it'll be okay. I only vomited once last night, but it felt as if it purged everything from my system."

Tom was already back out on the deck. "I'll drop by in a couple of days to make sure you're ready for the trip. Pat said she'd be by later today. She'll probably make you soup or something."

"For heaven's sake, there's no need for all this fuss. I'd rather be left alone." I felt the old irritation with people building inside.

"I know the feeling. But it will be hard to stop Pat." His white grin flashed. I felt mean.

"Thanks for coming to see me."

"Right. Look after yourself." He was off down the track.

I dozed on and off after that with the fan blowing over my hot body, and nightmares of boats and dead turtles lingering on the edge of my memory each time I roused. By midday I felt almost normal, and rather silly. Perhaps it wasn't the chicken. Perhaps it was psychosomatic, my way of avoiding the trip. I was a master at that—finding excuses not to do things that some part of me desperately wanted to do, and another part of me was too scared of. What if I failed?

Around two in the afternoon Pat showed up and took over. She'd been over earlier in the morning, she said, but I had been sound asleep. Within minutes she had me sitting down to a steaming bowl of the most delicious vegetable broth I have ever consumed. I wouldn't mind betting that Tom had experienced her ministrations in the past—either that or he's a good guesser. An hour after the broth I felt much stronger and hadn't thrown up or had stomach cramps, so she made me a soft-boiled egg and toast soldiers. When she left around four o'clock, I was almost my old self again, and felt an urge to write something. I sat down at the table and opened up my computer.

Toast soldiers with marmite. An egg so soft it was almost not cooked. A coddled egg, Mum called it. A large glass of hot, freshly squeezed lemon, sweet with honey. A fire in the open fireplace in our lounge even though it was not really cold, just one of those early-autumn, dreary gray days London is so good at. The tartan rug snuggled around me as I lay propped up with pillows on the couch, the tray of invalid food on my lap. Mum sitting on the floor, her back against the couch, her face lit by the flickering flames. Her blond hair smooth and shining. I can see her bright red jersey and soft gray wool skirt, her shapely legs, clad in opaque black tights, stretched towards the warmth. I must have been about ten. About two years after she and Dad split up and we'd had to move to the pokey flat above the shop. So long since I've thought about those rare good times when I felt that Mum cared about me. I knew she loved me, of course, but I mean cared about me enough to not go to work so she could be with me. She even read me stories that time when I was sick. I'd had measles and was home for two weeks. Mum had to take her annual holiday early to look after me.

Where was Dad then? I can't remember him ever coming to see me that time. I suppose he was off on his travels writing other peoples' stories. I remember Mum once calling him a celebrity father when he arrived late to pick me up for one of our wonderful weekend outings. Later I asked Dad what she meant, and he told me that it was because he wrote articles that people read, and he travelled and met lots of interesting people, and that Mum was probably a bit jealous. I was pretty hard on Mum. I know that, but we're so different. It's almost funny to think we're mother and daughter. Nothing she did interested me, and how she looked just rubbed in how I looked. To be fair, she wasn't one of those mothers who tried to force me to be something I wasn't. She didn't make me wear fancy clothes or tell me I was plain. In fact, I'm not sure now why she irritated me so much—why I blamed her for everything. I suppose it was just the usual mother-daughter thing, although I thought that wasn't meant to happen until kids got into their teens. I was a strange kid and that's all there is about it. A strange kid who grew into a strange adult.

My rumbling stomach stopped me writing any more. So I made myself some more toast and smothered it in the Australian version of marmite. I felt like having a bloody good cry but forced myself to open my Kindle and read something mindless instead.

NINE

———————

There I was, with Tom, on a deserted tropical island. I ran out of excuses and found myself getting into the dinghy two days after my vomiting experience. Tom's assurance that the sea was as calm as a millpond and the weather report was for hot settled weather for the next week was accurate; the hour-long trip from Turtle Island to the perfect little coral blip in the middle of a turquoise sea was completely smooth and quite delightful.

Tom kept his camping stuff and turtle tagging gear stored in two large tin trunks under the trees. Apart from that the only sign of human habitation was a one-meter-square canvas enclosure that hid a long-drop toilet. As Tom erected the single tent on a flat patch of grass under a Casuarina tree, my heart began to thump. I think he heard it, because he turned and leered at me.

"I never sleep in the tent. If you want to, you can. Or you can sleep under the stars. I've got two groundsheets, so our sleeping bags can be as widely spaced as you like."

"Oh. Do you put your sleeping bag straight onto the groundsheet? Isn't that a bit uncomfortable?" I was perfectly aware I was talking to cover my embarrassment.

"Good lord, woman. This is luxury accommodation, I'll

have you know. I have nice thick sleeping mats as well. And if it looks like rain I can rig up a tarpaulin overhead. But it won't rain in the next few nights."

The campsite established, we walked around the island—it took all of forty-five minutes. Like Turtle Island, the center was covered in Pisonia trees with their sticky buds, every branch overflowing with the squawking nests of noddy terns. Underfoot were the burrows of thousands of ghost shearwaters, and around the perimeter of the central forest, Casuarinas drooped their feathery branches. There was not another island in sight, nor a boat of any kind. When we arrived back at the tent, Tom opened up the insulated cool box he had brought with him—called by the Aussies an Esky, for some reason— and extracted all sorts of goodies. Then he laid and lit a fire in the circle of blackened stones in front of the tent, and within minutes had the kettle boiling. After two chunky cheese, tomato, and pickle sandwiches and some of Pat's yummy shortbread, I was ready for a nap in spite of two cups of coffee.

"The tide's not right for a nap," Tom said. "It will be full out at four o'clock, so if we want to get a dive in, we have to go now."

"You go. I'll stay here."

"Anna, this is one of the most pristine and stunning reefs you will ever have the chance to see. Get your wetsuit on and let's go."

"Tom, I can't dive. All I do is snorkel over the reef flats."

"I'll take you out over the reef edge. You don't have to dive."

"I'd rather just muck around in the shallows. You go off and dive. I'll be fine." And I did, all of a sudden, want to be out there, floating in the blue. But only where I could touch the bottom. I disappeared into the tent and got changed.

The coral was breathtaking—more colorful and many more species than around Turtle Island. I could see Tom out of the corner of my eye, flippering alongside me, as I mooched about over the coral flats. The water was getting deeper as we neared the edge of the reef and I had to slow my breathing. Time to turn back. Then Tom reached out and grasped my hand and I found myself almost pulled along beside him as he kept moving into the deeper water. And then we were over the side and the blue dropped away, down, down into the depths. Giant corals clung to the steep sides of the reef and hundreds of fish, from big to tiny, swam below me and around me. My heart was thumping and I thrashed my feet, trying to pull away from Tom and back to the safety of the reef flat. But he held my hand firmly and continued to pull me along beside him.

We had now turned and were swimming along the reef edge, with Tom on the outside, protecting me from the bottomless sea. With his free hand he pointed to this fish and that, and I looked. I stopped thrashing and hung in the water, the beauty below me making my heart sing instead of thump. I saw Tom forming the okay sign under the water, his thumb and forefinger joined in a circle, and I nodded, then made the sign back. He pointed down, and let go my hand. I watched him as he arrowed into the depths and disappeared into a cave I could now make out far below. It seemed like many minutes before he was at my side again, shooting the water from his snorkel.

We swam slowly along, and in front of us was a silver wall. It parted and formed again as we swam through it—thousands of sleek silver fish all turning as one. A large green turtle swam gracefully below us and then, out of the shadows came the streamlined shape of a small shark. My feet thrashed and I turned blindly towards the reef flat, water sloshing down my snorkel tube, and under the seal of my mask. I felt my hand being pulled back and I turned my head towards Tom. He was holding his fingers in a circle and I stopped thrashing and forced myself to blow the water out of my snorkel. I looked down. The shark was still there gliding below us, but rapidly leaving us behind. I could see the white tip on its dorsal fin. Tom stuck his head out of the water and I heard him say, "Harmless white-tip reef shark," and my heart slowed down a little.

Tom turned and I turned with him, and we swam back along the edge, Tom diving down every few minutes. But each time he returned he took my hand again. Soon he angled back over the reef flats, where the water was rapidly becoming shallower as the tide flooded out over the edge. I felt as if I had climbed to the top of Everest. That nothing could ever surmount this.

OUR REAL REASON FOR BEING ON THE ISLAND WAS TO carry out a nesting turtle count and tag any untagged turtles. Tom did this once a month during the nesting season. High tide was at ten o'clock tonight and the turtles would be nesting two to three hours each side of that. The previous month, Tom had counted over sixty turtles every night on this tiny island, and he expected about the same tonight. We would be busy. I offered to cook the evening meal but Tom said he had it all planned, and by half past six we were feasting on smoky steak, mashed potatoes, and salad. Four fragrant mangoes and a bottle of very pleasant South Australian cabernet sauvignon also disappeared. We agreed that two small glasses each would not be sufficient to muddy our scientific tagging endeavors. The sun set in a soft rose and apricot sky as the shearwaters flew back to their mates, landing all around us as we sat on a bleached log on the beach. It was dark when we split up at eight o'clock to start the turtle watch, me on the tent side of the island and Tom on the far side.

Tired and happy, I watched my twenty-eighth turtle slipping back into the water as Tom's slim figure appeared around the curve of the island. It was half-past one in the morning. I managed to stoke life into the embers in the fireplace and boiled the kettle, and we sat, barely speaking, and drank hot tea, contentment shimmering in the moonlit air. Tom spread out a groundsheet and placed the two sleeping mats side by side, but not touching. After changing into clean knickers and a very long T-shirt in the tent, and spreading out my sleeping bag on one of the mats, I wriggled into it. I could hear Tom moving about behind me somewhere, and then he was lying beside me, his sleeping bag unzipped. I turned towards him, feeling hot. I unzipped my sleeping bag, and threw the top aside. I could see Tom's smile in the moonlight. He had on an old T-shirt and I suppose his underwear, although I didn't like to look. He leaned over the gap between us and kissed me. His lips felt like a moth's wing.

"Goodnight, sweet Anna. Sleep well under your stars."

When I woke, I could feel the heat of the sun on my body. Tom's sleeping bag was empty and Tom nowhere in sight. He couldn't be far. I was bursting, and scuttled off into the bush. When I came back Tom was there, lighting the campfire. After that, the day went by like a dream. This time, when we went out over the edge of the reef, my heart didn't thump as much and I didn't thrash my flippers and try to flee even when Tom pointed out an enormous moray eel as it snaked from a hole below us. Before the tide fell too low to get the dinghy out over the flats, we puttered around the island and well out past the reef edge on the other side, where we were permitted to fish. Well provisioned as always, Tom produced a fishing rod for me as well as for him, and showed me how to attach soft baits to catch a fish for our supper. Within two minutes I had a bite, and then a fat coral trout landed flapping in the bottom of the boat. I was so excited, we almost capsized. I couldn't quite bring myself to kill the jeweled fish; the adrenaline rush from the catch was all I could handle. Tom declared that there would be no more fishing, as we had sufficient for our dinner, and we puttered around the remainder of the island.

Our turtle watch was an hour later than the night before, so we had a more leisurely feast. Over the best fish I have ever tasted, we talked. Protected by the flickering firelight, I told Tom about Dad, and how he died.

When, after completing our turtle patrol, we met up again around two o'clock, it seemed natural to put our sleeping mats close together and lie down side by side with our sleeping bags unzipped. Perhaps the tot of whisky we drank with our tea helped, and when Tom reached for me I moved into the safety of his arms without hesitation. When we were naked, I almost stopped him as he got up to scrabble in his pack for a condom. I didn't want him to go, even for a moment. But he had more sense. By the time he entered me, it felt as if there was not a centimeter of my body he had not caressed and kissed. I was a touch shyer, but later, after we had slept a little and woken again, our naked bodies a little cold even in the balmy tropical air, I took my turn to explore him. He was beautiful and young and smooth. I felt beautiful too.

In the morning, the morning of the day we were returning to the real world, we were quiet as we packed up. Tom wanted to take the dinghy out over the flats by one o'clock in order to make it safely over the reef flats at Turtle Island before the tide was too far out. We squeezed in one last snorkel before we left, and this time, with Tom at my side, I dove down into the depths and came up, heart pumping, and blew the water brazenly out of my snorkel.

❦

Dear Fran,

It's a while since I wrote, and ages since I got a letter from you. I think about you a lot, and miss your smiley face. I am loving it here, and can hardly recall, or even imagine anymore, what it was like living in Boston and working in that cold lab day after day. Last week I went to another little island with Tom, the man who does the turtle research. I told you how I'd been snorkeling over the reef flats, but now I have been out over the reef edge into the deep ocean, and even diving down. It is wonderful, Fran, and so freeing. I think I've almost got the best of the fear I've had of the sea ever since Dad disappeared when he was diving. I don't ever want to leave. What will I do when my year comes to an end? Only eight more months to go.
Love, Anna.

TEN

————————

Tom has gone, leaving an empty place in my heart.
A month earlier I would not have believed I had it in
me to think such a purple thought. He'd soon be back,
which made that thought even more melodramatic. It was
March, and the turtle-nesting season was winding down,
giving Tom the opportunity to spend some time with his
parents. It had been a mass exodus. Pat had gone as well to see
her grandchildren in Melbourne, and Bill and Violet had
taken their kids off-island for their twice-annual grandparent
bonding session. So with Bill away, Tom had left the data entry
up to me—I felt ridiculously proud of this. It also gave me an
excuse to loll about every day in his house, sitting at his
computer. One night, after Ben and I had finished the turtle
patrol—only twelve turtles up that night—I came back to
Tom's place and lay on his bed. My dreams there were always
of higher quality than the dreams I dreamed in my own bed.

We'd made love—how decadent that sounded, vibrating
around my mind—a few times since that first time. Four, to be
precise. It was nothing like I remembered, although I suppose
the likelihood of accurately recalling a sensory memory after
twenty-two years is not high. I knew his body so well now, but
so little about him. Looking around his house, there was almost

nothing personal to see. A few books, a pile of CDs, a change of clothes, and a black-and-white photo in a simple wooden frame. When I first picked it up I thought it was of Tom with a wife and two children. Tom caught on pretty quickly when it clattered onto his bedside table.

"That's me when I was a kid," he said, his voice carefully casual.

I picked it up again. The man was still the spitting image of Tom, but now I could see some subtle differences—the way identical twins become different as you get to know them. The pretty woman standing close to him had the look of a flower child, a hippie. Her dress was loose and flowing and her long black hair looked as if it had lost a flower. The Tom look-alike, Tom's dad I assumed, looked less dated, except perhaps for his rather long hair, and the two kids looked no different from today's kids: shorts and T-shirts and cheeky grins.

"I was about ten when that was taken, and Hilary must have been seven. She's married with two kids now. Lives in Melbourne. My parents still live in the house we grew up in, in Sydney." His face went still. "Dad's got dementia. Mum won't be able to look after him at home much longer."

I touched his arm but he shook his head. "Talking doesn't help."

I had managed to discover that Tom had had a vasectomy. He told me because he ran out of condoms; said he only used them to protect against STDs, and that he was pretty sure he was as clean as a whistle. That makes two of us, I said. Clean as the proverbial whistle. For some reason we found these revelations hysterically funny. Love is a strange beast.

Was I really contemplating being in love?

I asked him why and when, and he said he'd got the cut when he was twenty-five because the world was already overcrowded. I muttered my agreement. Not everyone had to have kids. I could imagine Tom carefully thinking it all through, and then just doing it.

WHEN I GOT BACK TO MY CABIN, IT WAS MID-MORNING. On my table was a note from Basil.

Cyclone warning. It probably won't come to anything but batten down the hatches just in case.

Holy cow, let's hope it doesn't come to anything. The island was only about three meters above sea level at its highest point. I looked up at the sky. The usual bright blue, and the trees dancing a little in the breeze.

I walked down the side track that led to Basil's house and found him battening down his hatches. He was hammering a piece of ply over a window. Two of the others were already covered up.

"This looks serious," I said as he climbed down from his ladder.

"It's impossible to tell if it will stay on track for this part of the coast, but if it does hit us it could do a lot of damage. Best to be on the safe side."

"How do you know about it? Does everyone else on the island know too?"

"They will by now. I got a radio message this morning. Heron Island and Lady Elliot are being evacuated, just in case."

"Well they have tourists on them. I suppose they can't take any risks." Moth wings fluttered in my throat.

"That's about it. We haven't got the same resources here. Jack's not due over until next week and the other boats we could scrape together aren't big enough to risk starting back to the mainland now. In any case, there are only a few people here so we should be able to ride it out. That's why I'm fixing up my place; it's the sturdiest house on the island. We can all squash in if necessary."

"I'm not sure how I could fix up my cabin. What do I do about those sliding glass doors? They take up the entire front."

"I'll come over after I've finished here and nail some battens across them. That will help a bit. Otherwise if it looks grim, come over here."

"When will we know? If it's going to hit us, I mean."

"Have you got a radio? Listen to that; it will keep you updated. We'll get plenty of warning."

I soon learned that Cyclone Hamish had been developing since the fourth of March, and was tracking down the Great Barrier Reef from Cape York. Today was the eighth of March, and as Basil had said, Heron and Lady Elliot Islands, not far south of us, were being evacuated. I checked the campground. Thank goodness the busy season was over; most of the students had left the previous weekend, reluctantly returning to a new university year. There were two tents left: Kirsty's and one other that belonged to two young scuba divers from New Zealand. The occupants were nowhere to be seen.

I walked over to Diane and Ben's cabin. Their windows were already covered, and the deck and surrounding grass were cleared of all the junk usually dumped on them. Kirsty was there too, sitting on the deck, and I found myself snapping at her. "You should be getting your tent down, not sitting around here."

"Keep your hair on, Anna," Ben said. "I'm going over there to do that as soon as I've finished here. Kirsty can't do it in her condition."

"Sorry, of course not. Sorry, Kirsty. I must be a bit uptight. I've been in Boston when we've had hurricanes, but it's a bit scarier being stuck on a lump of coral in the middle of the ocean."

Kirsty hauled her bulk out of the chair and groaned. She looked enormous. I hadn't realized how far on she was.

"Are you all right? You should have left the island weeks ago by the look of you. When are you due?"

"Not for another five weeks, so calm down. I'm leaving next week when Jack comes back."

"Where are you going to sleep tonight? You can't stay in your tent."

"Obviously not. I'm staying here with Diane and Ben. What about you? Will you be okay alone over there?"

"Of course. I don't know. I'll wait and see, I suppose. Basil seems to think we should all go to his house if it gets really nasty."

IT WAS GETTING NASTIER BY THE MINUTE. THAT morning I'd never heard of Hamish—shows how totally cut off I'd been from the world—and twelve hours later I was cowering on the top bunk, surrounded by my pitiful collection of things: computer, passport, books, first aid kit, Jeff's radio, my anorak, my boots, a large plastic bottle of water, head torch, gas lamp, two candles and a lighter, some cheese and a block of dark peppermint chocolate. It was hot and humid with the doors and windows tight shut. In fact, it was the first time I'd ever shut the sliding doors across the front of the cabin.

My migration to the top bunk was in case of flooding. Fifteen years earlier the island had suffered badly from a cyclone, and all the houses had flooded in the torrential rains, backed up by an exceptionally high tide and gale-force winds. It took years, apparently, for the vegetation and noddy tern numbers to recover. Not that it was going to happen this time, but better to be safe than sorry.

Basil came by—blew by would be more accurate—before dark to check on me. Apparently the cyclone had veered away from its beeline for us, and all we would get was the edge of it. That meant torrential rain and gale-force winds. Basil had the two New Zealanders from my campground with him; they were bunking down in his house that night. I declined his repeat invitation to join them. Especially now that I knew Hamish—such a gentle name—was not going to annihilate us.

But I was wavering. I wasn't sure the cabin would hold up if it got much worse: it was rocking and rolling with every howl of the wind. Even thinking was becoming impossible over the thunder of the rain. Perhaps I should make a dash for Basil's place. It was now or never. If I didn't do it soon I'd drown on the way.

Sliding off the bunk, I pulled on my anorak and boots. There was an almighty crash, and I waited a moment before turning on my headlamp and gingerly sliding the door open. I was almost blown over by the force of the wind as soon as I stepped out on the deck, and I grabbed one of the posts that held up the roof. Then I saw a light wavering its way towards me. *It must be Basil to the rescue.* I was ready to hug him. But it was Ben who loomed out of the gloom. He was shouting in my ear.

"It's Kirsty. She's in labor. You need to come."

"Oh, my god." *Please no, please no.* I could hear the mantra repeating in my head.

"Have you got any medical stuff?" Ben yelled.

"What sort of medical stuff?"

"Medical supplies, forceps. I don't know. You're the doctor."

"Shit." I forced my way back through the door and retrieved my first aid kit from the top bunk. A fat lot of use that would be.

Within seconds of leaving the comparative shelter of the deck I was soaked through. I may as well not have bothered with my anorak; it was useless. Never had I seen such rain. It was as if a dam had burst in the sky. Leaves and branches were whipping past us and sand lashed my bare legs and face. I scurried after Ben as he made his way along the beach. I peered towards the sea, certain I would see massive waves pounding the shore, about to engulf us. But I could see nothing through the rain curtain. Finally we got to Ben's cabin and fell through the door into the bright light.

"Thank god," said Diane. She looked crazy, her curly dark hair standing on end. I followed her into the adjoining room. Kirsty was squatting on the floor, gripping the side of the double bed. She was panting and clearly into a contraction. I could see her pale buttocks protruding below her pink-and-white-striped nightshirt. I shucked off my anorak and dropped down beside her, my heart contracting every bit as much as her enormous belly.

"We've boiled water and got all the towels and sheets we could find. I tried to get her to lie on the mattress but she wouldn't; she wanted to squat." Diane's voice was shaking.

The bed had been pushed against the wall, leaving about two meters of floor space free. There was a sheet spread over the floor.

Kirsty groaned.

"How far apart are the contractions?" I asked, hoping someone would answer.

"I've been timing them. They're about four minutes apart," Diane said.

"How long has she been in labor? Why did you wait so long before you came for me?"

"She didn't realize it was real labor until her contractions started coming quickly."

Kirsty's body relaxed and she collapsed back on her bottom and looked around at me. Diane squatted beside her and began to rub the small of her back.

"It was around dinnertime—about six o'clock—when I had the first contraction," Kirsty said, still breathing hard. "I thought it was one of those practice ones I'd read about. The baby's not due for weeks yet." She let out a shuddering sigh. "I didn't want to worry Diane and Ben so I told them I was going next door to Violet's to lie down. I was going to sleep over there because there's no room here."

Diane rubbed her back harder. "Never mind. It's all right now."

"I think I even got a bit of sleep but then the contractions woke me and they were a lot more painful. I was too scared to move, or go outside in that rain and wind. God knows how I got over here."

She grabbed my hand as another contraction took her over. "Shit, shit, shit," she screamed.

"Kirsty, I'm going to wash my hands and then I'll need you to lie on your back on the bed for a minute so I can see how dilated you are," I said as soon as the contraction was over. I snuck a look at my watch. It was close to midnight. She'd been in labor for six hours.

In the main room next to the bedroom, Ben had every saucepan on the stove. On the table was a pile of towels. I grabbed one and wiped my face, arms, and legs, and scrubbed my soaking hair. "Can you get me a bowl with hot water in it so I can scrub my hands? It's bottled water you're boiling, I hope, not the noddy-shit variety."

Ben looked at me. "That's meant to be a joke, I assume. Here you go. Do you want this carbolic soap? It stinks but I use it to get the fishy smells off my hands."

"Thanks. Do you have anything I can use for a lubricant? Vaseline? K-Y Jelly?"

"Both."

"Gosh, you are well prepared."

"Not for this, unfortunately. The Vaseline stops our wet-suits rubbing and the K-Y Jelly—well, I'll leave that to your imagination. Diane's also got some baby oil she uses on her legs."

"I don't suppose you've got any sterile gloves hanging around as well?"

"No, sorry. Tom has some at his place. Do you want me to hike over there and get them?"

"What on earth does he have gloves for?"

"He uses them when he's examining the gut contents of the turtles; he has to push a tube down them. And he does post-mortems on dead ones and he uses the gloves then."

"Right. Well perhaps once we see how long Kirsty is going to take, if you can get over there safely in this bloody cyclone you could get the gloves. But wait a bit. We might need you here." I was scrubbing my hands and arms furiously with the tar-smelling soap, using what looked like a clean nailbrush.

Kirsty was lying on her side on the bed when I went back in, her face screwed up in agony as another contraction ripped through her. When it was over I helped her roll onto her back. She winced when her eyes were assaulted by the bright over-head light as it swung wildly above her with every fresh howl of the wind.

"Can we light a gas lamp in here and turn the light off?" I asked Diane. She disappeared for a second and two minutes later Ben brought in the lighted lamp and vanished rapidly back out the door.

When Kirsty's legs were splayed wide, I aimed the beam of my headlamp between them, and with one hand pressing gently, low on her belly, I inserted a lubricated finger. The last time I had done this was as an intern, over twenty-five years ago, when I was on a three-week rotation in Obstetrics. Even then I'd observed only a handful of births and had been permitted to feel the cervix and feel how much it was dilated in only two of them. Dear god, I hoped I'd been paying attention. I felt a shiver of relief as my finger remembered what it was supposed to find. The cervix was about four centimeters dilated. It was all coming back to me. Ten centimeters and the baby's head should be engaged.

Before I could remove my finger Kirsty went into another contraction and I felt the powerful uterine muscle squeeze under my hand on her belly and travel down to my captured finger. I felt a rush of adrenaline. I had liked this part of doctoring. It was the dealing with the human emotions that I couldn't handle.

Diane and I helped Kirsty back onto the floor. I thought she might cope better in the doggy position. With pillows cushioning her knees and hands, she knelt there, her buttocks pointed towards me, and her enormous belly tight as a drum and almost touching the ground. Diane made up an ice pack from the bag of ice they had in their freezer and placed it on the back of her hot neck. It seemed to help.

For endless hours Diane and I hyperventilated along with Kirsty as she panted and groaned and wailed through contraction after contraction, ever stronger and closer together.

Every six or so contractions she changed position and squatted, holding on to the edge of the bed. In between contractions Diane massaged her shoulders and back and I massaged her perineum with baby oil. I had the scissors from my medical kit boiling in the kitchen, but no way did I want to have to do an episiotomy. I silently thanked the midwife who, all those years ago, had taught me how to soften and gently stretch the perineum so it would be less likely to tear when the baby's head was delivered.

Just after four in the morning Kirsty's water broke, gushing over my legs and shorts as I sat behind her kneeling body, my own legs splayed on either side of her. I inserted three fingers into her vagina and felt the baby's hard skull pressing against the fully dilated cervix. My heart was pounding in my chest.

"You're doing well, Kirsty," I shouted against the howling wind and torrential rain that had not abated one iota throughout the long night.

Another contraction shook her body. "I've got to push. Get it out of me. Shit, shit, shit, it hurts. I can't do it, give me something for fuck's sake." The contractions were coming fast now; she hardly had time to take a breath before the next one ripped her up.

"Why on earth do people think childbirth is beautiful?" I hoped no one heard my mumbled words over the racket outside. "The baby is coming, Kirsty," I yelled. "Hang in there, girl. Not long now."

"I've got to squat," Kirsty screamed.

"Okay. Let's get you up." I knelt in front of her and she grabbed my hands in hers and clung on like a vise. I could see her inflamed vulva pulsating and gaping with every contraction.

"Diane, push a pillow—two pillows—under her backside

and get Ben in here to sit behind her and support her back," I shouted.

Ben materialized, looking as scared as I felt. I got Diane to stand behind me and grab Kirsty's hands so I could concentrate on the delivery.

Another contraction, and I saw her vulva spreading in the light of my turtle-tagging headlamp as a glistening, dark shape pushed against it. "I can see the head, it's coming, it's coming," I shouted.

Kirsty let out a bloodcurdling scream. "I'm burning. It's burning me. I'm splitting open. I can't do this."

"Yes you can. You're nearly there." I saw the next contraction coming. "Push, Kirsty, push."

"*Eeeeoooowww.*" The primitive sound pierced the stuffy room, echoing the howling wind outside.

Half the head slid out into my waiting hands.

Diane was squealing. "It's coming. Kirsty, it's coming."

"With the next contraction, push like you've never pushed before," I yelled. There was an almighty crash on the roof, and the gas lamp flickered and went out.

"Lordy, what was that?" Ben's voice sounded alien in this women's lair.

"It's coming again," screamed Kirsty. "*Eeeeoooww.*"

The rest of the head catapulted out, facing the floor, and I cradled it in one hand and tentatively explored the tiny neck. It was clear. I had been petrified that the cord would be twisted around it. I moved my hand to find the shoulder. "One more push to get the shoulders out, Kirsty."

"Go, girl," Ben yelled as another contraction shook her.

One shoulder came out and then the other. The little head coughed, and coughed again. I gently rotated the miraculous body and it slipped easily around. Now I could see the scrunched up face. I reached for the damp flannel in the bowl beside me and wiped away the mucus. Its little cries grew lustier, the lower half of its body still inside Kirsty. She was sobbing so loudly that I could hear her over the racket outside. "One more push with this next contraction and your baby is in your arms," I said.

And he slithered out, all boy. I cradled him for a second while I wiped my finger inside his soft mouth to remove the mucus. Ben was laying Kirsty back and putting a pillow under her head. Diane and Kirsty were sobbing. I looked over at Ben and the light from my headlamp fell on his face. His hand came up to cover his eyes, and I reached up and dimmed the light, feeling as if I had intruded upon a moment too intimate for him to share. Gently I passed this perfect baby to his mother, the umbilical cord still attached. I could feel my own tears seeping down my face.

I got up and stretched. My back ached, my legs ached, but my heart soared. I grabbed a soft beach towel from the now very small pile on the bed, and tucked it over the baby's tiny body, still shrouded, like an infant ghost, in greasy vernix. I pulled the towel up around his head. He stopped yowling and, cracking open his blue eyes, looked at his mother. His rosebud mouth moved into a shape resembling a smile.

I looked at Ben and Diane standing behind the fledgling family, their arms around each other and tears still trickling down Diane's weary face.

"Thank you, team," I said. "Good job, as they say in the States."

"You were amazing," Diane said. "Thank god you were here."

"She would have done it fine all by herself if she'd had to." I laid a towel over Kirsty's lower half in a belated attempt to restore her modesty. "I'd better cut the cord. Ben, could you get those scissors and pegs you've got boiling away in the kitchen, please?"

Kirsty didn't even notice when I clamped the cord with the clothes peg and then cut it, severing the lifeline between mother and child. It was clear they didn't need it now. They were forever bonded. Kirsty continued to hold him while I tied a knot in the cord, close to his little tummy, hoping I was giving him a belly button to be proud of.

I pressed my hand gently on Kirsty's lower abdomen, jelly-like now. I felt the contraction and parted her legs as the placenta slithered out, just like that. If a neuroscientist with barely a jot of experience and no kids of her own had to deliver a baby in a cyclone, Kirsty was the mother to choose. A thin river of blood trickled from between her thighs, but then it stopped, even when I pressed again on her uterus. I examined the placenta carefully. It was bright scarlet, intact, and beautiful. Holding the amazing, life-giving sac in my hands, I went into the kitchen and laid it on a paper towel on the bench. In the cupboard I found an empty ice-cream container, and in that modest vessel I reverently placed the placenta with its twisted blue cord and put it in the freezer. *I'd better remember to label it later, or Ben and Diane will be opening it and wondering what the hell it is.* I'd once heard a story about an elderly woman who, slightly blind and perhaps a little confused, almost cooked her great-granddaughter's frozen placenta, mistaking it for liver.

THE DAWN, IF WE COULD HAVE SEEN IT THROUGH THE sullen black skies, should have been breaking by the time we had settled a tired and happy Kirsty in the double bed. The baby had attempted to suckle, with a little success, and Kirsty had consumed three cups of lemon and ginger tea and a large plate of scrambled eggs. In fact we had all scoffed large plates of scrambled eggs. The howling wind and torrential rain had continued unabated. And yes, corny though it may be, Kirsty had decided to name her newborn after the cyclone.

Hamish was even clothed. To our amazement, after she had been cleaned up, Kirsty calmly announced that she had a stash of size 000 baby clothes next door, including some triangular-shaped terry-toweling diapers sized especially for newborns. Violet had carefully washed and folded Danny's baby garments for Kirsty some weeks previously, and packed them lovingly into the bassinet—complete with bedding—she had used for her own two. Apparently she was quite definite about having no more kids herself. The cloth diapers were a glorious consequence of her and Bill's dedication to saving the environment. Pat had also knitted some tiny booties, hats and jerseys. Why did this not surprise me?

When Ben and Diane returned from their mission next door to get the baby booty, they also brought back diaper liners, baby wipes, Johnson's baby powder, and zinc ointment for tender baby bottoms, all of which they had "borrowed" from the top of young Danny's chest of drawers.

So at seven o'clock, with Hamish dressed in a doll's-size purple-and-green-striped all-in-one and tucked snugly into his bassinet, his clever mother asleep in the bed beside him, Diane and Ben braved the elements once more and returned to Violet and Bill's to bunk down in their bed. I opted to sleep beside Kirsty. I wasn't about to leave her alone to hemorrhage or develop some other unlikely complication.

The noise outside and the adrenaline still pumping through my system thwarted my efforts to fall asleep, in spite of my whole body feeling as if I'd just got off a plane after a twenty-hour flight. The events of the long night replayed in my exhausted mind and I smiled into the hot darkness as I remembered how scared I'd felt only fourteen hours ago as Cyclone Hamish racked up steam and I climbed onto the top bunk in my lonely cabin, my puny possessions around me. I breathed in deeply as the timeless smell of Johnson's baby powder curled about me.

———————

We were woken by the baby's mewling cries and
Basil's "Blimey." He was standing in the door of
the bedroom, water dripping from his oilskins and
his mouth wide open. As Kirsty had another go at nursing, I
made some coffee and relayed the night's events to him. It was
ten thirty in the morning and the rain had eased a little. Basil
hadn't been able to get any radio contact to discover where the
cyclone was but he was confident that it had passed us by.
Apart from tree limbs ripped off, including one large branch
across the roof of Diane and Ben's house—no doubt the crash
that had shaken the house during the birth—he had found no
serious damage. Apart, that is, from the noddy tern chicks.
They lay, many almost fully fledged, in their hundreds on the
sodden ground, tipped out of their nests by the wind. And
there was nothing to be done. The parents wouldn't accept
them back even if we knew what nests to put them in. It was
heartbreaking. Basil said that as soon as the wind died down
he'd shovel them into his trailer and find somewhere in the
center of the island to bury them, many of them still alive.

"On the plus side," he told me, "there are still plenty in
the nests. It could have been much worse. It's nature's way of
controlling the population; otherwise it would get so enormous

the island couldn't support it. In a couple of seasons they'll be back to their maximum numbers again."

Cold comfort for the agitated parents wondering where their babies had gone. I took a peek in the bedroom and smiled when I saw Earth Mother with her tiny infant lying across a pillow on her stomach, his rosebud mouth clamped over her nipple. Kirsty was a natural. She looked up and made a face.

"He's got a grip like a moray eel," she said. "It hurts like hell."

"I suppose it will take a while to get your nipples hardened. Perhaps you should rub them with Vaseline to stop them cracking?"

"Yeah. My fanny too."

"Is it sore? Silly question, I suppose it must be."

"It's not too bad, actually. But I'm having crampy contractions all the time; they're bloody painful."

"That's normal. Stops you bleeding. Have you checked that you aren't too much? A bit is normal, but not a flood."

"I've got some blood on the diaper I stuffed into my knickers—thank god for those, they have myriad uses—but not a lot. All good, really." She scrubbed at her eyes. "Sorry. I don't know why I feel weepy. He's perfect."

"I'd be worried if you didn't feel weepy. I feel like having a good bawl myself, and I haven't done anything to deserve it."

"Gosh, Anna, you saved our lives. What would I have done without you and Diane?"

"You would have popped Hamish out all by yourself, without any trouble. But I'm glad you didn't have to. It was very special to be part of it." I wiped my own eyes. "Give me a yell when you feel up to Basil coming and having a peek, now that he's recovered from the shock. He said he'd get his fish scales and weigh Hamish if you liked. We should do, really, just for the record."

"He can come in now. I'm sure he has seen boobs before, although perhaps not this huge."

HAMISH WEIGHED IN AT SIX POUNDS THREE OUNCES—A splendid size for a baby born five weeks early. After the weigh-in, we had a meeting—Diane and Ben, Basil, Kirsty, Hamish, and me. It was decided that Kirsty and the baby would shift in with me when the winds died down. She could sleep in the bottom bunk with the bassinet beside her, and I would take the top bunk.

She got pretty upset when we began to discuss her going back to the mainland, perhaps by helicopter when it was possible to fly safely. "But I have nowhere to go to," she wailed. "Why can't I stay here for a few weeks?"

"Where were you planning to go when you went back next week?" I asked her.

"I was going to stay at Mum's place in Brisbane until she got back. She's in the UK on a holiday jaunt and she's not coming back for another month. But I didn't know I'd have a baby with me. I thought she'd be back in time for his birth, and she could help me look after him."

I stopped myself rolling my eyes. "Okay. We'll see how you and Hamish are over the next few days, and if there are no problems you can stay with me until your mum gets back."

"Anna, you are the best. Thank you. I promise we'll be no trouble."

"I'll hold you to that. No crying baby in the night, no diapers to wash." I grinned at her. "You know what, I don't want you to leave. I've never had a little baby living in my home, and I think I've missed out badly."

"How come you know so much about it, then?"

"I don't. I just remembered it from the bits I learned as an intern, and from novels I've read."

Kirsty giggled. "We'll make a great team. Here, you hold him for a bit. How can he get so heavy when he's so tiny?" She passed him, fast asleep, over to me, and I held him close.

The wild weather went on and on. Kirsty and I moved to my cabin the next day and there we stayed, both dotty about the baby. I ventured out for a walk on the beach each day, a scarf tied around my head to lessen the pain in my ears as I bent double against the howling wind in one direction and flew back in the other. The reef flats, usually so serenely lagoon-like, had been battered by surf that even three days later still thundered up the beach in front of every high tide. The sand was littered with branches, and the sea had reached almost to my cabin, leaving a high-tide line of debris partway into the campground, but there was no serious beach erosion. I hoped the nests of baby turtles ready to hatch would have some way of knowing it was not a good idea to appear, and stay put. I certainly never saw any hatching over those wild days.

Basil and Ben had cleaned up the baby noddy terns—two full trailer loads. It was amazing to me that there were any left in their nests, but the trees on the inside of the island were still alive with resilient parents blowing in and out, feeding their young. Fortunately the shearwater chicks remained snug in their underground burrows, although I supposed some of the parents would have been lost at sea.

Basil made radio contact with the mainland on the tenth of March. Cyclone Hamish had forged a path parallel to the Great Barrier Reef and never veered inland to mainland Australia. Turtle Island and the other islands on the Capricorn reef had been spared this time. From Cairns to Brisbane, winds and seas were high, and all trains and planes had been cancelled for days. Jack would not be able to get over to our little island for a while yet, and it was still way too windy for helicopters.

But Kirsty didn't need any rescuing; she was as happy as a pig in clover. Hamish was a mellow little chap, sleeping and suckling in turns. Kirsty's nipples were still tender, and every time he latched on she would screw up her face. She said the pain was so bad her toes would curl. Her determination to breastfeed him never wavered. Not that there was any option; Violet had no stocks of baby formula in her pantry. Luckily Kirsty had an abundance of milk, and Hamish was feeding every two and a half hours. The whole thing was totally involving. I now understood why nursing mothers got nothing else done.

Daytime thoughts of Tom were fleeting, but at night, as I lay in my top bunk listening to Kirsty's soft breathing and Hamish's contented little slurping noises, I allowed myself to indulge a little. What would Tom think when he returned and found me playing auntie (I refused to be an honorary grandmother, as Kirsty had at first innocently suggested)? Would he become besotted as well? Unlikely. Perhaps he'd feel a twinge of regret about his vasectomy. He would have made a wonderful father. Even though I was glad he wasn't, as that would have made us impossible.

IT WAS ANOTHER FOUR DAYS BEFORE THE WIND completely died away and the days were blue again. We all pitched in with the island cleanup. The reef was a different story. Basil was receiving dire reports of extensive damage to the delicate corals of the reef. When the tide receded we could see the damage to the exposed coral, broken up by the days of turbulent seas. It would take a survey to find out if the damage extended to the coral in the deeper waters.

Now that Basil's Skype connection was back up and running, he was able to communicate with Jack. He would be returning to the island on his usual trip the coming Saturday. Violet and Bill and their children, as well as Pat, were due back then. Tom had told me before he left that he might return then as well, but no promises. It seemed like a lifetime since we'd seen them, not two weeks. Basil had been given strict instructions by Kirsty not to let the cat out of the bag about baby Hamish's unexpected arrival. She wanted to surprise everyone.

On Saturday I must have ventured out to the beach six times before I saw Jack's boat approaching. I went back to the cabin to get Kirsty, and she hauled a sleepy Hamish from his bassinet and secured him cozily in the long shawl she wrapped around her body as a baby sling. As we almost ran along the beach to the wharf, we could see Basil, Diane, and Ben already welcoming the people coming off the boat. I could hear Chloe's excited voice as her small figure jumped up and down. Then we were there, and Pat was following Violet and Bill onto the wharf, and there were hugs and oohs and aahs as Kirsty pulled aside the shawl to reveal Hamish's little face, sound asleep again.

My heart was thumping as I looked for Tom. A petite woman with a cloud of dark, wavy hair emerged from the wheelhouse. A late-season camper? And then Tom appeared, his hair on end and his dear face split into a grin as he looked at the excited welcoming party.

Ben was slapping him on the back and Kirsty was showing

him her treasure. I felt suddenly shy. I could hardly throw myself at him; we'd been pretty discreet about our affair. Hopefully no one knew about us. I could feel the heat rising up my neck as Tom looked past Kirsty and winked at me. I shuffled towards him.

"Hi. Tom. What do you think of our new islander?" I sounded ridiculous.

"He's a corker. Can't leave you lot alone for a minute without everything going west. Babies, cyclones. I dunno." He bent and kissed me chastely on the cheek. "You okay, Anna?"

"Yes. I'm fine. Great, in fact. I'm so glad you're back though." I could feel myself mooning at him. Thank heaven for my dark glasses.

"Anna, Kirsty, meet Collette. Collette Dubinois. She's here to check up on the turtle program." He turned to the woman. "I think you've met everyone else?"

"Yes. Hullo, Diane, Ben," she said, ignoring Kirsty and me. She looked like a young Elizabeth Taylor—an impossibly perfect face. I felt like an elephant.

"Hi, Collette," said Diane. "How long are you here for this time?"

"Eight weeks perhaps. I'll see." She turned to Tom. "Let's go and get settled in. I would kill for a cold drink."

"Right. I hope I've got something in the fridge." He nodded to Jack. "Do you want a hand first to unload?"

"No thanks. Nick's gone to get the tractor. I'll deliver your stuff and Collette's in a bit. Go and get the lady settled." Jack's grin looked distinctly lecherous.

"I'll see you later, Anna. I want to hear all the gory details." Tom smiled at me, hauled on his pack, and scuttled after Collette.

Hamish had woken with all the noise, and Pat had

extracted him from Kirsty's shawl and was cuddling him, a look of wonder in her blue eyes.

"Oh Kirsty, he's a miracle. However did you manage?"

"Anna did it. And Diane and Ben. It was in the middle of the cyclone . . ."

Her words tumbled out but I wasn't listening. All I could think about was Tom and Collette. Who the hell was she? Why hadn't Tom warned me he'd be bringing her back with him? Eight weeks here, staying with Tom? What about me?

PAT CAME AROUND LATER TO ADMIRE HAMISH, AND I asked her straight out who Collette was. The good news was that she wasn't Tom's love interest, and the bad news was that she was his boss. I hadn't known he had a boss, but according to Pat, Collette was a professor at the University of Queensland and one of the principal investigators on the turtle research program. I knew what that meant: she was the one who wrote the grant applications and published the research papers, and Tom was the minion who did the hard work. I'd assumed that Tom had his own research grant and danced to his own tune. He seemed too—I didn't know, confident, I supposed—to be a mere research assistant. And Professor Collette Dubinois who, according to Pat, fancied herself as descending from the French aristocracy, looked as if she couldn't tag a turtle to save herself.

The other bad news was that she got to stay in Tom's house while she was there. It was, in fact, not Tom's house but belonged to the Queensland Parks and Wildlife Service, along with Tom's boat. They provided the grant money and paid Tom's salary through Collette's grant. It took me right back to Boston, where I was Collette—albeit a rather larger and plainer version—and my lovely researchers were my Toms. I couldn't have done my research without their fieldwork, going into the homes of Huntington's disease families and assessing their terrible symptoms and talking to them about their even more terrible fate.

Damn. My fantasies about creeping over to Tom's place at night, pretending I was tagging turtles, were custard. For a moment I almost wished Kirsty could go home to her mother, but as if she had second sight, Pat handed Hamish to me, and my heart melted. Tom could wait. I'd have little enough time to cuddle this precious little warm body.

When Pat left, I went for a stroll along the beach with a vague idea that it would be perfectly natural to drop in on Tom. I should bring him up to date on the turtle numbers since he left. I supposed Collette would want to be in on our conversation, seeing as she was the one I'd apparently been working for—voluntarily, at that—and not Tom. Luckily I was spared this pleasure as I met Tom on the beach.

"Are you checking out the cyclone damage?" I asked when he came near.

"No. I'm coming to see you." He looked at me, his face aglow in the opalescent evening light. He touched my face. "I missed you."

My whole body was instantly infused with happiness. I felt like one of Pat's rum babas—a crusty golden muffin on the surface, but pop it in your mouth and it disintegrated, every morsel bursting with sweet warm rum.

We meandered down to the water's edge. The tide was full and the lagoon was still and blue and gold. It was hard to believe it had been a thrashing sea monster only days ago. We gazed at it in companionable silence for a while, and then Tom asked me about the cyclone, and the birth. It all came tumbling out. I hadn't realized I was still so emotional about it all. Tom listened with that wonderful, intent way of his—I could feel his total focus on me. There was no one else on the beach, and he took my hand. We found a spot under the Casuarinas, back a little from the exposed beach, and sat down.

"How was Sydney? How is your father?" I should have asked him earlier, not waited until I had told him every little detail about what had happened while he was gone.

"He's not good. We had to move him into a nursing home. Mum couldn't cope any more."

"I'm so sorry. Is she okay?"

"Not really. It was hard for her to let him go, but she's exhausted. Dad often doesn't recognize her any more, and even though he is so thin now, he's too heavy for her to lift."

"That's so sad. Dementia is a tragic disease."

"I tried to get Mum to come back here with me for a break, but she wouldn't. She'll be in at the nursing home for hours every day."

"It must have been hard for you to see him like that. Did he recognize you?"

"No. I don't think so."

I fancied I could hear the anguish in his voice and leaned over and kissed him. He lay down and I lay beside him. After a while he turned towards me and gave me his crooked smile.

"Sorry about Collette. I didn't know she was coming over. It's a good job Mum didn't come back with me; she wouldn't get on with Collette."

"Would anyone?" I couldn't stop myself.

"Wicked woman. You should feel sorry for her."

"Why?"

"She's so short."

"Silly."

He drew me to him. We kissed for a long time. I felt about seventeen. In the evening light, Tom looked about seventeen. This was happiness.

HAPPY ONE MOMENT, DOWN IN THE DUMPS, THE NEXT. Like I said, I felt about seventeen. Next afternoon I went over to Tom's to go over the data Ben and I had collected. We'd just sat down at his computer and opened up the Excel file when Collette appeared from her bedroom and, without so much as a hullo, asked Tom what he was doing.

"We're going over the data Anna's entered while I've been away."

"Is that necessary? If she's entered it correctly it will be self-evident."

I might not have been there.

"Anna is an experienced researcher. She's giving me much more information than can be conveyed by the numbers on the spreadsheet."

"Well, hurry up and get it done. I want you to go over the last six months' data with me. We won't be needing volunteer help from now on."

I turned around and glared at her. "My volunteer help wasn't for you, it was for Tom. If he still wants me to help, that's for him to say, not you."

"I approve the workers on this project, not Tom. We're grateful for your assistance but it's no longer necessary. Most of the work from now on will be data analysis and inter-pretation, and preparing research papers, and that is not a job for amateurs."

"For heaven's sake, Collette. Anna's given the project an enormous amount of time. She's not an amateur. She's a senior scientist; I told you that. She's written dozens of research papers. We'd be lucky to have her input if she wanted to help. She's already shown me how we can analyze some of the data better." Tom sounded very irritated.

"Tom, we'll talk about this later. I'm going for a walk and I'll be back in an hour. I want a meeting with you then." Collette flounced out the door and Tom and I looked at each other, not knowing whether to laugh or swear. So we laughed.

"God in heaven, what did I do to deserve her?" Tom said when we'd calmed down.

"Why ever did you take on the job in the first place? You must have had an inkling of what she would be like?"

"I inherited her, for my sins. I did my PhD with her predecessor, and later he employed me as his research scientist, funded out of his research grant. Three years ago he had a heart attack, out of the blue, and that was that. One minute as healthy as a horse and next minute, dead."

"That's awful. I'm sorry."

"Yes, it was. Anyway, Collette had been appointed as an associate professor in his department the previous year, and he'd kindly added her as one of the investigators on this project. When he died, she became the principal investigator. I only have to put up with her once or twice a year when she comes over here, and occasionally when I'm in Brisbane I have to suffer for a few days. I love what I do so I put up with it."

"Why don't you try and get your own research grant?"

"I'm no academic. It would be difficult to get a grant without having a tenured university post. And in truth, it's the fieldwork I love. I'm not sure I have the ability—or the desire —to do all the complex analyzing and write research papers, even if I could get a grant without having to be an academic as well."

"Of course you could. I'd help you."

"Dear Anna. I'm sure you would, but you're leaving in October."

"I could stay."

"Don't be silly. Turtle research is a bit different from the high-level medical research you do in Boston. And you'd need a PhD in marine biology, not neuroscience."

KIRSTY WASN'T HOME WHEN, STILL FUMING, I GOT BACK. She'd left a note on the table saying that she'd taken Hamish to visit Violet and she'd make dinner when they got back. I felt better. I would miss Kirsty when she left. She was the sort of young woman who carried happiness into a room, always laughing and seeing the good side. I got myself a beer and opened up my computer. I needed to vent.

When I get back to Boston, I'll track down my research assistants, and if they're still in the area I'll take them out for dinner and thank them properly. I know I didn't appreciate them enough. I just took them for granted. All their hard work with the Huntington's families. They probably knew I could never have done it myself. But I'm sure I didn't treat them like Collette treats Tom. How he puts up with her I can't fathom. She treats him like a slave; do this, do that.

This morning, Kirsty tried to convince me that Collette might turn out to be perfectly nice and that we could even become firm friends. Pigs might fly. When she was speaking to Tom like that and ignoring me, I was shriveling up inside. Not that I showed it. But it was there. I've felt it before with those sorts of people; the ones who suck the air out of the room. Like Professor bloody Knight. My esteemed PhD supervisor. Knight by name and dark by nature. All over me until he had me where he wanted—under him. Arrogant, cold man. I hope he rots in hell. On the positive side, he makes Collette seem like a silly little girl. And at least I no longer have to worry that Tom fancies her.

TWELVE

————————

The night sweats came out of nowhere, and came with a vengeance. Of course I'd heard them described by menopausal females—they seemed to talk of nothing else—but they are impossible to imagine if you haven't actually experienced one. It's like a burning from deep inside and within milliseconds your whole body is on fire. The speed at which it happens beggars belief. There is nothing for it but to rip off all your garments as fast as possible and get outside where there might be a cool breeze. Thankfully it was quite a lot cooler on the island at night now. The southern part of the reef didn't exactly have seasons, but by April it was beginning to get too cold in the sea to swim for long without a wetsuit. Still, I spent the night leaping out of the top bunk and trying not to disturb Kirsty as I hurtled outside, ripping off my T-shirt. I did disturb her, of course, and what with Hamish's three-hourly feeds we didn't get much sleep.

It was cruel, so cruel. It was bad enough being separated from Tom—in the biblical knowledge sense, at least—until either Kirsty or Collette had left. But to have slammed in my face my looming status as a wizened up spinster, irrefutably past the age where sex was a biological imperative, is brutal. From seventeen to fifty was not the sort of time travel I was interested in.

I looked back on my last birthday with amazement. It seemed a lifetime ago. It was a lifetime ago. I could barely remember what it felt like to be lonely any more. Not that I admitted I was lonely in Boston. I always told myself that I liked being alone. If I had to go back there, how would I live with myself, all alone? How would I live without these perfumed days? *Perhaps I'll make Eggs Benedict with bacon—tinned salmon won't cut it—for breakfast next week.* Kirsty would love it, and she didn't need to know it was my birthday. I didn't want anyone to know, especially Tom. How could he feel romantic about a fifty-year-old? Of course he knew I was forty-nine, but that sounded so much younger than fifty. I'd somehow have to hide the night sweats from him, too, if we ever slept together again.

HERE WAS I THINKING I HAD SUCCEEDED IN HIDING MY upcoming birthday when the Gossip Group showed up, laden with a giant paella overflowing with sea creatures, great bowls of salad, and warm, crusty, homemade bread. Tom was behind them with his offerings of five kinds of cheese, biscuits, fresh fruit, and an enormous box of dark liqueur–filled chocolates. And wine, of course, lots of it. All together, nine of us sat down to my surprise birthday feast—Violet and Bill, Diane and Ben, Pat, Tom, Basil, Kirsty, and me. Violet and Bill's two children were sound asleep on the bottom bunk, and Hamish snuffled in his bassinet. It felt like family. The one I'd never had. The candles flickered on the table on the deck, and the stars sparkled above in the dark sky. I found myself thinking of my last birthday, crying over red wine in a posh Boston restaurant with Fran. A lifetime ago. Dear Fran; if she were here now, tonight would be better than perfect.

"How did you know?" I asked them at some point during the evening.

"Remember that first time we came over here for our book group?" Violet said.

"The Gossip Group, you mean?"

"Whatever. We were talking about our star signs and we asked you what yours was. You didn't have a clue so we asked you when your birthday was."

"And you remembered?"

"Naturally. These things are important."

"Well, I'm glad. I didn't think I wanted to celebrate it, but it's lovely. More than lovely." I was a bit tipsy, we all were, but no one had to drive.

Then Kirsty brought out a chocolate cake, "Happy Birthday Anna" blazoned across it and candles—not fifty, but a fair few—circling the outside.

"Oh, Kirsty, it's beautiful. Did you make it?"

"I did. Over at Pat's so you wouldn't see it. Happy birthday, dear Anna."

Later I asked Kirsty how they knew I was fifty. I was sure I hadn't told them my age when I let slip my birth date.

"We didn't know your age until you told us tonight. Who cares about age, anyway?"

"Oh my god. You mean I could have kept it a secret, or pretended I was forty?"

"Yep."

"Damn." I was grinning.

"Right on, girl."

Pat as well as Tom had known I was forty-nine. Neither of them had let the cat out of the bag. But I was glad it was out now, and what's more, I didn't give a toss. If only fifty didn't come packed in night sweats and hot flushes . . .

⚜

COLLETTE WAS STILL ON THE ISLAND AND GAVE NO SIGN of leaving any time soon. I had felt a bit mean that she hadn't been invited to my party, but Tom told me to stop fretting; my party was for sharing with the people I really cared about. And two of those people were soon to depart. Kirsty's mother was back in Brisbane, and Kirsty and Hamish were leaving on Jack's boat when he returned after delivering the supplies next weekend. Kirsty didn't want to go, but her mother was desperate to meet her first grandson, and in truth, Kirsty couldn't wait to show him off. The only good thing about it was that Tom and I would have some privacy at last. But if I had the power to choose, I would have kept Hamish—and Kirsty of course—there with me. My heart clenched tight as I thought about Hamish growing up in Australia, while, on the far side of the world, I trudged on through life.

At six thirty on Sunday morning, four hours before he would be gone, Kirsty passed Hamish and a fresh diaper up to me on the top bunk. I had lain awake listening as she fed him, lying below me, not caring about the tears that wouldn't stop oozing from my eyes. I changed Hamish's sodden diaper and tucked him under the sheet close to me while Kirsty boiled the kettle for our morning tea and packed the last of their things. We didn't speak; we were both feeling the impending loss.

Everyone—barring Collette—was on the wharf by ten to say goodbye. In the four months she had been there, Kirsty had become part of the community, and as Pat said, Hamish, at only four weeks old, had a unique place here. No one else still alive on the planet had actually been born on the island. Even Danny, Violet's youngest, had first seen the light of day in Brisbane.

"Time to go, Kirsty," Jack said once he'd stowed all the gear on board.

"I know," she said, her voice wobbling. I handed Hamish to her and she did the hug rounds. Hamish's eyes were wide open, taking it all in. After every person there had kissed his downy head, Kirsty came back to me.

"He's yours too," she whispered, putting him in my arms. "You'll always be part of him."

I held him close one last time. His fingers closed around one of mine and he smiled his rosebud smile. I kissed him quickly and handed him back. With a hug, Kirsty turned and almost ran up the gangplank. I felt Pat beside me, her arm around my waist. Tom was helping Jack cast off, and for a second I imagined him leaving as well.

I don't know why I am feeling so upset about Kirsty and Hamish leaving. I've never been especially interested in kids; they seem like more trouble than they're worth. If I were his aunt or his grandmother I could understand it. Obviously my involvement in his birth, and then him living here with me, gives him a special significance, almost as if I were related to him. But even that doesn't seem enough to account for my sadness. It feels deeper than that. More like grief.

I'm far too inward looking these days. Too much time on my hands, I suppose. It's all mixed up with being fifty and these annoying night sweats—the end of my childbearing years. I've had the nightmare a few times recently, the one I used to have, eons ago, over and over, after the abortion. Am I grieving for that lost child? A little late for that. It's not as if I didn't grieve when it happened—when I organized it to happen—I was a wreck for weeks. My depression back then was so mixed up with my anger and hurt over being dumped by him—I still can't even think his name without spitting—that perhaps my grief didn't get its proper due. How dare he patronize me like that. I was so naïve, so trusting. It was such a cliché and I couldn't see it—PhD supervisor, older, attractive, powerful, married—and the sweet little student, desperate to be loved.

"Pregnant? Are you sure it is mine? How could you be so careless? If you want to get your PhD you'd better keep your mouth shut. If anyone finds out you'll be in as much trouble as me. Get it aborted and we won't say any more. Our little dalliance was over anyway. My wife and I are having another baby of our own and I can't afford to take any more risks."

He didn't actually use those words but that's what it felt like. I wonder if it were a boy or a girl? I've never allowed myself to think of it as a person before. Thank goodness for young women like Kirsty with the confidence and courage to hold tight to their child and thumb their noses at the lowlifes who use and abuse and leave them. I never had that choice. I'd probably have had an abortion in the end; the last thing I needed was a baby. But it should have been my choice, not his.

I felt better after my little catharsis. *My Life* would need a fair amount of editing before being published as an account of my experiences as a research scientist.

TOM APPEARED AROUND FIVE WITH A SIX-PACK OF COLD beer. "Thought you might be ready for a cold one. Want to sit on the beach?"

We sat in silence for a while, and my throat got tighter and tighter.

"That was a rough goodbye," Tom said.

"Yes. I knew it would be hard, but this is ridiculous." I

stared down at my fingers, sifting through the sand, and swallowed as Tom's hand closed over mine. I forced myself to look at him. "On the bright side, I have my privacy back."

"Just what I was thinking. How about I cook you some dinner and then we'll have a quiet night in?" He did his sneer imitation. I felt the warmth creeping back.

Half an hour later—it was not dark enough yet for us to feel hidden in my open cabin—Tom placed two enormous bowls of seafood risotto on the table and poured me another glass of wine. I was starving. I hadn't eaten all day.

"Aha, hawksbill turtles. Have you read this?" Having cleaned his bowl, Tom had picked up an article from the haphazard pile of papers and magazines on the end of the table.

"Yes. I borrowed it from your house. I was wondering why we get so few hawksbills nesting here."

"They prefer the warmer waters farther north." He picked up another article. "What's this?" His voice had changed.

"What? What is it?" I asked.

"It's a research paper on Huntington's disease." He sounded cold.

I looked at him, but he was concentrating on the reprint he held in his hand.

"Oh, that. It's the last article I wrote," I said, grinning as I remembered Kirsty hamming it up, reading the title out loud. It looked like a foreign language—"polymerase," "microglial," "direct mutation analysis." "Huntington's" and "disease" were about the only plain English words. "Good title, huh?"

Tom was silent.

A sliver of apprehension fluttered in my chest. I tried again. "I brought a few articles with me just in case I felt motivated enough to write a new grant proposal. But I haven't. It seems light years away, all that."

"You write grant proposals for Huntington's research?"

I was beginning to feel irritated. "I'm not completely washed up, you know. Is that what you thought? That I'd never do any research of my own again?"

"You told me you did laboratory analysis of neurological changes in the aging brain."

"Yes, I do. I did. But we mainly used Huntington's patients to test our theories. I told you that."

"No, you didn't. You never mentioned Huntington's disease."

"Perhaps you weren't listening. Does it matter?"

"Not to you, apparently. I suppose if the Huntington's patients are just convenient guinea pigs, it mightn't occur to you to mention them."

"That's unfair. We have enormous respect for our research participants. My research assistants spend hours with the families. They were never treated like guinea pigs." Anger—or shame—was burning my face.

"I'm simply surprised that you never talked about your work to me."

"Well, I'm very sorry. I've had other things to think about. It's not as if you share your life story with me. I know almost nothing about your past."

"There's nothing to tell. I talk to you about my research."

"That's because I'm interested in it, and I'm helping you with it. I'm trying to have a break from mine."

Tom pushed his chair back and stood up. He placed the article carefully on the table. "It's been a long day. I'll do the turtle patrol later; no need for you to help. The nesting season's about finished anyway. You'll be able to get on with your grant writing."

"And of course you've got Collette to help you now." I heard the hurt in my voice.

"Sarcasm is not your most attractive characteristic. I'll see you around."

I was shaking as I cleared away the plates and banged them in the sink. *If that's the way he feels, he can go jump.*

THIRTEEN

A letter from Mum had also arrived with Jack. Amidst the previous day's emotional turmoil I'd completely forgotten about it, but in the morning it was waiting for me on the table when I sat down to my bowl of muesli.

I'd had a hellish night. I missed being woken by Hamish mewling for his night feeds, and my mind wouldn't let me alone. It endlessly replayed and rescripted the previous night's scene between Tom and me. I still couldn't make sense of what had happened. One minute we were savoring dinner under the stars, anticipating being naked in that deliciously narrow bunk after so long apart, and the next minute Tom was freezing me out.

I swallowed, but the aching tightness in my throat didn't go away, and I shoved my muesli aside. How could he say those things to me? If he'd shown any interest in my research I would have talked to him about it. It had just never come up. I swiped at the damn article and it slid off the table, taking with it the whole tottering pile of papers.

Pushing away my chair, I went over to the stove to boil some water for a long strong coffee. Huntington's disease and everything to do with neuroscience could go to hell. I was here to get away from all that. I wanted us to talk about turtle research and the reef and the birds. Kicking the article as I passed, I took my coffee and Mum's letter out to the deck. Not that it would cheer me up. She wrote every month, wherever I was, and it was all pretty much more of the same. Her life, at seventy-three, was hardly riveting in spite of being married to a man thirteen years younger than her and living in a fisherman's stone croft at the coldest-most tip of the UK. Perhaps I'd write to her this morning. It would be better than thinking about Tom. I could tell her about Hamish. Poor Mum, denied even a grandchild. There was a photo in the envelope with her letter. The colors were faded but I could still remember the cute red-and-white-checked sundress I was wearing. I must have been about six. The Yorkshire Moors stretched into the distance, and Mum and Dad were standing behind me looking ridiculously young—twenty years younger than I am now. They looked happy. I supposed they must have loved each other in the beginning. I opened the carefully folded letter and felt a bizarre yearning to see Mum again as I imagined her writing this in her small, neat way, black fountain pen on fine, almost transparent airmail-light paper. She'd never succumb to e-mail. Reading her letter was like reading a beautiful book after flicking through a Kindle.

Dear Anna,

The weather is at last becoming a little less cold. The winters here are hard on my aging bones. To keep myself warm I've been going through boxes of old photos and letters, and putting them into some sort of order in a scrap book. You might be interested some day, when you're my age. I had it in the back of my mind that there might be an address for your father's relatives somewhere. It seems a good opportunity to try and make contact while you're in Australia. I always felt it was wrong of Harry to leave like he did. I don't know if he ever got in touch with them after he left. Whatever happened to him there can't have been so bad that everyone in his family deserved that. He once told me that he would try and find Mary, his sister, someday.

I stopped reading and got up to make some more coffee. I needed it. I hadn't expected this from Mum. I knew bits and pieces of Dad's story—it had seemed exciting to a nine-year-old. He'd run away from home, a farm in Victoria, when he was eighteen. When I asked him why, he told me that he had a bad fight with his father, and as his older sister had already left home, there was nothing to stay for. And he hated farming. He wanted to see the world. Of course I asked him about his mother. She'd died when he was seventeen; what of, I never discovered. Cancer, I supposed. Mum had told me that Dad's father was an alcoholic, and had abused Dad's mother, as well as both him and his sister. Dad had cut them out of his life as if they had never existed.

I returned to Mum's letter.

When Harry died, you were his only next of kin, and although we were divorced, it was up to me to contact everyone. I had no way of finding his family, and none of his work colleagues knew anything about them, so I suppose the family never found out he was dead. I should have gone through his possessions as soon as I got them to try and find his sister's address, but I couldn't face it. I was very depressed for a long time, and I had you to think about. Apart from clothes, all that he left were boxes of work papers and books, which I finally went through before I shifted to Shetland. I threw most of it away, apart from a few books I thought you might like to have. There was nothing much personal. No letters, a few photos, including this one of the three of us, and an old Australian passport with his photo as a teenager. I'll keep it here for you. I don't trust the post. Your father was an unusual man, so extroverted yet so solitary and homeless, somehow.

The address of the farm where he lived as a boy was written in the back of the passport. It's Dry Acres Farm, Thomson's Road, Healesville, Victoria. I looked up Healesville in the atlas, and it's not far from Melbourne. I know it's a long way from where you are but wouldn't it be wonderful if you could find it? Perhaps the farm was left to Mary. She would be in her late seventies by now if she were still alive. Even if she's not, whoever lives there now might know something about the Fergusson family. I don't even know if Mary married and changed her name.

Mum was losing it. The chance of Mary being at that ancient address was remote, especially as she fled from the farm before Dad did. I counted back; it was over sixty years ago. I felt my sigh before I heard it. The need to connect with the past—another sign of aging. Okay for Mum, but I was still a bit young.

How strange that Mum saw Dad as solitary. He seemed to me to fill every space he entered. But she was probably right; in some sense, he kept himself apart.

Like Tom. My breath caught. Perhaps that was why I was so attracted to him. They didn't look alike, but there was something. I closed my eyes and saw my father, smiling at me as he always did. I could hear his lovely voice. *"Anna my Anna,"* he said. *"Anna my Anna."* I opened my eyes and blinked in the bright sun. Dad's unusual accent came from his seventeen years in Australia and then his years of hobnobbing with English journalists—most of whom were Cambridge and Oxford graduates. And that was it, their likeness. When I'd teased Tom about his ever-so-slightly Queen's English vowels, he'd blamed them on his school—a private grammar school in Sydney. I needed to clear my head. My letter to Mum could wait. Stuffing a packed lunch and my swimming things into my daypack, I set off along the beach to Shark Bay, hoping I wouldn't meet anyone, especially Tom. I still felt too raw. The hot, humid weather had given way to what passed for autumn here, a balmy 25 degrees. At Shark Bay I floated about over the lagoon for an hour before feeling chilled, and, as always, it worked its magic. I was feeling optimistic by the time I'd scoffed my sardine and onion sandwiches. We'd sort it out. It was just a lovers' spat. I shivered in the warm sun at the thought of even being entitled to a lover's spat. I decided to wander across the end of the island, through the trees, towards Tom's house. If he was there I bet he'd act as if last night never happened. That was fine by me. I was too old for these roller coaster feelings.

I almost missed her, caught upside down between two thick branches protruding from a half-buried Casuarina tree. It was the very end of the laying season and over the last few nights no more than one or two turtles had come up. I had heard that turtles occasionally got caught up in branches if they ventured too far up the beach to find a spot to dig their nest. Bill had informed me of the research ethics: if a turtle got trapped during nesting, the researchers had to leave her there. Rescuing her would be meddling with nature. Bill obviously thought it was bollocks.

The big mamma looked at me from her awkward position, her watering eyes opening blearily before closing again. God knows how she had managed to end up in this position. She must have flipped right over on her way down the beach and been caught up in the partially buried tree limbs.

It was already two in the afternoon, and her underside had been exposed to the sun for far too long. She flapped her front flippers weakly, and I saw the glint of a tag. It was too sad; this was surely her last nesting of the season, and she didn't deserve to die. Anyway, who would know if I managed to get her right side up and point her down towards the sea? The tide was still well up and she'd have no trouble swimming off if she was uninjured, and I couldn't see any obvious signs of damage.

But she was caught fast, and no matter how I pushed and pulled I couldn't budge her. She was clearly weakening, and her flapping had almost stopped. As giant tears dripped from her closed eyes and dropped, shimmering onto the sand beneath her, I felt like crying with her. Surely this wasn't right? Tom would help get her out if he found her here, research rules and Madam Collette be damned. I pulled my towel from my daypack and rushed down to the sea to soak it. I draped it over her great body, carefully covering her head and trying not to think how like a corpse this made her look.

"What are you doing?"

I jumped a foot in the air and turned around. Tom was standing there, frowning.

"I can't get her free. She's dying." My words rushed out, and I could feel myself preparing for battle.

"Poor thing." Tom pulled the towel back from her head and I saw her eyes open and wearily close. "We're not meant to interfere if it's an *act of nature*." He said the last three words as if they were in inverted commas.

"But that's crazy. The purpose of all your research is to save them, stop them going extinct. What's the point in letting her die?"

"The research bosses have their reasons. I'll give you the manual to read later. In a word, if we interfere, it will bias our research results."

"And bloody tagging them and disturbing them when they're laying, and jumping on the males from bloody boats when they're mating isn't interfering?" I was screeching like a fishwife.

"Calm down, Anna. You'll have Collette here and then we really will have to leave her stuck." He was yanking on one of the tree limbs as he spoke. "You pull her back while I try and pull this branch away from her."

She wouldn't budge, and after another five minutes of concentrated effort, Tom decided to go back to his house and get a saw. While he was gone I talked to her—soothingly, I hoped.

Even cutting her out was tricky, as there was not much room to maneuver between the tree limb and her shell, and it took another fifteen minutes or so for Tom to saw the branch off. But at last she was free and we heaved her up the right way and pointed her towards the sea. She lay there, not moving, her eyes closed.

"It's too late. She's dead." I sat beside her and stroked her glistening shell.

Tom had taken the towel back to the sea, and was now squeezing it over her head. "Give her time, Anna. She's exhausted and dehydrated. But Eve's a trouper. She'll be right in a while." Tom was standing behind me and I could feel his hand on my head and sliding down my plait.

"Eve? Is it really Eve?"

"Yes. I'd know her barnacles anywhere. And I checked her tag just to be sure. I even know her number by heart."

I swallowed, trying to act my age. "Can't we do something? How do you know she's still alive? She doesn't look it."

"Patience. Why don't you soak the towel again, so we can keep her head cool?"

I got up and ran to the sea, knowing full well that Tom was trying to keep me busy to stop me blubbering like a child. It was bad enough losing a turtle in this cruel way, but to lose Eve would be terrible. She was a touchstone, a symbol of everything that this place had come to mean to me. I squeezed another towel-load of water over her head, and I saw her reptilian eyelids move. "Oh, Tom, she's not dead. Thank you, thank you."

"Who are you thanking?" I heard the smile in his voice.

"Nature, the turtle god, you, I don't know." My mood had catapulted from the depths of despair to exhilaration in a millisecond.

Eve blinked, and two large tears crept from her eyes.

"Don't cry, Eve," I said. "You're going to live another fifty years, I know it."

She flapped her front flippers a few times and then launched herself forward and made a slow path to the sea. We followed behind, silently cheering her on. Tom was holding my hand. She slid into the gentle waves at the edge of the lagoon and lay motionless for minutes, her head almost submerged.

"Shall we push her deeper?" I whispered.

"No, let her do it in her own good time. She needs to get her bearings first."

We sat in the sand behind her and waited. And in her own good time she lifted her head and gazed over the wide lagoon to the edge of the reef and the deep sea beyond, then pushed herself deeper and deeper until she was back in her element and swimming effortlessly into the blue. I turned to look at Tom and he took my face in both hands and kissed me sweetly on the lips.

"Are we friends again?" I murmured when he let me go.

"Always. I'm sorry about last night. Sometimes I get in these moods, and I'm not good company."

"I don't mind. You can be moody with me; you don't have to leave."

"I'm a loner by nature, Anna, and sometimes I have to be alone."

"Oh." I ran my fingers across his chin, rough from a day's stubble. "That's okay. I'm a loner by nature too. Since meeting you I had almost forgotten that."

Tom grabbed my hand and kissed it. "Come on, loner. Let's go back to your cabin and begin last night again."

✂

11ᵗʰ April, 2009

Dear Fran,

It's a new day and I am feeling like a new woman. At the end of the week I am going with Tom back to Lost Cay. The baby turtles are coming out in their hundreds now, and Tom wants to do a survey there to see how many nests hatch over a twenty-four-hour period, to compare with our numbers on Turtle Island. I can't wait. The snorkeling on Lost Cay is amazing, and this time I'll be able to go out over the reef edge without being a trembling wreck.

So much has happened lately that I don't know where to start. I'm up one minute and down the next. Kirsty and Hamish left and that was a down, but at last Tom and I could be together again and that was an up, or should have been. But before we got very far we had our first fight, and that was an even worse down. Then today he helped me free a turtle who'd got caught up in a tree (don't ask!) and we made up, and after that it felt as if something shifted in our relationship. It feels more real to me now. I think I'm beginning to understand him and what he needs and doesn't need. I don't want to be like Mum and lose him, as Mum lost Dad. Tom reminds me of Dad in some ways, especially in the 'don't crowd me' way. I hardly need to tell you that crowding people hasn't been one of my problems, but it isn't so easy with Tom. I want to be near him all the time. I have to admit it, Fran, and you are the only one I'd admit it to, but I think I love him. I know this is crazy, but I can't control it. What's more, I don't want to control it. Ha! That's got to be progress. I can almost hear you cheering.

I didn't dare contemplate this before because we're so different and I'm so much older and plainer and more nerdy than him. But I am beginning to think perhaps age really doesn't matter so much. After all, look at Mum. She's thirteen years older than her husband and it doesn't worry them a jot. And all this turtle tagging and snorkeling has changed me physically as well. I'm pretty fit now and so brown I could be an Aussie. And don't frown like that. I know being brown is bad for you, but at my age who cares? It makes me look good, and I feel almost attractive—in fact I truly do feel attractive, when Tom looks at me.

I'm wondering if I should stay in Australia when my year here ends. I could perhaps get Australian citizenship given Dad was born here. Do you think I'm mad?

Write, dear Fran, and tell me how YOU are.

Love, Anna.

FOURTEEN

If I'd been a bloke, as they say in Australia, I'd have woken with a boner this morning. The very thought of being alone with Tom on Lost Cay turned my insides to goo. Literally. I spent an inordinate amount of time on the loo, telling myself it was just nerves and a serious case of adolescent excitement and not food poisoning like the last time. Too bad if it was; nothing would stop me going. We were to leave on the high tide at eleven. Only two hours to go.

I was at the wharf thirty minutes early, my promised curry packed into a plastic container. Tonight we would eat well. A bin full of diving gear and an Esky were already stashed in the stern of the boat. I saw Tom striding out of the trees and the butterflies intensified. It took me a while to catch on to Collette's presence as she scurried along behind him on the narrow path, her pack on her back. Surely she wasn't coming too?

"Morning Anna," Tom said, sounding a little sheepish. "You're early."

"Am I? I wasn't sure of the time."

"It's not really appropriate for you to come with us," said Collette, and I swear she was looking down her nose at me, in spite of my having a good thirty centimeters on her.

"That's not what Tom thinks," I shot back.

"Collette knows that I asked you to come, so let's get off."
Tom was already stashing his pack in the boat. "I'm going
back to get the water containers, so you two get your stuff into
the boat." He disappeared along the track, leaving Collette
and me stuck there.

I shoved my small pack into the dinghy and watched as
Collette struggled to heave her rather larger one over the side.
No way was I going to help her.

"Given Tom agreed that you could come, I'll go along
with it just this once, but you must realize that the University
cannot be responsible for your safety," Collette informed me in
her surprisingly deep voice.

"Don't worry, I can look after myself. If a shark eats me I
promise I won't hold you responsible."

We stood in silence until Tom returned, his face tense and
his crooked smile missing. The ride I had been so looking
forward to seemed to take forever. Tom sat at the back gun-
ning the boat into the waves, and I sat at the front with my
face turned towards the horizon, my butt leaving the seat and
crashing back down with every massive bounce. After a bit, I
stopped being scared shitless and began to enjoy it. A wave
broke over the bow, saturating me, and my dark glasses misted
with spray. It was exhilarating. With luck, Collette might
bounce right off into the sea. I didn't look behind me. I'd had
enough disappointment for one day.

Lost Cay was even more beautiful than I remembered. We
were there before one o'clock, and set up camp—two tents.
*God forbid that I have to share with Madam. Will Tom take me into his
tent in front of her? Oh please, yes. That would be the perfect revenge.*

"You two can have a tent each. I'll sleep outside," said Tom.

"Me too," cooed Collette. "You know I always like to sleep
under the stars, Tom."

"Whatever. I'm off for a dive while I can still get the tinny over the reef." Tom was hauling his wetsuit from his pack.

"Excellent idea. Give me a minute to get my gear on and I'll be with you," said Collette, ducking into the tent she had claimed with her pack.

"Are you taking *her?*" Even to my hot ears I sounded like a petulant child.

"You can come too, if you like. There's no charge."

"I can't dive, you know that."

Tom looked at me, and his eyes softened. "I'm sorry, Anna." He was whispering. "I couldn't stop her coming. The boat is paid for by her grant, and as far as she's concerned so is my time. And she obeys the rules: no scuba diving alone."

"You usually dive alone."

"When the cat's away . . ."

"I'll walk around the beach and see if any hatchlings are emerging. Isn't that what we're meant to be doing?"

Tom grinned. "I'll take you out for a snorkel later; there might be time for a quick one when we get back. We'll be gone no longer than an hour, I promise."

I watched them clamber back into the dinghy, Collette looking sexy in her sleek black-and-silver wetsuit with her dive tank on her back. Why hadn't I learned to scuba dive?

I set off around the island, and came across one nest of turtles emerging on the beach on the far side. That kept me occupied until they returned. As I sat there watching the babies erupting from the sand and scuttling towards the sea on their little clockwork flippers, I sensed Dad beside me, probably because I'd been thinking about how he had gone diving alone. If he'd obeyed the rules and dived with someone . . . I shook my head and concentrated on counting the baby turtles.

The dinghy was speeding back over the lagoon when I got

back to our camp. They'd been gone only forty-five minutes. Tom leapt out of the boat and dragged it into the shallows, shouting to me as he did so.

"Anna, get your wetsuit on, quickly. There's a Queensland grouper out there. You've got to see it. It might be gone tomorrow and you won't get another chance; they're bloody rare around here. We'll just make it before the tide's too low."

I stood still, just for a moment, poised on the verge of crying off. Then I saw Collette smirking in the boat. Within minutes I was back with my wetsuit half on, clutching my flippers in one hand and my mask and snorkel in the other. Tom stuck out his hand and steadied me as I clambered into the boat, then he pushed it into the deeper water, vaulted in, and we were off. I looked down as we crossed the reef edge, my heart in my mouth. It was only minutes before Tom cut the motor and heaved an anchor overboard. In the sudden silence I looked at him as the dinghy bobbed gently on the small swell.

"You'll need a weight belt," Tom said, maneuvering the thing around my waist. "Get your flippers on and you can lower yourself over the side, feet first."

He was all efficiency and I was all a liquid mess.

"You stay here, Collette, in case we drift and you have to come and get us." His tone made it clear that Collette had no option.

"Are you certified, Anna?" said Collette.

"Not that I know of," said I.

Tom snorted. "We're not using a tank. She doesn't need to be certified, for Christ's sake."

"I don't think it's a good idea. This is university equipment."

Tom ignored her and pulled the weight belt tight. "Okay?"

"Won't I sink?"

"That's the idea. It will make it easier to dive down. I'll be beside you; I promise you will be fine. Wait 'til you see this beauty." He was as excited as a small boy.

"What is it we're looking for again?"

"You'll see it. Now over you go."

I held my breath, slipped off the side and sank below the surface. I could feel the panic in my chest, but then I was up again and Tom was beside me, helping me with my mask and snorkel. He winked at me, and then pulled his on and flippered off. I stuck my head under and the underwater world opened up in all its glory.

We swam away from the boat, side by side, and I concentrated on breathing normally and looking at the fish swimming in their myriads below us. The sea bottom seemed a long way down but the water was crystal clear and I could see a large blue starfish on a patch of white sand between the coral outcrops. I felt Tom take my hand. We must have swum out of the reach of Collette's beady little eyes.

Something strange was happening—a stillness in the water. Then I realized that the fish had disappeared. We were swimming alone. Spooked, I pulled back and Tom stopped and stuck his head out of the water. I followed suit, flapping rapidly in my effort to stay vertical and in one place. I hadn't quite mastered treading water with flippers on. I looked around and saw our boat far, far away. How could we have come such a distance? I tried to cover my panic. Tom had removed his snorkel and was saying something.

I took my snorkel mouthpiece out and instantly got a mouthful of water, which made me flap even harder. I was about to sink. Then I felt Tom's arm around me, holding me steady.

"Take it easy. Tip the water out of your snorkel and put it back in," he said.

I managed that and breathed again.

"I'm going to take you over to a big bommie and on top of it is a massive fish. We won't go too close, but it won't take any notice of us so don't freak out. The other fish don't like it. That's why the sea around it is empty." Tom had sunk back into the water and I had no option but to follow him. What I wanted to do was to flipper as fast as possible the other way, back to the boat.

Tom was pointing ahead and I peered through the fish-free, shimmering water to a large dark coral outcrop rearing up from the deep: the bommie. It must have been twenty meters or more high. Unlike every other bommie I had seen it had no fish darting in and out around it. Tom was hanging in the water and I could feel him fizzing. He jabbed his finger towards the bommie again and I nodded. What was I meant to be seeing? He was pulling me along again, and as we got closer, the top of the bommie became a giant fish. A great brown ugly fish just sitting there, his enormous mouth open. My heart was thundering, and I started to turn away, flee as far away as I could get. But Tom held firmly to my hand and pulled me back. He turned his head and made the okay sign with his free hand. My heart slowed down a little and I forced myself to give him the okay sign back. Together we floated just below the surface, and I gradually calmed down. The monster hovered there above the bommie, glaring at the world. It looked at least three meters long, and it would take two long-limbed men to embrace it around its middle. Not that that would ever happen. Even a couple of Aussie blokes wouldn't be that crazy. Its repulsive, drooping, wide mouth opened wider, and my heart rate accelerated again. If it sucked inwards, I could disappear right down its slimy throat.

Tom looked at me and I could see him grinning around

his snorkel. He made a diving motion with his hand and raised his eyebrows above his mask.

I shook my head desperately.

He shook his head back and jabbed himself in the chest and made the diving motion again, and then the okay sign.

I breathed through my snorkel and returned the okay sign. Tom released my hand and swift as an arrow dove down and swam towards the bommie. My heart was still thumping but it was definitely in my mouth now. I tried to stay in one place, concentrating on keeping my snorkel end free of the waves, which had become choppier, and conscious of my weight belt holding my body below the surface. I knew if the monster went for Tom I'd never get back to the boat by myself.

Tom had surfaced again, far too close to the side of the fish. Now I could see him diving and swimming just above it. Men are so mindlessly stupid.

Then it moved. A giant wriggle. Its great mouth shut and opened again. I could feel the force of the water pushing out to where I floated, twenty meters away. It could have me in a heartbeat. I held myself there with phenomenal courage and looked for Tom. He had scuttled away bloody fast and was back at the surface. He made one last dive down to the monster and skimmed alongside it, then continued towards me. I waited for the monster to lunge after him.

I felt like a pro as we flippered away from the fish-free zone and back into the friendly bustle of the healthy reef. Even the sleek shape of a small white-tipped reef shark minding its own business a few meters below us caused only a brief palpitation. Within minutes we were back at the boat and Tom was shoving my butt from below as I heaved myself over the side. Even Collette seemed nicer, leaning over and grabbing my shoulders to haul me in. As we sped back to Lost Cay, weaving in and out of bits of coral piercing the rapidly receding waters over the reef flats, I sat in the middle of the boat and grinned at Tom. *Wow* was all that I could think. *Wow.*

Things felt a little easier between Collette and me after that. At least we managed to be courteous. Over a sandwich and a good billy of strong tea, we listened as Tom, still on a high, told us stories about the legendary Queensland grouper. Only twice before had he seen one, and never had he been so close. He was skeptical of tales about them eating divers in one gulp, but it seemed entirely possible to me.

We patrolled the island in the afternoon and again at dusk, looking for signs of recently emptied nests, and between us discovered six more eruptions. After a fine dinner prepared by me—my pre-cooked rogan josh and rice—accompanied by Esky-cool glasses of In Vivo, a special New Zealand Sauvignon Blanc I'd purchased online, and a surprise I had intended to share only with Tom, we roasted marshmallows on sticks and squashed them between wafer biscuits. Their revolting sweetness enhanced the sense I'd had lingering at the back of my mind all day: being with Dad in this same sort of place, doing these same sorts of things and feeling happy.

High tide was at midnight, so around ten Tom and I took off in one direction to circuit the island and look for laying turtles, and Collette went in the opposite direction. I don't know whether she had finally caught on to us, but she didn't argue when Tom suggested she walk the other way.

Tom and I found no late nesters, but sat for a while under the slender moon and watched the sea, just in case. In the silence I turned to him, and was stopped by his profile, chiseled against the lighter night sky. He looked like Michelangelo's David, admittedly the only Greek god I'm even remotely familiar with.

Kiss me. The thought was so intense, so real, so out loud, it was as if a wizard had tapped me on the head, endowing me with an instant understanding of the psychotic seduction of auditory hallucinations.

Tom turned, perhaps captured by the same wizard, and breathing his breath, I wondered if perhaps I'd spoken out loud after all.

"How can you stand being bossed about by her?" I asked him when I'd climbed back out of my seventeen-year-old psyche.

"She's not so bad when you're not around. You bring out the worst in her. Competitive bloody women."

"I'm not competitive."

"No?"

"No."

"Okay, keep your pants on."

I smirked. "I want to take them off." Seventeen again.

"Shameless woman. Collette will be around this side soon. I'm not sure she's quite ready for that."

"We could go into the bushes."

"But we won't. She'd know something was up if we'd disappeared from the beach."

"So what? Are you ashamed of us? Is it because I'm too old?" My wanton feelings had evaporated.

"No, don't be silly. I'm not interested in everyone gossiping about my private life, that's all."

I stood up. "Let's get on, then." I walked away from him, the shimmering ocean blurring. I saw Collette's midget shape at the far end of the beach and scuffed along the sand towards her.

We all slept under the stars that night, apart in our thoughts. In the morning, after another beach patrol for laying mothers and exploding nests—none of the first and two of the second—we packed up the tents and went for one last snorkel.

This time we swam out over the lagoon to the reef edge, Tom a little ahead and Collette to my side. Swimming along the edge of the reef, I watched as they dove down and explored bommies and caves, seeming to hold their breaths for longer than humanly possible. How beautiful they looked, as if they belonged in this deep blue. Tom came up to me and took my hand, and the pulse in my throat pumped with joy. He indicated that I should dive with him. I breathed in and headed down. Tom pointed into a hole halfway down the reef face and I saw the snakelike head of a large moray eel dart out and in. I jerked Tom's hand and flippered back to the surface, spluttering as I tried to clear my snorkel. Collette's head popped up beside me and she raised her hand in the okay sign. I signed back. Okay.

Tom was beside me and down we went again. This time I saw more, and when I came up, spluttered less. As we were circling a bommie on my fifth dive, the sun-washed corals darkened, and at first I thought the sun must have gone behind some clouds. Where the clouds had come from I wasn't sure; it had been a cloudless sky two minutes ago. Tom was gesturing up and I turned my head and almost forgot not to breathe. Above us a massive silhouette blotted out the surface of the water. We were under a ship. But it flapped its great wings and sailed gracefully over us, its long tail streaming out behind it. I watched it, mesmerized, as we rose to the surface, and without even thinking, I blew clear my snorkel.

"You are blessed," I heard Tom say, his mask and snorkel pushed to the top of his head. "A giant manta ray and a Queensland grouper, all in twenty-four hours."

When we got back to Turtle Island, Tom stayed in my bed all night, and as we ate our muesli sitting on my deck in the morning, Basil walked past and gave me a huge wink.

FIFTEEN

———————

Dear Anna,

I miss you. I hope it's all going well with your new friends on your island.

This is difficult to write and I probably won't even send it, but perhaps putting it down on paper will be therapeutic somehow. You are so sensible, and if you were here I could talk to you, but you're far away and I can't even phone or e-mail you easily.

There is only one way to say it. Greg is in trouble. A PhD student of his has put in a complaint about him: that he put pressure on her to have an affair. She wants a different supervisor and says she can't work under Greg anymore. I found out because she wrote me a letter. I tried not to believe it, but deep down I knew it was true. Years ago a student accused Greg of sexual harassment, but he denied it, and the university backed him and got the student to withdraw her complaint. So this time I looked at his e-mail; I guessed his password because it's the one he uses for everything. I felt like a heel, but I knew he'd deny it if I confronted him without any evidence other than the student's word. I found all I needed. He's such an idiot. He had e-mails from her and to her. They've been having an affair for at least a year. He must have broken it off about a month ago because there was one e-mail from her that made that pretty clear. She was terribly upset and angry, and accused him of getting "into the pants" of Zoe Walters; she's that new lecturer in his department. I printed them all, so he couldn't deny it.

When I confronted him, of course he did deny it, but then I showed him my evidence. He was furious that I'd gone into his e-mails, and ripped them out of my hands. I didn't tell him I'd kept copies, hidden away. I feel sick that I've had to stoop so low. He stormed out and when he came back, hours later, he admitted the affair but not the new one with Zoe. I don't believe him for a second. She's very attractive. Then he told me that he knew the student had put in a formal complaint and he'd hoped it would all be sorted out without me finding out, because he didn't want to hurt me. He was confident the university would be able to quieten her, and transfer her to a different supervisor. Poor girl. I almost feel sorry for her. But not really, because of her letter to me. It was vicious. Greg insists he never put any pressure on her, and that it was all her fault. She was all over him, begging for it, so he said, and he resisted for as long as he could.

That was all three weeks ago, and now it has gone public. It's all over the university. I can feel the tension wherever I go; everyone not knowing where to look, what to say. The boys are in shock. I threw Greg out after I went to see Zoe. I know her quite well; she's been over here for dinner a few times. She told me they had a brief fling when they were at a conference a couple of months ago and had seen each other once or twice since, but she told him to get lost when she found out about the student's complaint. She told me I should get rid of him, and that everyone in the department knew about his string of affairs. Apparently I'm the last to know. How could Zoe sit there at my table, eating the food I had prepared, playing footsies under the table with my husband and pretending she was my friend? How can a woman do that to another woman?

Anna, did you know Greg had affairs? I don't think so, because you would have told me. You didn't have anything to do with the English Department, so probably not. What should I do? One minute I want to divorce him immediately and the next I can't stop crying. We've been married for twenty-five years this year, and I thought we were so lucky to have got here intact, unlike so many of our friends. We've had plenty of rocky moments, but on the whole we had a comfortable life. He's been a good father, at least when we go to the lake. He and the boys go fishing and boating together. He's never been violent or abused me, not even verbally. Even up until all this happened, he could be loving. We didn't make love much anymore but I thought that was just our age. I never missed it. In fact I was happier than he was to do without. Perhaps that was the problem. He needed more than I gave him.

I'm sorry to burden you with all this, dear Anna, but you'd find out when you came home anyway. Please write and tell me what you think I should do. He says he is sorry and wants me to give him another chance. He even said he'd go to marriage counseling. He's always been completely cynical about any sort of therapy so I suppose that must mean something. Is it better to work on our marriage and get through this, or go through the horrors of divorce? The financial implications of that are too scary to even think about.

Love, Fran

I dropped Fran's letter on the table and sat there, stunned. How dare he. How bloody dare he. I never liked him. Patronizing, arrogant shit. He'd certainly made it crystal clear that I was not attractive enough, too tediously boring, for him to even bother to be polite to. But I thought he loved Fran. It was beyond me what those young women saw in him. He was about as sexy as a, as a . . . I thought for a while . . . a slug. Rather an emaciated slug at that. Tall, skinny, pale, bespectacled, with longish puce-colored graying hair, and even a straggly beard. The stereotypical English professor. I occasionally caught a glimpse of the sardonic wit he was supposedly famous for. He was known as an entertaining lecturer. Entertaining lecherer. Very entertaining, obviously.

It was impossible not to make comparisons. I knew what the PhD student was going through. How well I knew. At least she wasn't pregnant. I crossed my fingers. I hoped she wasn't pregnant.

Had Phillip been as slug-like as Greg to everyone else back then? He had been younger and fitter, and surely more attractive to look at. But he had a wife who was presumably as lovely and innocent as Fran. Perhaps he'd been right to drop me like a hotcake as soon as I got pregnant and wanted more, and before his wife found out. Did she ever find out? At least I never told her. I was beginning to wonder if any male could be trusted.

I shook my head. Stupid generalization. Tom wouldn't behave like that, and nor would Dad. He had girlfriends after he and Mum split up, but he wouldn't have cheated on her. I could feel a little worm of doubt squirming uncomfortably in my gut. If he hadn't had another woman to go to, why would he have left us? Perhaps Mum had found out like Fran—like Phillip's wife.

I stuffed the letter back in the envelope and threw it across the room.

"Leave him, Fran. Leave the lying, cheating scumbag. He was never worth you. You'll be *much* happier without him," I muttered, my jaw so tight I could barely get the words out. I couldn't face replying right away. I needed to calm down a bit first. Tonight would be soon enough. Jack could take it to the mainland to post when he left tomorrow.

I checked the time. The tide would be just about high enough for a snorkel in the lagoon. I needed to wash these feelings away.

"Yoo-hoo."

Pat. I couldn't help grinning. She always hollered like that when she got near my cabin.

"Hi, Pat."

"Hi, you." She came up the steps onto the deck, a book in one hand and a plastic box in the other. There would be goodies of some sort in the box. Pat never arrived empty-handed.

"What's up? You look a bit pale." She dumped the box on the table.

"I just had a letter from a friend back home, and she's having a bad time. Her shit of a husband has been having affairs and she's chucked him out." I hadn't intended telling anyone about Fran and here I was spilling the beans to Pat within seconds of her arrival.

"Oh, that's awful. Poor woman. Is she a close friend?"

"Yes, my best friend in Boston. Fran. She's the doctor."

"Of course. It was her son who put you on to coming here. We owe him for that."

"You remembered that? Thanks for the vote. I owe him too, for that. And I owe Fran. I would never have considered such a crazy thing if she hadn't encouraged me."

"How is she coping? You'll be feeling a long way from her, now she needs you."

"She's not coping. I've never known her not to cope, and she's had a few hard things to get through before. Do you think I should go back to Boston?"

Pat patted my hand as she walked past me into the cabin.
"Cuppa and chocolate cake first. You look like you need it,"
she said, filling the kettle and plonking it on the stove.
It really helped, having a chat. Pat was the only woman,
other than Fran, that I'd ever wanted to talk to about personal
things. I suppose that's why I was so surprised when she told
me about her marriage. I was hopelessly naïve about human
nature. I'd rather ignore it and hope it goes away. But being
there had changed me. The islanders were so unafraid to let it
all hang out. I didn't know if that was a small community
thing or an Australian thing. A bit of both, I suspected.

Pat always seemed to me to be so balanced, so content, so
loving. I imagined—well I didn't imagine, but I assumed—that
her marriage would have been just like her, and when her
husband died she would have been devastated for a while but
then picked herself up and got on with life. And she had done
that, and she was all those good things, but she told me, at first
calmly, and then, as she talked more, not so calmly, that her
husband had cheated on her more than once. She had stuck
with him the first time, thrown him out the second time then
taken him back, and taken him back again after a third affair.

"But why?" I asked, gobsmacked.

"Because I couldn't imagine life without him, I suppose.
He seemed truly repentant each time, so I forgave him."

"Three times?"

"I know. It's stupid. But finally, after the third time, he
agreed to counseling and he really tried to change. I had to
change as well. Like your friend, I hadn't been taking the
intimate side of our marriage seriously enough."

"And did he change? Did it last?"

"He did. And as far as I know he had no more affairs. If
he had, that would have been the end. He knew that."

"How old were you when all this was going on?"

"I was in my mid-forties when I first found out about him. It was another ten years before we worked it all out and I began to trust him again."

"How old was he when he died?"

"Exactly my age now: sixty-six. I was sixty, so we had about five content years. When we were first married we were blissfully happy for a while, and even when the children were small we were mostly happy."

"Looking back now, do you think you should have left him for good when you first found out abut his philandering? Ten years of misery seems a high price to pay for a few reasonable years at the end."

"You're thinking about Fran, and what would be best for her."

"I suppose so."

"Well, only she can decide that, and even then she'll probably never know for sure whether she made the right decision. For me, I think I did what was best. Going through a divorce would have been much harder, and the consequences much worse. At that age, splitting the family finances is hard to recover from, and although our children were adults with their own lives by the time it all came to a head, they would have been terribly upset. They loved their dad, and I didn't want them to see that side of him."

"They didn't know?"

"No. Well, if they did—if they suspected—we never discussed it. Gordon and I were both masters at putting up a front."

"That can't be healthy, surely?"

"It wouldn't do today, but it served us well." Pat grinned. "And we had some fair dinkum fights when we were alone."

"How did you feel when he died so soon after you came right?"

"Sad, very sad. And lonely. We'd been married thirty-eight years and I still loved him."

AFTER PAT LEFT, I SAT DOWN TO WRITE TO FRAN. I wanted to write a real letter, not something written on the computer and printed out; that seemed too impersonal. But I couldn't get the words right, and the floor was soon littered with balled-up paper. I wanted to tell Fran to give the cad the boot and begin again, but Pat's story kept intruding. They were quite similar in many ways, Pat and Fran. Who was I to judge what was best? The only serious relationship I'd ever had had been a disaster, and it was me who'd ended up a mess. Even though I was only twenty-five, I never had another serious relationship. Not until Tom, that is, if what we had could be called serious. Perhaps Fran needed to have a partner, and at fifty, if she lost Greg, she mightn't find anyone better.

Tom's shadow falling over me was a welcome relief, and when he raised his eyebrows at the paper strewn across the floor, I shut my pad and by way of explanation told him I was writing to a friend who'd been having some problems. Being Tom, he didn't question me and handed me one of the beers he had brought with him, icy cold from his fridge.

Later than night, as we lay like a pair of commas in the narrow bunk, I finally let it all out. I felt nervous. What if he didn't share my disgust? He was, after all, a man.

Tom didn't say much, but he held me as if he knew how I felt. When I insisted he tell me what he thought, at first I found his sentiments unhelpful.

"Greg *is* a cad, and Fran deserves better. But even cads

can have good characteristics, and almost anyone can change if they truly want to. Me, I find it impossible to judge relationships other than my own"—he tickled me—"and even that's not an easy call. It's hard to fathom what draws some couples together in the first place, let alone what keeps them together given all the trauma most relationships seem to go through."

"So what can I say to Fran?"

"What do you think she wants you to say?"

"What I honestly believe?"

"Perhaps. Or perhaps she hopes you'll support her in whatever she wants, even if it sticks in your craw."

"How can that be true friendship? That's as bad as lying to her. It's treating her no better than bloody Greg."

"You're probably right. I'm no psychologist. I guess I was thinking that given how deeply you care about her you'd want what's best for her. Not what might be best for you in the same situation."

"Mmmm. I think, Tom Scarlett, that your definition of an honest opinion is different from mine."

"I suspect Fran wants your support, not your opinion. But I don't know her, and you do."

Long after Tom's breathing softened into sleep, my head churned with one carefully worded phrase after another. When Tom woke at four and found me gone, he got up and made me a cup of tea, kissing the top of my head as he placed it beside me.

"Thanks. I'm sorry I woke you."

"No problem. I'll get dressed and go home; leave you to your thoughts."

"No. Please don't go. I need you to stay. I've finished my letter now."

"Well done. A letter written at this time of the night is sure to be from the heart."

"Would you read it and tell me if you think it is okay?"

"No, Anna. I've no doubt it will be what Fran needs from her best friend. I can tell by your face."

"What about my face?"

"It looks soft."

SIXTEEN

———

Early May and the island was emptying ahead of the cooler weather. The noddy terns had disappeared and the last of the adult shearwaters were leaving, abandoning their fledged chicks, who were still learning to fly. Turtle hatchlings had hatched and swum away, not to be seen again until they were dinner-plate size. Collette, as well as Diane and Ben, had just left. Everyone was at the wharf to say goodbye—to Diane and Ben, at least. I wasn't sure they would have come out for Collette. But she seemed pleased. She'd probably never had a goodbye wharf session when she'd left before. I hugged her, briefly to be sure, but it was spontaneous. What's more, she hugged me stiffly back and thanked me for all my help. I could feel Tom and Pat's grins through the back of my head. Saying goodbye to Diane and Ben was a wrench. We'd shared Kirsty's birthing and the miracle of Hamish's arrival, an unbreakable bond.

Still, I felt as light as a reef heron as I waved them goodbye, watching Collette's petite shape diminish to a mere dot as the boat sped away. Tom hugged me from behind and whispered in my ear.

"Big bed tonight, woman."

We were well and truly a public item now, but he'd not been willing to go as far as sleeping with me in the room next to Collette.

WHEN PAT ARRIVED THIS MORNING THERE WAS NO *YOO-HOO*. I was finishing breakfast, sitting alone on my deck. I spent about three nights a week in Tom's big bed, but the other nights we stayed apart. I'd convinced him that I too thought this was a marvelous plan. In truth I would have succumbed to six—seven?—nights a week together, but I knew Tom wanted his time alone.

I looked up from my Kindle when Pat's shadow fell across me. I had never seen her looking her age before.

"What's wrong?" My stomach went rock hard.

"I've got a lump," Pat said, her hand touching her breast.

"It's probably a benign cyst," I said, feeling my own breasts tighten.

"I know. But it worries me."

"When did you find it?"

"Last night, when I was showering. It feels big, Anna. Would you have a look and see what you think?"

"It's not my area, Pat. I have no experience at all."

"But would you check anyway? It's a time when a husband would be helpful, just to confirm that it's not my imagination."

"Oh Pat, of course I'll check you. I examine myself often enough, and I had a benign cyst removed years ago. It was no big deal but I was pretty anxious until I got the biopsy results."

We went into my tiny bathroom and Pat removed her T-shirt and bra. She had a firm, fit body; her breasts were still perky. Not the droopy appendages so often seen on images of aging women, especially those with an unshakeable belief in breastfeeding. Even Pat's tanned skin had somehow triumphed over the leathery wrinkles we were supposed to suffer if we exposed ourselves to the merciless sun.

Fran once told me that she could tell whether a patient, worried about cancer, was sick simply from the way they looked. Except for her tired eyes and cautious expression, Pat glowed with health. She was pressing on the side of her left breast and I replaced her fingers with mine. I could feel it immediately: a firm lump, perhaps a centimeter in diameter. I tried to recall what mine had felt like, but could only feel the hollowness that the discovery had brought.

"Can you raise your arms above your head?" As I performed the ritual breast examination, I forced myself into doctor mindset. "I can't feel any other lumps, but I'll be able to do a more thorough exam if you lie on the bunk." I poked my head out of the bathroom door and checked that there were no onlookers walking along the path outside my cabin. "It's all clear. Basil's not lurking." My feeble comment wasn't worth Pat's small grin.

She lay on the bunk and my hands completed their exploration. I draped her T-shirt over her chest.

"What do you think?" Pat's voice was steady, but my gut knew her apprehension.

"Truthfully, I have no idea. It could be benign or not. I can't feel any other lumps though."

"So I need to see a doctor pretty smartly."

"Yes, I think so. A specialist might be able to tell from the feel of it whether it is only a cyst or some other benign condition, but I suspect they'll want to do a needle biopsy anyway, just to be sure."

"Does that mean going into hospital?"

"No, it's just a simple procedure in the surgery, using a local anesthetic. When I had mine, I had to wait a few days for the results."

"Damn. I thought I'd been too lucky with my health."

"You certainly look fantastic. I'd put my money on this being benign. You simply don't look as if you could have a thing wrong with you."

While Pat dressed, I made coffee, and we sat on the deck in a patch of sun.

"Is there any history of breast cancer in your family?" I broke a long silence.

"Not that I know of. My mother died quite young, but from cervical cancer. Is that related?"

"I don't think so."

"Oh well. I'll just have to deal with it. I'll use Basil's Skype to phone and get a doctor's appointment for next Tuesday. I should be able to make that if I go back to Gladstone with Jack on Sunday, and fly to Brisbane on Monday. I've never been to a doctor up here. Mine's in Melbourne."

"Perhaps you should go there instead of Brisbane? At least your daughter's there."

"I don't want to scare her. She's got a lot on her plate at the moment. There must be a specialist service in Brisbane?"

"I'm sure there is. Why don't I look it up on Tom's Internet, and see what I can find? Then you could make an appointment directly with a specialist and not see a GP first."

"Thanks Anna. You'll be a better judge than I about who to see."

I was back at Pat's house an hour later, armed with the latest information about Brisbane specialists. I had even made an appointment for her at ten o'clock on Tuesday morning—easily changed if Pat wanted some other time or doctor. When

I walked into the kitchen and saw her at her bench, kneading a big lump of dough, I felt suddenly embarrassed. Who the hell did I think I was, taking over and even making appointments for her?

I didn't deserve the relief I felt when she thanked me with not a hint of annoyance.

"You're a blessing, Anna," she said. "I was feeling so alone last night, and now I'm not." She came over to me, her eyes shining with tears. We reached out for each other and as I held her and she held me, I couldn't tell which of us was trembling. We were the same height and build, and as toned as our bodies were, our hug was warm and safe. When I could feel the trembling no more, we reluctantly drew apart, our eyes meeting in a smile of recognition.

"I'll come with you," I said. "That's if you'd like me to."

"Yes, I would like you to. I can manage on my own, but if you really want to, I would like that."

"I've spent no time in Brisbane, so we'll see the sights. If they want to do a biopsy, no way will we hang around, glooming about, waiting for your results."

"Oh, Anna. Whatever did I do before you came?"

"Come on, Pat, you never stop doing stuff. I've made no difference at all."

"You've stopped me feeling lonely. I've had no real friends since I got married. Too damn busy."

"We're two of a kind then. And I didn't even have a husband to talk to. Fran was my only friend, but she had her own life—that marriage thing for her as well—and we didn't see much of each other."

"I'm starting to look forward to this Brisbane trip. Can we go back to Tom's and book our flights online?" Pat's face was looking younger.

"What about your bread?" I glanced over at the dough lying half kneaded on the bench top.

"Give me a sec to stick it in the hot water cupboard to rise. When we come back it will be ready for the oven."

THE WEATHER IN BRISBANE WAS PERFECT. WARM ENOUGH to wear a short-sleeved top, no humidity, no wind, and a clear sky. We had booked into a small hotel in the CBD, close to all the shops spread along the beautiful river. We'd decided not to talk about the lump anymore. Of course, it was there, lurking below the surface, but it didn't stop me enjoying myself. Pat enjoyed herself as well; either that or she was a bloody good actor. We arrived at our hotel around lunchtime on Monday, and began with a riverside lunch of calamari salad matched with a delicious Riesling, and continued from there. Mud crabs were the tough choice for dinner, in a very posh water-front restaurant. We laughed and played and generally acted like carefree tourists. I slept like the dead that night. Pat, I suspect, might not have.

The specialist oncology center we bowled up to next day was as luxurious as a five-star hotel. Not everyone in Australia has private medical insurance, but I was glad Pat did. Who needs to wait for hours with dozens of other sick and scared people, in a dreadful mustard-colored waiting room in a public hospital, for a ten-minute consultation with a harried specialist, if you can do it in comfort and style? Real coffee—cappuccino, latte?—served with crisp almond biscuits while you wait, the latest glossy magazines to read, soft lights, beautiful furnishings, charming, attentive staff. I needed all the trimmings to take my mind off what was happening for Pat when she disappeared for ninety minutes. She was calm when she returned, and told me her specialist was wonderful and she'd already had a mammogram and an ultrasound. Her needle biopsy was scheduled in an hour's time. As I had thought, the specialist had made no diagnosis but had told Pat the lump could well be benign. We filled in the time by strolling through the clinic grounds, admiring the tropical plantings alive with parakeets and the unseasonal water lily blossoms on the ornamental ponds.

The biopsy was over in thirty minutes and the waiting began. The specialist had told Pat she would phone her with the results between three and four on Friday afternoon. I was impressed. Not only was this a fast turnaround for a lab result, to give an actual time when Pat would hear back from the specialist was textbook perfect. I knew how important it had been for our Huntington's families. When a non-symptomatic family member who did not know whether they harbored the Huntington's gene decided to get tested, they first went through a long process of counseling, followed by the test. It took a while for the results to come through but at the time of the test an appointment time for four weeks later was set with the Huntington's disease social worker, and that was when the results would be given. Removing the uncertainty about exactly when one's fate would be sealed reduced the stress immeasurably.

And so it was for Pat. We shopped, took ferry rides, went to the stage version of the Abba musical *Mamma Mia*—which we both admitted we enjoyed in spite of never liking musicals —walked five kilometers along the river, and had our hair cut at an expensive hair stylist's.

My idea of having my hair cut was a trim every four months. This hairdresser, a thirty-something young woman with a mass of red curls that looked as if they'd never seen a hairbrush, weighed my great hunk of hair in her hand and said, "This is aging. Why don't you go for a shorter cut? It would look great with a nice rich color through your hair. It's so thick it would be a breeze to look after."

The image of Polly popped into my head. Model thin with that cute boy look. I was sure Tom had been attracted to her, in spite of his insistence that she was like a sister. But my fantasy that a new hairstyle would turn me into a Polly type was rapidly vanquished as my face, reflected cruelly back at me from the brilliantly lit mirror, became increasingly convict-like with every snap of the scissors.

Three hours later we left the hair salon, Pat with her hair a soft gold-brown, feathery about her face, and me with a sleek, dark brown—with highlights and lowlights—glossy cap. My head was so light I thought it might blow off in the tiny breeze. I felt giddy.

"It's gorgeous, Anna," Pat said kindly.

"Are you sure?"

"Yes, I'm sure. Tom will love it."

"I'm not worried about Tom."

"Of course you are."

"Why on earth did I let that woman talk me into this?"

"It will grow again, if you don't like it. Give yourself time to get used to it. When was the last time you had short hair?"

"Never, in my memory."

"Well then, it's high time you tried something new. Let's buy some new clothes to go with our new hair."

I hugged her, hoping she hadn't noticed my watering eyes. How could I bang on about losing some of my hair when Pat was worrying if she might end up having a boob removed?

On Thursday we met Kirsty and Hamish for lunch at an airy eatery on Southbank. What a treat. Hamish had grown in the short time since we'd last seen him, and was even more delightful. Kirsty had enrolled in a distance learning program training to be a veterinary nurse, and asked me if I would think about looking after Hamish for two weeks in late July while she went on an intensive live-in course that was part of the program. Her mum was back at work and couldn't get more time off after her long overseas trip. Kirsty would bring Hamish over to the island and collect him later.

Hamish chuckled at me as I considered—for about two seconds—her request.

"But you'll have to stop breastfeeding." Pat's words fell like stones into our pool of friendship.

Kirsty fussed with her salad. "I thought I'd start weaning him soon. He already has a bottle sometimes."

"I only fed my two for three months; that's what the experts said back then about the minimum time. I'd had enough by then of being the only one who could do the night feeds," Pat said, her tone giving nothing away.

"That's still the advice. I would go longer but I really need to get a qualification so I can get a job I like as soon as he's old enough to go to crèche." She turned to me. "Thanks Anna. You're a gem. I don't know what I would do if you couldn't take him."

"I'd be nervous about it if I didn't have Pat and Violet to back me up," I said as Hamish curled his fingers around mine. "I think it's great that you're doing the course."

"I'll make sure Auntie Anna doesn't spoil him," said Pat, winking at Hamish.

IT WAS NOT QUITE SO EASY TO FORGET ON FRIDAY, BUT we gave it our best shot. Unfortunately we made a bad decision when we decided to go to a late-morning movie to fill the hours. The only movie on that wasn't full of car chases or vampires was one called *My Sister's Keeper*. Neither of us had heard of it, and we had no time to read more than the briefest of descriptions—something about families—before it began. I'm not one for weeping in movies, but this was a corker: about a teenager dying of leukemia, and her younger sister's fight to stop her mother using her blood, bone marrow, and kidney for spare parts. I wondered about leaving early when it became clear what was going to happen, but Pat was glued to the screen. Along with the only other four people in the theater, we shuffled with our heads down to the women's restroom as soon as the movie was over and grinned at each other as we dabbed at our red eyes.

"That was a bit heavy for a midday movie," I commented as we emerged into the sunshine.

"Lovely though," said Pat.

The phone in our shared room rang at three o'clock, and I knew my prayers weren't answered when I heard Pat saying, "Yes, I have my friend here with me so I'll be fine. Thanks, Doctor. I'll see you tomorrow at ten."

Neither of us slept that night. All the doctor had said was that it was a Grade 2 primary breast carcinoma—that is, a bit faster growing than a Grade 1 and not as nasty as a Grade III —and that as it had been detected early, Pat's chances of cure were excellent. Dr. Pascoe would go over all the treatment options tomorrow. We resisted the temptation to Google them.

Pat asked me to come in with her when she saw the specialist at her Saturday morning clinic—no waiting around until Monday there. My opinion of the clinic and especially Dr. Pascoe escalated as I listened—and learned—while she talked calmly about Pat's options, showing no discomfort when

Pat became tearful at one point, and giving her all the time and space she needed. Pat wanted to have the surgery in Melbourne so she could stay with her daughter, and I knew that leaving this doctor for a new one would be hard. Afterwards we bought a picnic lunch and found a peaceful spot in the botanic gardens to eat it, or play at eating it. Pat had some big decisions to make, and by the time we had finished lunch and we had both read and reread the information pamphlets, she had decided to go with a full mastectomy rather than the breast-conserving surgery, saying she was long past worrying about having perfect boobs. She had even decided not to have a breast reconstruction; a prosthesis would do her just fine. She was more concerned about living, she said. As a bonus, a mastectomy would mean she was less likely to require radiotherapy, although chemotherapy looked like a certainty.

Her next and perhaps hardest task was to phone Susie, her daughter. While she did this back in our hotel room, I walked along the river again, trying not to cry. I was already thinking about going to Melbourne with Pat, and so as not to intrude too much on her family, spending a few days trying to trace my father's sister.

We flew to Melbourne on Sunday, and I rented a car at the airport and dropped Pat at her daughter's home before booking in at a motel. The front door opened as we reached it and two small girls, mirror images of each other, jumped up and down, their curly heads huge halos about their faces, their innocent ecstasy a joy available only to young children and one-man dogs. While they shrieked, their mother and grandmother clung together in silent love.

I declined Susie's invitation to stay for dinner. Her sweet face—a younger version of Pat's—was strained, and I could hardly bear to think how she must feel. I did accept the traditional cup of tea, and for ten minutes Susie and I struggled with trivial conversation, both avoiding the dark fear weighting our hearts. Pat had long ago been spirited away by the seven-year-old twins, and as I rose to go, Peter, the son-in-law, appeared through a door and, putting a close arm around Susie's waist, gave me the loveliest smile.

"Go and say goodbye to Queen Pat," he said. "Just follow the squeals."

I did as he suggested and waved from the door at Pat, sitting center-stage on one of the beds with a crown on her head and a smile on her face, surrounded by the butterflies, ballerinas, and books of her granddaughters' bedroom.

—————

SEVENTEEN

I'd never e-mailed Tom before, and my insides were quivering when I sat down at the computer in the motel's reception area that evening. In all the thousands of e-mails I had sent hither and thither when I was in Boston, not a one had been personal. Once I got in the swing of it I found it quite freeing. I read it over a few times, and removed a few soppy bits before finally sending it. I could see how this could become rather addictive. I'd never before understood the fuss made about the time wasted in these trivial pursuits. I contemplated e-mailing Fran, but couldn't face it. Pat's problems were enough to worry about without refueling my anger over the Professor's disgusting behavior.

On Monday, I bought a map and found roughly the whereabouts of the farm where my father grew up. I thought the best first step would be to see if a farmhouse still existed at that address. I'd decide if and when to go there after I knew the date of Pat's operation. I wanted to stay around until that was safely over.

"Wednesday, first thing," Pat told me next evening. "The specialist is almost as nice as Dr. Pascoe," she added, "in spite of being a man."

He was certainly wasting no time. Pat went into the

private hospital—larger and more generic than the Brisbane one—on Tuesday morning, and I stayed with her while she underwent a barrage of tests. Her family arrived after the kids got out of school, expanded now by Troy, Pat's bachelor son, direct from his engineering job in the massive Perth mining industry. In spite of Pat's obvious joy when he walked into her room, she looked exhausted, and I thought I could see fear cowering beneath her smile. Perhaps it was my fear. I left, no longer fitting in. I could hear their cheerful and positive chat as I walked away, down the long corridor that smelled like every hospital I'd ever worked in—an evocative medley of floor polish, antiseptic, and illness. It occurred to me that this smell—I could never think of it as a scent or a perfume— called up powerlessness and apprehension in most people, yet power and excitement in the soul of the dedicated doctor. Perhaps all those years ago when Fran and the others in my medical year lengthened their stride when they were assaulted by the odor, it had signaled QUIT to me as I lagged behind, my stomach in knots.

The next time I saw Pat she was back in her hospital room, and I was permitted ten minutes. It is a mystery how in the space of a few hours the human body can morph from tanned and muscled to wan and hollow. She managed a smile, and I sat beside her and said nothing much. We both knew the surgeon had been pleased with the way the operation had gone; he had biopsied the lymph nodes under her arm and the tests carried out during surgery had shown they were blessedly clear of malignancy.

ON SUNDAY, AFTER TWO DAYS OF MISERABLE RAIN, THE sun peered out and I drove to Healesville, on a search for my own family. In truth, my heart wasn't in it. Pat was still in hospital and "doing well." When I visited the evening before, she had been sore and tearful. The dressings had been changed earlier in the day and she had seen the operation site. She remembered feeling the same depression a few days after each of her two children were born. Perhaps, she said—and I thought she was joking—it had something to do with losing body substance—the child in the womb, or the boob. My throat ached with love as I drove along, her final words playing with my mind. *But by the time I got home from the hospital with my babies, what I felt was wonder.*

Taking Highway 34 east out of Melbourne, the fickle sun, now sailing through a blue sky, soon had me donning dark glasses as the glare ricocheted off the wet bitumen. I turned on the radio and found some classical music. After a while I almost began to enjoy the sensation of being on the road in a Melbourne that was still surprisingly quiet, even for a Sunday. Melbournians apparently weren't yet ready to trust the sun's staying power. Driving through Coldstream, I took a right towards the Yarra Ranges, finally leaving the built-up sprawl behind. I passed the sign welcoming me to Healesville, and stopped in the main street of the charming rural town my father must have known well. After a first rate espresso and a greasily yummy pie, I headed out of town past more cafes, antique shops, and galleries.

I didn't believe Thomson's Road would exist, in spite of seeing it on the map, but there it was, right where it was meant to be. The dusty, unsealed road wound up and down small rises and around numerous bends, and I was about to give up, satisfied that I had at least tried, when I spotted the faded words "Dry Acres Artists' Community" on a large sign nailed to a rustic farm gate. I stopped the car. The greasy pie had expanded and was being remixed in my stomach. I contemplated turning back.

Artists' community? Was this where the family farm used to be? The farm was probably farther along Thomson's Road. No doubt the artists would be able to tell me. Perhaps this was one of those sex-crazed seventies cults and they'd lock me in a cellar and brainwash me.

This jocular approach didn't work and my stomach kept churning. I got out and lifted and pushed the gate open and drove through, and got out again and shut it, cutting off a quick exit. Bouncing along a rutted track that led to a jumble of buildings in the distance, I looked around at the green freshness of a peaceful valley. I was expecting dry acres, but perhaps they only appeared during the high summer months. I stuck my head out the window and breathed in the sweet air. A stream chuckled quietly alongside the track and a skylark was singing somewhere in the blue. Ghost gums were scattered randomly across the paddocks, their brilliant white trunks indescribably beautiful in the winter light. As I slowed to negotiate a large puddle, a white and yellow cloud of sulphur-crested cockatoos erupted out of a tree and flew into the air, their loud screeches echoing around the valley.

I parked in the small visitor's car park and went into a little café that opened off what looked like an old shearing shed. Inside the café, I could see through to a big space where pottery and wooden bowls and the like were displayed and a few people wandered about. A sign above the archway entrance proclaimed *Walk through to see artists at work*. The delicious smell of fresh coffee and home baking was tempting, but the greasy pie churned again as I approached the young woman behind the counter.

"Good morning." She smiled. "What can I get you?"

"Well, nothing right now, but perhaps I'll come back later. I was just passing through and wondered if this was where Dry Acres Farm used to be. My father lived there when he was a boy. His family's name was Fergusson. I don't suppose they still live around here?"

"Oh yes, George left to go back home about half an hour ago. You could probably find him there."

"George?"

"Yes, George Fergusson. He's one of our craftsman."

"Gosh. Fancy a Fergusson still being here."

"Well there you go then," she said cheerfully, as if people wandered in and found long lost relatives with the same name every day.

"Where's his house?" I asked, sitting down quickly at the nearest table.

"You can't miss it. Take the path around to the back of the shearing shed, and his is the nearest house immediately behind here. Just follow the steps up."

"Thanks. And then perhaps I'll come back for a coffee," I said, trying for normality.

"You probably won't need to. George makes a pretty good cup himself." Then her smile disappeared and she said in a quiet voice, "I don't suppose, then, that you know about Selina?"

"Selina?"

"His wife. She was in a car accident three months ago."

"Oh dear. I'm sorry. Was she hurt badly?"

"She died. It was awful." She looked as if she might start sobbing any moment.

"Oh dear," I said again. "How is George coping, do you think?"

"He looks dreadful, poor dear, but he's hanging in there.

He keeps pretty busy helping out here, but he hasn't had the spirit to get back to his painting yet."

"I'm sorry. Was Selina quite young?"

"No, not really. About fifty, I suppose. But everybody loved her. She and George were two of the original founders of the community. Selina organized all the social things, and she started the crèche and the community meals every Friday night, and none of it works properly any more without her." The tears were trickling down her cheeks now, and I definitely thought it was time to leave. George, whoever he was, would not appreciate a visit from me right now.

"I am sorry. Perhaps I'll come back another time."

"No. Don't do that. It will be good for George to have a visitor."

Damn. I escaped the curious glances of a couple enjoying their coffee and found a brick path that curved around the back of the building. As the young woman had said, the house was easy to find. Slightly dilapidated-looking, it was a low, graceful, wooden building with a wide wraparound veranda, furnished with comfortable-looking chairs. An elderly Old English Sheepdog rose to its feet and lumbered towards me. I felt better. Anyone with a dog like that must be okay.

The door was standing open, and I could hear a vacuum cleaner going. I knocked and called out, "Is anyone at home?" feeling silly, as obviously someone was. The vacuum cleaner stopped and a tall man lolloped down the passage to the door. I nearly passed out. For a second my father stood there. Older, much older, but almost my father. I was shaking so much I had to grip the doorframe.

The reincarnation of my father grabbed my arm. "Whoa there. Take it easy." He lowered me down onto the step and I sank my head between my legs until the blood returned.

"Better?" he said. His voice was reassuringly Australian. If this imposter had sounded like Dad, with his charming Oxford-cum-Australian accent, he would have had his work cut out to convince me he hadn't returned from the dead.

"Sorry," I said, hauling myself up and staring at him. Inside I was twelve again, screaming at the strangers telling me my father had drowned and I'd never ever see him again.

"Come inside and I'll get you a drink of water. Then you can tell me who you are."

I followed him into an enormous room filled with sunlight, dominated by a large, circular, freestanding fireplace in the very center of the room, cleverly designed so that the flames could be seen and felt from all sides. The massive stone chimney rose up through the apex of a heavily beamed vaulted ceiling, and a low, wide bench, clearly hand carved, circled the fireplace. Gulping down the water he shoved into my hand, I concentrated on a large pottery vase filled with grasses and berries sitting in the center of the table until my head stopped spinning. I looked around. It was a beautiful room. As well as the fancy fire in the center there was a monster wood range on the far wall, also glowing red. On the hob, a coffee pot was burbling merrily, and the aroma of fresh warm bread filled the room. A family home.

"Perhaps you should tell me who you are," he said, pulling out a chair and pushing me onto it.

"I'm Anna Fergusson. I came here looking for my father's relatives. Harry Fergusson."

"Stone the crows. The mysterious missing Harry. He's your father?"

I nodded. "You look so like him. That's why I felt faint. When you appeared at the door, I thought I was seeing a ghost." I sat on my hands to stop them shaking.

The ghost laughed. Not just laughed, laughed his head off. "You're obviously a relative," I said, when he'd calmed down. He grinned, and offered a slim brown hand. "George Fergusson. Mum told me I looked like Harry but I didn't realize we were that alike." I shook his hand, my stomach churning with excitement now. "Mary? Is Mary your mother?"

"She is. Your father's big sister. I'll go and get her. She's out in the garden."

"I don't believe it," I said.

"I'm sure she's there. At least she was last time I looked." His laugh again. "Mum's seventy-eight so your father must be about seventy-six. I hope I don't look that old."

"Not quite. Although you look much older than Dad was when I last saw him. It's strange to think how he would have aged. Not that you look old."

"Your father's not alive, obviously. When did he die?"

"He drowned when I was twelve, and I never saw his body. They never found his body."

"Jesus. Look, just sit there and I'll get you a cup of coffee, or would you like a whisky or something?"

"No thanks. Coffee would be good. Black, please."

He put a coffee down beside me.

"How come you're a Fergusson?" I asked.

"Mum never married. My father was around from time to time, but she liked her independence. I don't think she ever even considered giving me his name. I'll go and get her," George said, and was out the door.

A blast of cool air heralded his return, and I looked up over my mug. A tall woman followed him in, taking her wide-brimmed hat off and shaking free her curly white hair.

"Anna, meet Mary Fergusson, my mum," George said.

"I can't believe you're sitting there after all these years. Harry's daughter." Her voice faltered and George put his arm around her and guided her to a chair.

"I'm sorry," she said. "It's a shock—but a wonderful one."

"It's me who's sorry. I should have written or phoned first, but I didn't even know if Dry Acres Farm would still be here."

"You look like him, tall and dark. The Fergusson look," she said, her face still pale.

"I suppose so. George—I thought I'd seen a ghost for a minute."

Mary glanced at George, and the color returned to her face. "Yes, he was so like Harry when he was a boy." She turned her bright eyes on me. "What happened to Harry? He left here when he was eighteen and he wrote once from England. After that we never heard from him again. We tried to find him but it was hopeless. Nobody would help us. He was old enough to leave and that was that."

George had piled the table with thick-cut bread and various other stuff, and he pushed a plate and knife over to me. "Help yourself, Anna. Try our homemade pickles. Nothing like a doorstop sandwich when you're in shock."

He was right: I was hungry. It was warm and soothing in the big room, and the three of us buttered, filled, cut, and ate for a while in silence. Then I told them about Dad's diving accident and never finding his body. After a while Mary got up and left the room. She was probably too upset to sit there with me. Five minutes later she was back and handing me a small photo and a yellowed envelope. I looked at the family photo. My father as a teenager was easily recognizable. No one in the photo was smiling.

"That's me beside Harry with our parents, not long before Mum died," Mary said.

It was the first photo I had seen of my grandparents. My fair-haired grandmother looked tiny and frail standing in the middle of her dark-haired family.

"The men all look the same," Mary said. "I'm not surprised you thought George was Harry."

"What are their names?" I asked, not looking up.

"Papa was another Harry, and Ma's name was Clemency. Didn't Harry even tell you their names?"

"I'd forgotten. I did know but he never talked about them." I touched my grandmother's face. "My first name is Clemency, but I've always been called Anna. It's my second name."

"Harry loved Ma. I'm glad he named you for her." Mary's hand rested on my arm.

"Did she have cancer? She doesn't look very strong here."

"She was tiny but she had plenty of guts. She had to, living out here in those days."

"Was she sick for a long time before she died?" I don't know why I kept on with these questions. I could feel the tension radiating off Mary.

"Harry didn't tell you." It was a statement, not a question. "Ma took too many sleeping pills one day when she was a bit confused. By the time we found her it was too late."

My mouth was dry. Was this my grandmother's only way to escape her alcoholic husband's abuse? I took a swig of my coffee, and wished George would say something to break the silence. I looked across the table at him, but he was sitting mute, staring into his own coffee. Poor chap was probably thinking about his own wife's tragic death. "That's very sad," I finally managed to croak. I took a deep breath. "Dad did tell my mother that he didn't get on with his father and that's why he left home. Was my grandmother—did my grandmother have problems with my grandfather too?"

"No, they adored each other, but I think Ma was alone too much with Papa always working out on the farm, and she had no friends way out here. She would be all right for a while and then she'd get very depressed and sometimes she wouldn't leave her bed for days. Papa tried everything to cheer her up, but we had no money so it was hopeless. He couldn't even take her away for a holiday."

My long-held beliefs about my grandfather tottered. "Dad told my mother that his father liked his drink. Do you think that was why he and Dad fought?"

George snorted.

"Have I got the wrong end of the stick?" I said.

"Grandpa was dead against the demon drink," George said, and grinned at me.

"I must have remembered it wrong. Was he one of those stern religious types?" It was stifling with both fires going. I ripped off my sweater, fighting the hot flush enveloping me from the waist up.

"Harry—your dad, I mean—could always spin a tale when it suited him." Mary's voice sounded almost exasperated. "Papa was as gentle as a lamb. He *was* religious, but not the stern type. He probably should have given young Harry a few good hidings. It might have sorted him out before it was too late."

"You weren't exactly the obedient little daughter, Mum," George said, winking at me.

I tried to grin. "I can imagine Dad being a bit of a wild lad. He could never stay in one place for long. I think that's why he and Mum broke up."

Mary's dark eyes were soft as she looked at me. "Harry was more than just wild. He caused Ma and Papa a lot of grief. He had a spell in borstal for converting a car when he was thirteen, and when he came out he was even worse, always in fights and getting drunk every weekend. He was on the fast track to prison, according to the police." She patted my arm awkwardly. "I'm sorry, Anna. It must be hard to hear that if you didn't know."

"It is a bit of a shock," I said. "He wasn't like that at all when he was my dad."

"Perhaps leaving Australia was the right thing for him to do. It forced him to grow up," Mary said.

"Do you know why he left? Was there anything in particular?"

"He got a girl pregnant when he was seventeen. She was underage, only fifteen, and she had an illegal abortion. She nearly bled to death, and Harry had to get a doctor. Luckily the doctor was the same man who looked after Ma, and I think to save her from more grief he didn't report it. He told Ma and Papa, though, and they were terribly upset. The girl recovered, and her family banned her from seeing Harry again, and that was that. But when Ma died not long after, I think Harry thought it was his fault. Ma doted on him."

I couldn't think of a thing to say.

"That's an unusual pendant," Mary said after a long silence, and I realized I was playing with it again.

"Dad gave it to me on my last birthday. My last birthday before he drowned, I mean. It's the only jewelry I possess. I'm not really the type."

Mary leaned over and weighed the entwined silver dolphins with their opal eyes in her hand. "It was your grandmother's. She only wore it on special occasions, and they were pretty rare." She let it fall, and it shivered into place.

"I didn't know. I'm sorry." I didn't meet her eyes.

"I thought it was lost. I even wondered if Papa had put it around her neck when he buried her, but he said he didn't."

"She must have given it to Dad, I suppose." I felt the heat again, rising up my neck beneath the stolen pendant. I fiddled with the tiny catch, wanting it off. "You have it. I didn't even know her."

"Leave it on. She'd have wanted you to wear it. You're her only granddaughter."

I forced myself to look at Mary, and she smiled at me.

"Read the letter," she said.

I pulled out the single page. I had recognized Dad's hand-writing on the envelope, addressed to Mr. Harry Fergusson, Dry Acres Farm, so I knew it was from him.

Dear Papa,

I am in England. I worked my way over on a container ship from Melbourne. I've already got a job here and am getting settled. I'm sorry I left without saying goodbye to you or Mary, but I didn't want you to try and stop me. I'm sorry for all the trouble I've caused you and the unhappiness I gave Ma. You were both good parents and didn't deserve me. All I can do is promise to make a better life for myself here and be a better person. I don't think I'll be coming back there, at least not for a long time. Try and forget me. Please give my love to Mary when you see her and tell her I'm sorry for not being a good brother.

Harry.

My father's sorry letter. Not even "Love, Harry" at the end.

EIGHTEEN

On the plane from Melbourne back to Gladstone and my island I fought to forgive my father. What was it about men? Were they all liars, or just the ones in my life—and Fran's professor, and Pat's husband? But I still had Tom. I closed my eyes and saw his face smiling his crooked smile. I pressed my legs together and, for an indulgent few seconds, enjoyed the tingling, zinging sensation that hollowed my belly.

"Coffee or tea, Madam?"

As I sipped the dishwater coffee, I took out the little photo Mary had pushed into my hand. Now that I knew, I could sense the despair in my grandparents, standing together dressed in shapeless gray clothes, with their out-of-control son and feisty daughter looking sullen beside them. Clemency. My fingers rubbed her pendant. What on earth were her parents thinking when they saddled her with that name? Did she feel clemency for her wayward son? I tried to feel a connection with her. It was easier than finding a connection with the land of my father. Neither Dry Acres Farm—or its reinvention as the Artists' Community—nor the pretty town of Healesville lit a spark in me. Did Dad feel the same way?

Mary and George were good people, and I had ended up staying the night and driving back to Melbourne the next morning. I heard all about George's grown son, and the tragic story of his wife's death. But although I felt sad for him, and even though we looked so alike, we didn't feel like family. Not close family, anyway. Perhaps the hole Dad left when he disappeared was too deep to be filled so easily. I suspected our promises to keep in touch would become cards at Christmas.

Pat felt more like family to me. She had been discharged from hospital two days earlier and I'd had dinner with them all the previous night at Susie's. When we hugged goodbye, Pat told me she would be back on Turtle Island the minute her chemo was over. Her first cycle was scheduled for the following week, and I offered to stay and ferry her to and from the hospital, but Susie and Troy had it sorted between them. Pat insisted that it was time for me to return to the island. "And Tom," she added with her old grin. If love and optimism could banish any lurking cancer cells, Pat would be flippering over the coral again long before I had to leave. Four more months, and then back to Boston. I stared out the window at the white beaches fringing the green and brown land far below.

I HADN'T TOLD TOM I WAS COMING BACK, SO MY DIS-appointment when he wasn't waiting for me on the wharf when Jack's boat docked was ridiculous. I was rubbing the damned pendant again. I'd take it off for good as soon as I got to my cabin.

Unpacked and uncertain, in the late afternoon I wandered through the trees towards Tom's house. My hand reached for the missing pendant. What on earth was the matter with me? Why would anything have changed? I turned along the sidetrack and stopped. There was a man in a chair on the sandy grass in front of the house. He was performing some sort of contorted dance—either mad as a hatter or high as a kite. I moved behind a tree and peered out like a kid. It was a wheel-chair, not a chair, and the man was gesticulating and grimacing, his chair rocking with the force of it. My scalp prickled. Why was this man, so clearly unwell, outside Tom's place? I wanted to turn and run, but was stuck there, mesmerized and repelled by the familiar gestures. I had organized my lab so I could avoid direct contact with the participants in my research, but it was never 100 percent foolproof, and I had, over almost quarter of a century, been forced to watch the painful twisted movements of many Huntington's disease victims.

I crept out from my cowardly hiding place and the man's movements stopped abruptly. I could see him, his head twisted to one side, looking over at me. I walked sheepishly towards him, praying that Tom would appear and not leave me alone with whoever this was.

"Hullo there. Don't be scared. I don't b-b-bite or scratch." His voice was deep and surprisingly melodious.

"Hullo," I said. I took the long, thin hand he was waving in my direction, and shook it up and down before letting it drop.

A smile took over his face and he lurched back in his chair, almost tipping it over. I grabbed it and held it steady and he laughed. "It's okay. It's more stable than it looks." His deep voice cracked and wobbled up a few notes.

"I'm Anna Fergusson. I'm a friend of Tom's but I've been away."

He spluttered and a glob of spit dribbled from the corner of his mouth. I swallowed my own saliva and moved back a step before I could stop myself.

"Morrie Spencer. Nice to meet you"—his head jerked again and he waved towards me—"Anna."

"Is Tom around?" I said loudly, feeling stupid immediately. I smiled at him, forcing my eyes to join in.

"No. He's escaped to some other island. He'll be b-b-back tomorrow." His voice had become deep again. It was rather pleasant. I tried not to look at him as he waved a large white handkerchief over his face, trying to mop up his dribble.

"Sorry," he said when he had finished his mopping. "I've got Huntington's disease and sometimes it's a b-b-bugger to stay clean."

"Don't worry about it," I said, feeling like a total shit. At least I was controlling my urge to shout at him as if he were deaf. "Are you a friend of Tom's?"

"Yes. For a long time." He flapped his long arm back towards the house. "He lets me st-st-stay here every year. It's my holiday."

I could have hugged him. My head was zinging, my heart was singing. Tom wasn't jealous when he saw my article, he was just choked up about his friend. "Well, it's a nice place for a holiday," I almost sang at him.

"The b-b-best. I used to go out in the tinnie with him but it's a ba-bit hard now. Last time I went I fell out and Tom had a helluva time getting me ba-ba-back in." He threw his head back and I caught the twinkle in his eyes, but the belly laugh that went with his expansive posture came out as a wheezy whooping. I found myself chuckling with him, the vision of Tom and his gesticulating friend floundering in the sea dancing before my eyes.

"How will you manage tonight by yourself, if Tom's not here?" I asked when we had stopped laughing.

"It will b-b-be pretty funny, but I'll manage. Tom's left me a meal all nicely laid out on a plate." He twisted and writhed and gasped for air. "Cold meat and spuds and a nice salad. I'm not a total b-b-basket case yet."

"Of course not." I was blushing and blustering. "I was

wondering if you wanted some company? Perhaps I could even make something hot if you like." The words tumbled out of my mouth without my permission. Morrie did his head on the side smile again and I grinned back. He was nice, and didn't seem too cognitively impaired. It would be interesting to spend some time with him. He might even let out some secrets about Tom's past.

"Tom told me about you, Anna. He can't have b-b-been expecting you back."

My face got hotter. "No, I wanted it to be a surprise."

"Is Pat back too?" His head jerked again but I caught the concern on his long face.

"No, she's staying with her daughter while she has chemotherapy."

"She's a strong woman. I haven't seen her for a couple of years"—he gesticulated wildly as his voice faltered—"she was away when I was here last year. B-b-b-but she'll be baaa-be fine."

I felt the prickle behind my eyes and blinked furiously. "I know she will. She has to be."

I GOT BACK TO MY CABIN AROUND TEN O'CLOCK, exhausted. Whether it was from watching Morrie, or from the effort it took to understand him and make conversation, I didn't know. Probably all of those things and a few emotions thrown in for good measure. Guilt and shame are likely tiring. After a shower—so good to get back to the bucket on a string after the fast hot wasteful showers in my Melbourne motel—I hauled out my computer. Tired as I was, I needed to write down what I was feeling. If I didn't I'd never sleep, or if I slept I would regret it when the horrible dreams I deserved came to punish me.

1ˢᵗ June, 2009. I arrived back on Turtle Island today, looking forward to seeing Tom. I needed him to help me balance. I've been away for eighteen days but it feels like forever. First Pat, then finding Mary and George and discovering that Dad wasn't the honest, perfect man I thought he was.

Who am I to cast the first stone? My own disgusting behavior is what's eating into me now. I had a good time tonight with a man who has quite advanced Huntington's disease. Morrie is one of the funniest people I've met in a long while, and it has nothing to do with his movements. He's a natural comic. It's a long time since I laughed so hard that I got stitch. Why have I taken twenty-five years to find out what all my research assistants have known from their first days with people like Morrie? I'm appalled at myself. I've always been ashamed —secretly of course—by my avoidance of contact with the very people who have given themselves so willingly to my study. I have always known it was terrible to use them like that, and that to excuse myself by employing wonderful, humane research assistants was a copout.

There is nothing, nothing in my background that can explain or excuse my feelings. I have thought about this often enough. The only thing even vaguely related is a time when I was perhaps four or five when we visited a friend of Mum's and she had a teenage daughter who was severely disabled. She was hauling herself around the kitchen on her bottom and grunting. I remember being terrified of her. Hardly an excuse for my adult behavior. It doesn't explain why I'm so useless and awkward around any patient and even their families if they need to talk. What I would give for just a tiny bit of the easy manner of Pat's Dr. Pascoe.

I was on the verge of admitting it all to Morrie, and asking his forgiveness on the behalf of everyone with Huntington's, but I managed to stop myself. Imagine laying that on him. He might have made it into a joke but I think he would probably have taken me seriously and let me weep and wail and feel sorry for myself, and then he would have said something wise and healing. I wonder if he's always been so lovely, or if it is living with that horrific disease that has made him so sanguine.

I did tell him I had done some research on Huntington's. After Tom's reaction when he found my article, I didn't want to seem to be hiding anything. Morrie had no such reaction. He thought it was great and made some joke about that being why I was so skilled at dealing with him. Or perhaps it wasn't a joke. He said it was good to have another friend who wasn't frightened by the way he danced about. I think he was perfectly aware of my shameful feelings when I first saw him.

By the time I had our dinner on the table, I hardly noticed his gyrations. I was laughing so much most of the time my gyrations were not much different. All these years I have missed getting to know my own research participants, and hear their amazing stories from them and not from my research assistants. Morrie told me a little about his own family. His mother died of Huntington's ten years ago, and his father of a stroke two years after. He's an only child, so he lives in a home for the disabled in Sydney. He was a schoolteacher, but that all came to an end five years ago when his symptoms got too bad. He was only thirty-eight. He and Tom have been friends since they were kids. Why didn't Tom tell me about Morrie, at least once he realized I had worked on Huntington's? Did he sense, somehow, my fear?

I SLEPT LIKE THE DEAD, AND WOKE TO A KISS. TOM'S dear face was there, level with mine as I lay on the top bunk. I wanted to pull him up beside me, but the room was blazing with light, so I thought better of it. Safe on the floor and still half asleep, I nuzzled his warm hand as it slid around the back of my neck to my cheek. The feeling was new and delicious. Then I remembered. "Oh god, my hair."

"Why did you cut it all off?"

I looked up at him. Was he upset? "It was weighing me down."

"But why so much, so short? Such beautiful hair."

"You never told me that."

"Anna, you didn't need me to tell you. You could see for yourself every time you looked in the mirror."

"I thought you'd like it short. The hairdresser said it would make me look years younger."

"The hairdresser, huh."

I pulled away from him, feeling my happiness draining away. "I thought you liked short hair."

"Anna, why do you put yourself down all the time? You're a beautiful woman. I'd rather you hadn't cut all your wonderful hair off, but then I'm a man; we're suckers for long hair."

I swallowed, but the sick feeling stuck there. Tom was smiling at me and cupping my head in his hands.

"It's only hair, Anna. Long or short doesn't change who you are. Your hair has nothing to do with your beauty. You would be just as beautiful to me if you shaved it all off. You turned me on with long hair and by god you turn me on with this short sexy look." He hugged me tight but not before I caught the shine in his eyes.

"You were quite a hit with Morrie." His voice was muffled, buried in my hair.

I sniffed, and pressed into him. *Morrie. Such a beautiful, confident person, and I think the length of my hair matters.*

❄

THE NEXT TWO WEEKS WERE SO MUCH FUN. I HAD NEVER laughed so much. We'd had plenty of serious conversations too; Morrie was quite a philosopher. Tom told me that Morrie was brilliant at school and university, and everyone thought he should do something brainy, like nuclear physics, but all he wanted to do was teach kids. Of course he would have known he was at risk of getting Huntington's, so perhaps he figured there was no point in doing something that involved years of study. I bet he had been a wonderful teacher—still was. I had learned more about American politics from him than in all my years living in Boston. Then there was botany, and geology, and psychology, and literature. He seemed to have read every single classic, and lots of contemporary fiction too. So much for all the theories about poor attention span in Huntington's. Chess was another of his skills, and we'd had some great games. He had a chess set with large magnetized pieces that stuck like glue to the metal chessboard. I had fallen for him, totally.

The only thing we didn't talk about was Huntington's. I didn't bring it up again, and nor did Morrie. I almost expected him to, as he seemed exactly the sort of person who would want to know everything possible about the latest research. I asked Tom about it one night when he was walking back to my cabin with me, and he wasn't very forthcoming. He was quite short with me, and said he assumed Morrie was sick to death of the topic, especially as no research was going to make a jot of difference to him. It made sense when I mulled it over later. It wasn't as if Morrie had any kids of his own, or even any siblings to worry about.

Pat was set to come home the next day. We'd e-mailed a

lot and talked a few times on Tom's Skype, although Pat refused to try the video link. She said she looked awful, and that her hair was falling out in great clumps. She was between chemo cycles and I think wanted to give Susie a break, as well as have a break herself from exuberant grandchildren and noisy Melbourne.

Shaving our heads was Tom's idea. So there we were on the wharf, waiting for the boat to arrive, hats pulled over our heads. Not just Morrie, Tom, and me, but Violet and Bill as well. Basil was very cocky about his au naturel bald pate. Violet's kids wanted to have their hair off too but Violet drew the line at that. As she said, little Danny's hair had only just begun to grow a few months ago.

When Pat walked down the gangplank with her arms outstretched and her wide smile, we all whipped off our hats and threw them in the air. We must have looked like a strange alien species with our white scalps and brown bodies. Her eyes were shiny by the time my arms were around her, but Morrie soon had her laughing. Later, she asked me to shave off what was left of her hair. She looked much better then. We had an early barbecue at Violet and Bill's place that evening, and Jack and his son arrived with their heads shaven, both of them still with their bushy red beards.

I moved in with Pat that night. She tried to make me believe she would be fine by herself, but her eyes were dark holes and her complexion, usually so brown, was almost yellow. She ate no more than a lettuce leaf and a bread roll at the barbecue, and in spite of taking her medication to stop her nausea, vomited twice in the night. I felt so helpless patting her back as she retched over a bowl, the cold sweat pouring off her. At last she slept, and I watched over her for a long time, my body aching for her.

———————

NINETEEN

When Pat left for Melbourne to face her next two cycles of chemo, she looked more like herself, her skin almost brown again and her eyes rested. More importantly, she was in good spirits, and determined to beat this thing. I was trying to be as positive.

Tom and I hadn't seen much of each other in the "biblical" sense, although he and Morrie spent time with Pat and me every day. As Pat's boat disappeared over the horizon, Tom took my hand and led me to my cabin. I thought he was going to take me to bed, right then, but he pulled out my wetsuit and told me to put it on; it was time for a long, healing snorkel over the reef edge.

So right as always, and after dinner with Morrie at Tom's house, he came home with me. Making love had never been so sweet. In the morning, very early, we walked along the beach, stopping every few steps to gaze at each other in the luminescent pink dawn.

"I don't ever want to leave here," I whispered. "Never, ever."

He put his fingers over my lips. He looked so sad that I was afraid.

"What's wrong?" I asked.

"Don't say that, Anna," he whispered. "We have this. That's enough."

I felt the prickle behind my eyes. "You feel the same way; I know you do."

"I'm not into permanent relationships. It wouldn't work."

Tom's face was swimming. "I don't want you to marry me. I just want to stay here and be with you, that's all." I was past being embarrassed by having to beg.

He touched my cheek. "I'm honored and flattered. But you need to return to your own world. This is a lovely interlude. Don't let's spoil it by trying to turn it into something it could never be."

I could hardly speak, the pain was so intense. "I'm too old for you, is that it?"

"Never too old, Anna. Never think that."

I could feel my hysteria burning inside me. "So what now? Perhaps I should leave early."

"Don't be silly. I want us to keep enjoying each other's company until it's time for you to go back in October. A perfect year."

"A perfect year, a perfect year." My head was throbbing. I wanted to scream. But all I could see was his face, so dear.

"Anna, calm down. We can write to each other." He grinned. "We can even e-mail."

"I don't want to e-mail or write if that's all you think we are: a sweet little interlude. Thank you for nothing." I turned away from him and walked blindly back along the beach, hoping he would come after me and tell me he was teasing.

He didn't, of course. All day I fumed and hoped and told myself I didn't care, and refused to allow my eyes to so much as water. I sat at my computer and tried to write but that made me feel worse. I thought about descending on Violet, but descending would be the operative word, the way I was feeling. The evening came and went, and I forced some toasted cheese sandwiches down with too many glasses of wine. After dark I crept around the beach, all the way to the track leading to Tom's house. I could see a light through the trees and I sat on the sand and tried to pluck up the courage to go the extra few meters, calling out cheerfully as I walked in on their game of chess or whatever they were doing. But it might have been a thousand kilometers for all the progress I made.

Back in my lonely cabin I lay awake torturing myself. I was hot with shame—how could I have exposed myself like that, how could I have made such a stupid assumption that he felt about me like I felt about him? I was cold with fury—he'd led me on and used me, just like all men. Good riddance. I was lucky to escape. I was prostrate with grief.

Another day and night went by somehow. How can two people avoid each other so totally on such a small island? Where were all my friends when I needed them? I knew I was being irrational: Pat and I had eaten at Violet and Bill's the night before she left. Basil went by a couple of times and waved. I waved back, all smiles. I didn't even have my hair to hide behind. It had regrown to the short, prickly, ugly stage, and I wondered whether I should shave the fuzz off again. I'd almost certainly end up cutting myself. Another reason for needing Tom.

I wanted to see Morrie. He'd be leaving soon and I'd never see him again. It was so unfair. Why should I have to give up my friendship with Morrie because of Tom? I went as far as their house again on the third night, determined to march up to the door and ask to see Morrie. He could hardly get across the island to see me, not without Tom's help, anyway. I could hear music and Morrie's deep voice, and knocked tentatively. Then I heard Tom's voice and the pounding of my heart intensified. Tom was talking to Morrie. He hadn't heard my little knock. Catching my breath, I scurried away.

I heard his wheezing before I saw him and rushed out onto the deck. Morrie was outside on the path, slumped over in his wheelchair. I was beside him in a heartbeat. Sweat poured off him as he jerked his head up and his arms shot out.

"Morrie, what is it? How did you get here?"

"Hot." He flapped his arms near his face. "This chair not the b-b-best on these tracks."

"I don't believe it. Don't tell me you wheeled yourself across the island."

He nodded.

His cheeky grin was missing. Something was terribly wrong. "Is it Tom? Has something happened to him? Where is he?" I couldn't breathe.

"Water please," Morrie wheezed. "Tom is okay. Came to see you."

"I thought . . ." I maneuvered his wheelchair backwards up the two shallow steps onto the deck and into the shade and got him a glass of water. He drank it with great gulps and splutters, most of it landing on his lap and on me.

"Slow down," I said, alarm spiking through me. I knew only too well how easy it was for Huntington's patients to choke.

Morrie coughed and gurgled and then quietened. I filled the glass again and held it to his lips, feeding him small sips.

"Thanks," he said, and at last I saw his smile.

"It's a pleasure," I said. "Shall I mop your poor hot head and hands with a cold flannel?"

His head nodded wildly.

"Why did you come all this way?" I asked when he was cool again.

"I missed you. I wa-was worried." He looked at me with his head twisted to the side, and I could see his eyes were watering.

"Oh Morrie, I'm sorry."

"We need to t-t-talk about T-tom," Morrie croaked.

My stomach lurched. "I thought you said he was okay?"

"He's a m-m-mess. He needs you."

"He as good as told me he didn't love me and he didn't want me to stay here with him." I could hear the self-pity in my voice.

"He loves you all right. It's himself he doesn't love." Morrie's voice was suddenly deep and strong.

I was shaking. "What do you mean?"

"He's always insisted that no one knows. He thinks people will pity him."

"Knows what?"

"Huntington's. He's m-my cousin." Morrie's body contorted and I sat and waited, his words sinking in.

"You mean on your mother's side?" I seemed to be floating, looking down on us sitting there.

Morrie's head shot back and then forwards again. "His dad and my mum."

"Does his father have Huntington's?" I already knew, of course. His dad didn't have Alzheimer's, he had Huntington's dementia. It was all clear now. Tom's upset when he realized that was my research area, and his fear of long-term relationships. All I wanted was to hold him close.

"Yes," I heard Morrie wheezing. "He's in the final stages."

"Tom. Does he have the gene?"

"He'll have t-t-to tell you, not for m-m-me," Morrie said, his eyes so sad.

I bent over and took his twitching dear head in both my hands and held him still. Then I kissed him gently on his lips, my eyes blurring. "Thank you," I whispered.

Morrie blushed. "I l-l-ove Tom. He needs you, but he won't admit it, the s-s-silly shit."

I MADE POACHED EGGS AND TOAST SOLDIERS AND FED first Morrie and then myself. We both felt better after that. Then I wheeled him back along the track through the trees, astounded at every tree root and shearwater hole by his superman feat of getting himself to my place. The house was silent when we reached it; Tom wasn't back from wherever he had gone in his dinghy that morning. I helped a tired Morrie onto his bed, and left him with a promise to return that evening in time to make us all dinner.

The minute I got home, I grabbed my snorkel and flippers and was soon floating around the lagoon, willing the beauty and peace of the underwater world to permeate every cell of my body.

Tom greeted me with a chaste kiss when I arrived around six o'clock with my bag full of steaks and lettuce. I looked into his face, wanting to see my desperate desire for peace reflected in his eyes, but all I could see was bleakness.

"I'm sorry," I whispered. "Please tell me we are all right again."

He reached out and touched my cheek. "I'm sorry too, to hurt you. I've been miserable without you."

My heart and stomach soared together. "Me too. Can I come in?" I could see Morrie behind Tom, grinning at me, his head on one side.

We made the dinner together, and it was a nice evening,

but we didn't talk about Tom, or his father, or Huntington's. When the dishes had been washed, we played a game of cards, but none of us had our hearts in it and we gave up after one hand. Morrie was yawning and wheeled himself off to bed soon after, leaving Tom and me sitting in an uncomfortable silence.

"Do you want to have a walk on the beach?" I asked.

"I suppose so, but I don't want to talk about me and my family. That's my business, and Morrie had no right to tell you."

"He told me because he was worried about you. How could you keep it from me?" I whimpered.

"It's not you. I keep it from everyone. That's what I decided to do years ago and nothing's changed," he mumbled.

I tried to catch his eye but he was looking at the floor.

"Tom, please let me in. It doesn't matter to me if you have Huntington's."

"Bullshit." His voice rose. "Of course it matters. You do research in the damn area. You know what it means."

"Yes, and that's why you need to believe me. Have you been tested for the gene?"

He stood up. "Anna, leave it. I'm not one of your research subjects, and you can't bully me into talking about it."

His words hit me like a sledgehammer. I closed my eyes, willing them away. I could hear Tom's rasping breath as he walked the floor. After a while, I stood up, still shaking, and forced myself to speak calmly. "We're both tired. Perhaps I should go home and you can get some sleep."

"Yes, I'm stuffed. Thanks for coming around." His voice had softened and he dipped down and brushed my lips with his. "I'm glad we're back together again, but please don't push me to change."

✄

But we weren't back together again. The elephant in the room and on the beach and everywhere we were wasn't Huntington's but Tom's mistrust of me. Of course, the specter of Huntington's was there too, seeping through my head in the early hours of the morning. Did Tom have the gene? Did he even know? I let myself imagine how it would be if we did stay together and how I would cope as he became more and more disabled. I told myself it was better that I'd never have to find out. I could go back to my life in Boston, and in time my year on Turtle Island would be a happy memory, no more.

But none of it worked. Even floating about in the lagoon no longer gave me peace. Surely I was too old to feel like this over a relationship. I hated it, and it brought back memories of my year of depression after Philip rejected me and I lost— aborted—my baby; depression and anger and pain that took me places I didn't know could coexist with life. I didn't want to go anywhere near there again.

Before that, the only other time I had felt so depressed was after Dad drowned. I wanted to hide away. In hindsight, Mum did her best, and I suffered through some painfully useless sessions with the school counselor. In the end I simply learned to live with my new, withdrawn self. Before that I was someone else entirely—not exactly a social butterfly but at least a kid who could enjoy life when the opportunity arose. I blamed Dad's death for turning me into a sullen teenager and a studious medical student whose idea of fun was reading the occasional novel.

Perhaps by the time I began my PhD, flush with the relief that I had found something to do that excited rather than scared me, I was ripe for seduction. God knows why Philip even bothered; perhaps he got off on seeing me blossom under his smooth hands. But at least I'd discovered I could still feel joy, even if it was tainted with guilt and sandwiched between large chunks of misery as I waited yearningly for the crumbs he threw me.

I was no psychologist, but even I could see the pattern here. I was an intelligent woman. How had I gotten myself into this situation again? Damn Tom, damn bloody Huntington's, damn, damn, damn.

If it hadn't been for Morrie, I think Tom and I would have avoided each other more and more until we morphed soundlessly into mere acquaintances. In a strange way, Morrie was like a child we shared: we had to play our parts for his sake. Of course, he was far from a child, and our act didn't fool him. Morrie didn't interfere or try to mediate. I almost wished he would, but he had known Tom all his life, and I suppose he knew how stubborn he was. And he knew what it was to be haunted by Huntington's. Dearest Morrie. I wanted to shake Tom and say, "Look at Morrie. If that is you some day, how could you think I wouldn't still love you and want to be with you and share my life with you?" But I didn't, and I couldn't.

But Morrie's visit was almost over, and Tom was going back with him on Jack's boat to see him safely on the plane to Sydney. I considered not going to the wharf to see them off, knowing I would almost certainly never see Morrie again. I didn't think I could nod casually to Tom as he boarded the boat, acting as if he were nothing special to me. But when the time came I forced myself to join everyone else. It was such a thing on the island when anyone who belonged to the inner circle left, to be there to wave goodbye. And Morrie was definitely one of the most loved. I knew Jack had a quick turn-around this time—just long enough to dump the supplies onto the beach and grab the mail and any passengers, and he would be off again, back in time for his mother's birthday on the mainland that night. Even Jack had a mother.

So when the boat docked and Kirsty strolled down the gangplank, Hamish in a baby backpack, I was, by chance, waiting for them. I hadn't forgotten my promise to look after Hamish in late July so Kirsty could go to her vet nursing practical course, but I had thought she would contact me with an exact date. There was the difference between her and me. One of many. Pulling Hamish out of his backpack, she passed him to me. He chuckled as I took one chubby hand and kissed it. He remembered me. Kirsty hugged me, and then took Hamish back, squeezing him so tight that I almost grabbed her arms to loosen them.

"I thought I'd be able to spend a night with you before I had to leave again," she said. "Damn Jack's mother. Why couldn't she have her birthday some other time?"

"Why didn't you tell me you were coming? I'm not prepared, and Pat's not here to tell me what to do."

"Don't be a wimp. He's a lamb. I've brought everything you'll need: formula, bottles, diapers, his teddy, even a portable cot. You'll be fine. It's me who won't be."

"How long will you be away?"

"Two weeks. A lifetime." She hugged her baby close, and he squirmed in her grasp.

"Why don't you stay?" I asked, knowing I should be supporting her to go on her course, not making it harder.

"Anna, you promised. I have to do this. If I don't, I'll end up in some low-paying shop girl job, and I want more than that for Hamish."

"Sorry, you're right. We'll be fine. The two weeks will fly past, you'll see."

I became aware that the beach was covered with boxes and Tom and Morrie were beside me. Tears streaming down her cheeks, Kirsty thrust Hamish back into my arms, kissed me and then her baby's downy head, and turned and almost ran up the gangplank onto the boat. I looked down at Morrie, my eyes stinging as I saw his dear face twitching to one side as he flapped his hands at me. I bent awkwardly, but with Hamish in my arms my kiss didn't have a hope of making a landing. Then the baby was taken from me and I knelt down beside Morrie's wheelchair and grasped him around his middle. Squeezing my eyes tight shut I hugged him, and his arms closed around me before flying off again.

"Bye, my Anna," he said, his voice deep and strong. "I won't forget you, especially if you write to me."

I risked looking at him and he looked back, his eyes swimming.

"Bye, Morrie. Thank you for everything." I swallowed. "Love you." Then I was standing, and Tom was putting Hamish back in my arms. He bent and I felt the touch of his lips, and he and Morrie were gone, onto the boat.

TWENTY

I once read somewhere that women over sixty read more books than any other group. Because of a genetic flaw, men aren't big readers, and women aged between twenty-five and sixty are too busy being mothers and then career women to have time to read, even though they would love to. Since arriving on Turtle Island I'd read no more than ten of the sixty books I'd so diligently downloaded onto my Kindle before I left Boston, thinking I would have endless blissful hours to indulge. In the first five days of life with Hamish, I managed exactly one page of the novel that had been gripping me before his arrival—reading at that point being my only release from thinking endlessly about Tom and me. I was lucky to get through one sentence in the few seconds before I fell asleep each night, only to be woken around two o'clock and then again at six o'clock for Hamish's next bottle.

I'd never felt particularly tired when I was patrolling the beach every night and tagging turtles, although admittedly I'd slept late in the mornings. But this was another thing altogether. Four-hour blocks of sleep, punctuated with hot flushes, left me exhausted. But I wouldn't have changed it. The hot flushes I could do without, but the night feeds were strangely precious. Sometimes I woke before Hamish and willed him to open his eyes so I could lift his warm, sleepy body out of the cot and cuddle him close.

Days were filled with goodness knows what: crawling around on the floor, admiring Hamish's attempts to roll over; walks on the beach with babe in his backpack; cups of tea with Violet while her kids cooed over Hamish and he chuckled back. No time to fret over Tom. By half past six every other evening, I was sitting in Tom's house in front of his computer, awaiting Kirsty's Skype call. She'd left strict instructions about this in a note I'd found in Hamish's case of diapers, bottles, and formula. Although Kirsty had looked a bit teary when she waved her baby goodbye, she was loving every moment of her course and, although she wouldn't admit it, I think she was enjoying living it up with the other students in the evenings.

ON SATURDAY HAMISH WOKE WITH A SNIFFLE, AND BY midday he was fractious and off his bottle. I spent most of the afternoon walking the floor with him while he cried. Putting him in his cot made him cry louder and when I bravely tried to leave him there and sat on the deck where he couldn't see me, he kept on crying. When he began to sound choky, I wrapped him up, hot though he was, put him in his backpack, and walked to Violet's. She of course had some liquid baby Panadol, and within thirty minutes he fell asleep on my lap. Buoyed by Violet's assurances that it was just a cold and to give him more Panadol in three hours, I inserted him into his backpack again and took him home. Fortunately it wasn't a Skype night, so I didn't have to drag the poor little mite to Tom's, nor did I have to worry Kirsty. With luck he'd be a box of birds by tomorrow; I believed babies were like that.

By ten that night he was burning up and I was sponging

him with lukewarm water, trying to get his temperature down. Then, without warning, he arched back in my arms, stiff as a board. His eyes rolled up and he began to jerk. Medically trained I might be, but a seizure in a little baby was frightening. It seemed to go on forever, but was probably no more than a very long two minutes. My head full of meningitis and god knows what other baby ailments, I continued to sponge him, thankful that no meningitis-type rashes were appearing, and attempted to get some water into his crying little mouth. After the third attempt the teaspoon of Panadol I forced into him seemed to disappear down his throat instead of coating his chin. Wrapping him in a towel I walked the floor again, his downy head flopping on my shoulder as he snuffled and whimpered.

"Are you okay?" Tom's voice said.

I started, and Hamish let out a little squawk. Turning around, I saw his dark silhouette on the deck. "Where did you come from?" My knees felt as if they were going to deposit me in a heap on the floor.

"Is the baby sick?" he asked.

"Yes, he's got a fever and he had a seizure a while ago. It was terrible."

Tom was beside me, one hand on Hamish's head.

"What's all this, young fellow," I heard him whisper. "You look done in," he said to me, pecking me on the cheek.

"Thanks. It's been a long day. How did you get here? I didn't think you'd be back until next weekend."

"I caught a ride on a friend's catamaran. They were sailing up to Cairns and didn't mind going off course."

"Didn't Collette want you to stay in Brisbane so she could boss you around?"

"Very funny. No, once I'd waved Morrie goodbye I couldn't wait to get out of there. I'm no city slicker."

He'd taken Hamish from me and was rocking him gently back and forth, so I eased my aching body into a chair, groaning as I undid the knots in my neck and shoulders. My eyes focused on a pukey stain down the front of my crumpled T-shirt, and then my utilitarian knickers swam into view. I leapt out of the chair, almost knocking Tom over, and grabbed a pair of shorts lying on top of the pile of clothes at the end of my bunk. When I emerged from the bathroom, my hair combed, feeling slightly less exposed and less smelly, Tom was pouring water from the kettle into two cups. Hamish was sound asleep on his shoulder.

"What made you come and see me at this hour of the night?" I mumbled as the scalding tea burnt my parched throat.

"Just felt like it. I wouldn't have disturbed you if your light was off."

I sniffed. Perhaps I was getting Hamish's cold. "I'm glad. You seem to have a way with babies as well as turtles."

"Call me baby whisperer. Do you think it's anything serious, with the seizure?"

"I hope not. He was very hot so I'm praying it was a once-off febrile seizure. God knows how I'll tell Kirsty. She'll never leave him with me again."

"Bollocks. But I bet she'll want to get over here. Perhaps you don't need to tell her just yet, if he's okay tomorrow."

"I couldn't do that. She would definitely never forgive me, and I wouldn't blame her. Is that really how you think?"

"I don't know, Anna. I'm just a bloke, remember." Tom carried the still-sleeping baby over to the cot and laid him in it. "I'll leave you to get some sleep. I'll come by first thing in the morning in case you need anything."

"Don't go, Tom. I'm sorry."

"Nothing to be sorry for."

"Please stay. I felt so alone before. What if he gets worse again?"

"I'm sure you'd cope."

I could feel him looking at me.

"Are you crying," he asked.

"No." I sniffed again. "I'm just tired and worried."

"Okay, I'll stay."

Tom took the first watch, and I woke two hours later when Hamish's cry penetrated my dreams. He was burning up again, and we sponged him down and Tom managed to get some Panadol into him. When at last he was asleep, Tom insisted I go back to bed so I would be able to take over the next day. Two hours max, I said, telling him to wake me at five at the latest. But it was well past dawn when I opened my eyes and heard Tom murmuring to Hamish.

"Is he sick again?" I gasped, sliding off the top bunk.

"No, just hungry, I would imagine. He's been sleeping like a baby." He handed him to me. "You change him while I warm up his bottle."

He felt much cooler, and as I changed his almost dry diaper, thinking we had to get some liquid into him, he chuckled at me. We fed him a few ounces of milk at a time, which he managed to keep down. As I tucked him up in his cot, already asleep, the smell of bacon and eggs was heaven.

Perhaps it was my lightheaded relief, but as we scoffed down the feast, I said, without any preliminaries, "Tom, do you have the Huntington's gene?"

Tom's fork, halfway to his mouth, halted, and then continued on its way. I held my breath. He didn't look up, and I watched him as he finished every last smear of egg yolk.

"Why can't you tell me? Don't you think I deserve to know?"

Tom placed his knife and fork carefully on his plate, and looked at me. "What difference would it make?"

"Well, it wouldn't," I said. "Not to how I feel about you. But if you did have it, perhaps I could help you."

"Anna, I know you're an expert on Huntington's, and if I do want to know anything, I promise I'll ask you." He sighed. "It's not about facts any more. I've watched Dad get worse and worse, and Mum trying to help him. I know as much as I want to know."

"You haven't been tested, have you?" I almost whispered.

Tom shook his head.

"But you might not have it. Don't you want to know?"

He pulled a twenty-cent coin from his pocket and held it in his palm. "You call. Heads I don't have Huntington's and tails I do."

"Don't be silly."

"Silly is about right. Having the test is no different from tossing a coin. Even odds that I'll be home free. But what if it's tails, Anna? Is that better than hoping for a few more years that I might be heads?"

"I'm sorry. I shouldn't have asked." My stomach turned over.

"It's crazy, but even if I discovered I didn't have the gene, I'd feel terrible. Somehow, that would make it more likely that my sister had got the short straw."

"She hasn't been tested either?"

"No. Hilary and her husband didn't want to know, even when they decided to have kids. Instead they used IVF, using fertilized eggs that tested negative for the gene."

"But she would know, surely, if some of her eggs had been positive, or if none of her eggs had carried the gene?"

"They asked not to be told either way. That would have been no better than tossing a coin."

I could feel my mouth actually drop open.

Tom grinned. "Hilary's not to be messed with. She wanted her own kids, and she didn't want them worrying all their childhoods about having to look after her when she got Huntington's. She says that if she does have it, she wants to enjoy life first."

"That's incredible." I struggled to keep the disbelief out of my voice.

Tom started clearing the table as if that was that. I rehearsed my next sentence carefully, and as I dried the dishes he was so competently washing, I let it out. "I'm sure you know this, but just in case . . . The whole thing about 50 percent of the children of a parent with Huntington's having the gene doesn't mean that if you don't have the gene, Hilary does. It's a statistical thing over a whole population. You could both be free of the gene, and in another family both children might be unlucky." I dried the plate for the third time, not brave enough to look at Tom.

"Just like getting heads twice in a row in that coin toss. Yes, Dr. Fergusson, I do understand. I know I'm not being rational." He smiled at me—a genuine smile—and the flare of annoyance his words had spurred in me flickered and died.

He left soon after, leaving me to deal with a whirlpool of feelings: overwhelming relief that Hamish, in spite of a runny nose, was back to his happy self, and frustration, helplessness, misery about Tom. I had to face him again that evening when Hamish and I went to keep our Skype date with Kirsty. Hamish was perfect, grinning when he saw his mother's face on the screen, and I almost didn't tell her. But I had to, of course. I tried to downplay it, but explaining a febrile seizure isn't easy to downplay to a first-time mum. It took a while to calm her, and in the end it was Tom's matter-of-fact contributions that did the trick.

"Kirsty," he said, inserting his face next to mine, "Hamish is okay, but if you carry on like this you'll upset him. Get a grip. We sponged him down, gave him Panadol, and he is as right as rain. Heaps of babies have a febrile seizure and it does them no harm at all."

I'd told her something similar, but there you go. When did anyone listen to me? By the end of the conversation she'd agreed not to move heaven and earth to get back to the island before next weekend, on the condition that we Skyped every night.

Tom asked me to stay for dinner, and afterwards, with Hamish asleep in a tumble of blankets on the deck, we talked. Perhaps the wine helped, but it seemed to me that Tom was relieved that it was out there, that elephant, clear for both of us to see. Watching his face as he told me his story was gut-wrenching—his father's slow and dreadful deterioration, his mother's exhausted efforts to care for him, his sister's determined efforts to remain optimistic about her own chances.

"How long do we have to wait until he dies, Anna?" he asked me. "How much more agony must he and Mum go through?"

"I don't know," was all I could offer. "I don't know."

"WE COULD DO WITH A THIRD MAN ON THE TURTLE rodeo." Tom was standing on my deck, a silhouette against the bright morning light.

"I thought you only did that in October. What do you mean, a third man?" I felt a pump of adrenaline.

"A third person. You'll do, given the lack of alternatives. Are you game?"

"They're not mating again now, are they?" I was peddling for time.

"No, but we do a rodeo midyear as well. You'll like it better because we don't have to rip the lovers apart. The idea is we cruise around the lagoon looking out for turtles grazing, and grab them. That way we can get an idea of who stays around and who buggers off for the winter."

"Sounds like an excuse to me. You're just bored."

"Well, it is a little dull around here, with no one interesting to play with," Tom said.

Hamish chuckled from his rug on the floor.

Tom caught the tea towel I threw at him and ducked inside, grabbing me around my waist and swinging me into a three-step. I realized I had the radio blaring on the concert program, and it was playing a Viennese waltz.

"What would I have to do?" I asked when the music stopped.

"Be another pair of eyes when we're looking for turtles, and help Bill haul the turtle up the side of the tinnie and tie its flippers to the boat. Then help tag and measure it, just like you did with the females when they were laying. It will give these puny arms some muscle." He pinched my upper arm and I tensed my puny muscle.

"Okay. I'll give it a go," I said, already feeling the nervous energy that being out in a boat evoked. A good feeling, sort of —a lot different from how it used to be. "But I'll have to see if Violet can look after Hamish."

"You'll need your full wetsuit, and I've got some gloves you can wear."

"Gloves?"

"It's hard on your hands." Tom stooped down and picked up Hamish. "I'll drop Hamish off at Violet's—she's waiting for him. She reckons you've had more than your fair share of time with him." He grabbed a diaper from the pack on the table, and waved Hamish's hand at me. "I'll see you at the wharf in half an hour."

"Today? Holy cow, you could have given me more warning."

His eyebrows went up. "How long do you need to pull a wetsuit on? Do you need me to help?"

"Get outta here. I wanted more time to get used to the idea, that's all."

"Bugger me, I'd never have guessed." He stooped and kissed me. "You'll love it. Trust me."

"WATCH YOUR ARM." BILL'S YELL JERKED ME BACK, AS the enormous loggerhead turtle snapped the air, just missing my left arm. I almost fell on my butt into the bottom of the boat.

"Shit, Anna, that was close," Tom muttered from the water where he was valiantly pressing the turtle against the side while Bill maneuvered a rope around one of its flippers. "It could have taken your arm off."

"Sorry. I was so busy concentrating I didn't think." I edged back towards the flipper on my side and had another go at lassoing it, this time keeping my arms away from the massive jaws. An enormous dark eye looked balefully at me. I got the rope secured and sat back, feeling pleased with myself. Only a few loggerheads came up on the beach and this was the first one we'd caught today. It seemed much bigger than the greens.

"Good job," Bill said.

Once the loggerhead was released, decorated with a shiny new tag, Tom hauled himself back into the tinnie. He frowned at me, and then smiled. "We're a bit sensitive about turtle bites. I had a student assisting me a few years ago who wasn't so lucky."

"You mean he lost his arm?" My stomach turned over.

"No, but she got a nasty bite and had to be helicoptered to hospital to have it cleaned and stitched."

"Oh. Is her arm all right?"

"Fine."

"I didn't realize you had women helping you on the rodeo."

"For my sins, sometimes that's the only option." His wink in Bill's direction was not subtle.

I flexed my biceps, snug and unblemished in Pat's wetsuit. "Hmmm. Well, what are we waiting for. Let's get the next bruiser."

WE STOOD TOGETHER, TOM AND I, TO WAVE KIRSTY AND Hamish goodbye. Violet, Bill, and the kids were there too, and Basil as well. Family. But Pat was still missing and I knew I would feel her absence terribly with Hamish gone. Still as a stone, I glued my eyes to Kirsty and Hamish standing by the railings at the back of Jack's boat. My nose was tickling, my eyes were watering, my throat was clamped tight, my heart was bleeding.

"You'll see them again," Tom said, his arm tightening around me as the boat became smaller and smaller, and still I didn't move. We were alone on the wharf now; everyone else had returned to their lives.

"Will I? Even if I do, it won't be the same. Soon I'll be back in Boston and Kirsty will be busy with her own life. I'll be forgotten."

"That's up to you. If you want to keep in touch, you can.

No child can have too many people to love him." Tom turned me away from the sea and looked into my eyes. "Be happy that you had this extra time with him, and fell so hard for him. Surely that's better than not knowing he ever existed."

"It's better to have loved and lost than never to have loved at all," I said, forcing my lips into a smile. I felt Tom's finger wiping away a rogue tear, and my smile reached my eyes.

TWENTY-ONE

D ecision time. The Huntington's Disease Association had offered me a two-year research grant that would pay a small salary while I analyzed and wrote up some of the data gathered by my group over the last few years. Research labs always seemed to accumulate masses of data that never got written up, and my lab hadn't been an exception. Once the main articles were published and the main questions addressed, another project would take over, often leaving potential riches lying in filing cabinets or on computers. It seemed unethical to discard it—all that time given to our projects by Huntington's patients and their families, the countless hours of work by my research assistants, and the thousands of dollars supplied by my previous granting body. It's probably a fantasy—given that I'm no longer on that cutting edge—but perhaps I could find something useful, something new, that might help families like Tom's.

These days, when I thought about it at all, I wondered if research on how to cope with having Huntington's mightn't be more useful than working out ever-finer details about the genetics and pathology of the disease. We knew how to stop it —do what Tom's sister had done and make sure no more babies were born who carried the gene. It might be more constructive to pursue research on how best to persuade potential carriers with strong religious or moral beliefs to consider contraception, abortion, IVF, or genetic testing for the sake of their descendants.

Or perhaps I should become an activist, fighting to legalize euthanasia for patients like Tom's father. Morrie had told me that a few years ago, when he realized he could no longer teach, he asked Tom if he would help him commit suicide when the time came—when Morrie was no longer able to enjoy anything about his life. I didn't know, when Morrie told me, that Tom was his cousin, so I didn't realize what it must have meant to Tom to say yes. He did, of course, say yes.

I read the grant letter again. Coward that I am, I had been hoping that none of my many research grant applications would be successful. Yet here it was, the perfect solution. I could return to my nice apartment in Boston and become a recluse once more, with no need to connect with a single patient, a single family, or even any research assistants. Heaven, surely?

After a week of private agony I wrote an acceptance letter and put it on the table, ready for Jack's boat in the weekend. Then I almost ran down to the wharf where Tom and Bill were waiting for me, the third member of the turtle rodeo team. As we bounced over the choppy swell, I braced myself at the bow of the tinnie, the salt and wind and sun whipping my hair into stiff peaks and filling me up.

The next morning I looked at the letter as I ate my muesli. Even the address on the envelope gave me the shits. I picked it up and with my strong, turtle-lassoing hands, ripped it in half. It was the last thing I wanted.

❄

THE SAND FELT DECADENTLY WARM AGAINST MY SKIN AS I lay, stomach down, on the sand of Shark Bay. It was lovely on the island in late July—by midday, hot but not too hot, and at night, pleasantly cool. Like the air, the sea never really got cold, but for we permanent residents—how good that sounded —by July a wetsuit was definitely required for swims longer than thirty minutes. By October it would be bathwater warm again.

I couldn't—wouldn't—think about that; how could I be leaving in less than three months? I wriggled farther into the sand, and reached around my back to release the strap of my bikini top. *Perhaps I should take it off?* Who would have thought I'd ever have the courage to wear a bikini? I'd never even worn one when I was young. This one, almost skimpy and sensual black, had beckoned to me from a shop window when I was in Brisbane with Pat. Naturally, she'd encouraged me.

She'd be home soon, her chemo completed. I closed my eyes and visualized her as she used to be—her healthy brown body, still mostly firm even at sixty-six, looking amazing in her turquoise bikini. Would she have the courage to wear it now?

That morning I had been up early walking the beach, and out beyond the reef had spotted the spout of a humpback whale. Then through my binoculars I'd seen it again, and felt the joy bubbling up as her great hump appeared followed by a smaller one—her baby. Most days I saw them now, often with calves. Our sea, so warm compared with their icy Antarctic feeding grounds, had called them all this way to give birth. Mothers and babies—Kirsty and Hamish, Mother Humpback and Junior, shearwaters and noddy terns and their cute chicks, Eve and her hundreds of turtle hatchings. It was awe-inspiring what mothers would do for their offspring. I turned over, my bikini top discarded. I stroked my warm, flat stomach, and a tear slid down the side of my nose and landed in my ear. My breasts tingled and I could almost feel them swelling as my nipples reached for the sun.

SINCE HAMISH LEFT, TOM HAD, LITTLE BY LITTLE, BEEN opening up about his father. He was a gentle man, a boat builder by trade but never happier than when on a wild beach or a lonely river, fishing.

"He sounds a lot like you," I said.

"I suppose so, before the Huntington's at least."

"And after?" I ventured when the silence had lengthened into minutes.

"I hope not; I tell myself that forewarned is forearmed." He looked at me. "Do you know any research about the psychiatric symptoms of Huntington's—do they pass from father to son too?"

"I don't know, I'm sorry." My gut squirmed with guilt; I couldn't even help him with this.

"You don't have to be sorry. At least you're honest."

"What happened?" I wanted to take his hand, but I didn't.

"He changed gradually, I think, but I didn't notice. I was too tied up in my selfish teenage dramas."

I resisted asking him, but I wanted to know him as a teenager. Later, perhaps.

"One day, when we were eating dinner, Dad exploded: threw his full plate at Mum, screaming and shouting obscenities. We were in shock. He blundered about the room and Mum yelled at us to get out. I stood my ground but I was scared shitless. Hilary dived under the table, and Mum was trying to calm him down. He started to hit her and I managed to pull him off. I was sixteen, and already nearly as tall as him.

After that, he became worse and worse. Sometimes he'd go for days without any problems and then he'd fly into a rage. How Mum stood it, I don't know. Finally, one night, after he turned on me, she called in the psychiatric crisis team, and he spent a few nights in the psychiatric ward. At first he was diagnosed as paranoid schizophrenic, but the drugs didn't help. It wasn't until he started the movements that it finally clicked that he had Huntington's."

Tom's expression almost made me feel sorry for his father's doctor.

"Grandma's still going strong and is as sane as you, so he must have inherited it from my grandfather." Tom sighed. "Trouble was, he died when he was thirty, before he had any symptoms."

How often I'd listened to stories like this from my research assistants when they returned from a particularly harrowing family meeting. As soon as I began to curl up inside I would shut off my emotions and listen to the words spilling from their mouths, telling myself, I suppose, that that was the proper, objective way for me to behave. But this was Tom, and I could smell his fear—not of his father but of his own future.

MY T-SHIRT AND SHEETS WERE SATURATED WHEN I WOKE, my heart pounding as if I had run a marathon. My pleasant dreams vanish within minutes of waking, however hard I will them to stay. The ones I want to forget refuse to go. In the dream there was Morrie, and then he became Tom, his face contorted and screaming as he jerked in his bed, trying to rip his arms and legs from the straps that held him down. I was terrified, and desperate to escape before he got loose and grabbed me.

Every day since I found out that Tom might end up with Huntington's, I had insisted—to him, but more importantly to me—that it made no difference to how I felt about him. When he told me he hadn't been tested, part of me was relieved. But how long could I keep believing he couldn't possibly have it, and that one day a light would come on in his dumb head and he'd see that we were destined to spend the rest of our lives together?

So there I was, sitting at my computer at three in the morning, hoping that writing would be easier than dreaming and would somehow magically help me face the feelings creeping from the darkest corners of my psyche.

I'm good at denial. After Dad drowned, for months I refused to believe it, imagining bizarre scenarios where he returned after being washed up on a desert island, or after being rescued by an African freighter and taken to shore where a primitive tribe took care of him until his memory returned. I thought I had stopped believing in fairy tales thirty-five years ago.

Is this what I've been doing with Tom? Kidding myself that even if he does get Huntington's I will want nothing more than to stay with him and look after him until he finally chokes to death on his own spit? I, who for twenty-five years have had every opportunity to get to know and feel comfortable around Huntington's patients but have failed completely? Those few weeks with Morrie played right into my fantasies, but he is unusually free—so far—from cognitive and psychiatric symptoms. The physical contortions used to be hard enough for me to deal with, and at least Morrie has helped me overcome that fear, but as I know from my own research, it is those other mind-altering, soul-shattering changes that really challenge families, and especially partners. Tom knows me better than I know myself. Perhaps I don't have it in me to love anyone unconditionally, not even Tom.

In the morning light, I read what I'd written and felt sick. Facing the truth was something I had had little practice at. It is one of the fallacies harnessed to introversion, that the inward-looking types are the ones who know themselves best. But without others to care about, and who care for you, there seems little need for honest feelings.

I would tell Tom, somehow, that he was probably right about us—that we would never work long-term. And then I'd stop worrying about it and enjoy being here until it was time for me to leave. But I definitely wouldn't accept that grant. I had learned that much—I did *not* want to return to lab research.

Pat came home the other day. Her chemo had knocked her about and she was reed thin, her skin dry and pasty. But she was happy, so happy that the chemo was over, and was positive that she was cured. Her first checkup would not be until after I left, and she told me very firmly that we were not going to talk about cancer at all from now on. I wanted so much to help her find herself again, as she helped me find myself when I first arrived. We did talk a lot, and I was humbled by her willingness to look at how she had changed and to embrace it. She still found the physical changes confronting, but said the psychological challenges have so enriched her life that her brush with mortality had almost been worth it.

"I thought I couldn't love my children and grandchildren any more, but how wrong I was," she told me. "Before, I loved spending time with them, but, for my own sanity, not too much time. Now the time I spend with them is even more precious, and I leave them for their sanity, not for mine." Her laughter was genuine, as always, but I didn't doubt the truth of her comment. How wise she was, knowing when to let go, and having the strength and generosity to put the needs of the people she loved above her own. I needed to have that to hang on to as I read the letter that Jack had brought. Fran had made her decision: she was going to stay with the Professor. She thanked me for my understanding letter—said that it had helped her. Her other friends had all told her to kick him out, and she had been so confused she almost did. Then my letter came and my "sane and sensible logic" gave her the courage to stick with him. I felt like such a fraud. How could I have been so . . . so . . . dishonest?

I WAS PLAYING HOSTESS. IT WAS TOM'S BIRTHDAY, AND I was trying not to dwell on his age, even though forty sounded a damn sight better than thirty-nine to me. We'd been working hard to enjoy each day as it came: no pressure, no dwelling on the future. Even when I wasn't with Tom or Pat, I was filling every moment with something—reading, snorkeling, helping Tom with data analysis, whale watching, even writing bits and pieces about my life as a scientist for my unlikely book. Occasionally I allowed myself to think about what I might do, career-wise, when I returned to Boston. Perhaps I could retrain as a real doctor so I could help real patients? But tonight was for Tom, and I had been cooking up a storm for him and the rest of my island family. It was meant to be a secret, but I knew he knew that something was up when he told me he was going off sailing for four days, including the day of his birthday. As I stuttered out some reason why that wasn't a good idea, I caught the twinkle in his eyes.

Basil arrived almost an hour early, when I was panicking about all the last-minute things I had to do, but everything got put on hold when he handed me a slip of paper with a phone number on it and I saw that it began with 44. "Your stepfather just Skyped," he said.

"Pardon? You mean Magnus? He's my mother's husband."

"Oh, well, he said he was your stepfather. It's your mother; she's not well."

"No. What's the matter with her?" I looked at the half-prepared salad on the bench, and pushed back my irritation.

"He didn't say and I didn't like to ask. He sounded upset, though, so I said I'd get you straight away."

"It must be bad for him to call. What am I going to do about all this?" I waved my hand at the chaos on the bench and table, then sat down in the nearest chair, suddenly dizzy.

"I'll stay here and finish the salad at least. Don't worry, if it's not all done by the time everyone gets here, we'll all pitch in. You get off and talk to him. Turn my computer off when you've finished. It's probably not too serious or he would have said." Basil patted me awkwardly on the shoulder, and I took a few deep breaths and stood up.

When I got back, Pat and Violet had done everything and the table looked wonderful, set for six—Violet and Bill, Pat and Basil, and Tom and me. Bill was reading the two kids a story before they hopefully went to sleep in my bunk beds. Basil was sitting on the deck with a beer, and Tom had yet to arrive.

"All okay?" Basil asked, and I nodded, not quite ready to speak. He handed me a beer as Violet and Pat came outside, motherly concern on their faces. I drank half the beer and felt better.

"Mum's had a heart attack, but it's not too bad apparently.

She's still in hospital and the cardiac surgeons think she needs a double bypass."

"Oh, Anna, that's worrying," said Violet.

"She was always so fit. She's never smoked, always had a healthy diet. Just unlucky, poor old thing," I said, drinking the rest of my beer.

"How is your stepfather taking it?" asked Pat.

"Upset, I suppose. It was hard to tell because of his accent. There was no video link so I couldn't see his face. Apparently he was Skyping from a computer in the hospital."

"Poor man," said Pat.

"He wants me to go there. He thinks Mum wants me there."

"Of course she does. You're her only child."

I went inside so I didn't have to look at Pat. "We were never very close. Double bypasses aren't that risky these days," I said to the empty room.

Behind me I could feel the silence.

"Let's get on with the dinner party and I'll worry about it in the morning. I can't do anything now." The plates clattered as I pulled them out of the cupboard. "Tom will be here any minute, and I don't want him to know. It would only spoil it for him."

I GROANED AND CLOSED MY EYES QUICKLY AGAINST THE blinding sun. My head was hammering and I pulled the sheet up over it.

"She lives. Here Anna, drink some water. I'll get you some Panadol."

The sheet was pulled away from my face and I peered at Pat through the smallest slit in my lids I could get away with. "I don't think I can sit up." I groaned again as the demons stamped up and down on my poor brain. Pat was lifting my head and I felt the glass on my parched lips. I gulped and a shot of cold water exploded into my mouth and shot out again as I spluttered and coughed.

"Oops, try again," Pat said, her hand firmly under my head, which wanted desperately to collapse back on the pillow.

"Here, I'll hold her up higher," said Tom's voice. I felt his arms around my back, lifting me into a sitting position. I couldn't see him; he was behind me, and there was no way I could turn my head. I needed to hold it rigid; even the slightest movement resulted in a burning sword thrust. This time I managed to get some water down my poor throat. I felt the rest of it on my chest, and in sudden horror I looked down, hot swords forgotten as my nakedness assaulted me. I jerked the sheet to my chin, and looked at Pat, Tom now beside her in full view. "Where are my clothes?" I snarled.

"Soaking in a bucket as far away from the cabin as we could get them," said Tom, his grin very, very wide.

"Shit. I was drunk." I shrank back down in the bunk, my entire body blazing. "Who undressed me?"

"It took both of us. You were like a rag doll," Tom said, still grinning. "A very smelly one."

"Sorry, Anna. We gave up trying to get a T-shirt over your head. It seemed better to cover you up and let you sleep." Pat's tone sounded much more sympathetic than Tom's.

I sneaked a look under the sheet and did the whole body blush again. I was totally naked, totally.

"God, I'm sorry. I can't believe I got that drunk. Whatever can Violet and everyone have thought?"

"They left before you were too bad, so don't fret," said Pat.

"Yep, by the time you were unambiguously legless, Pat and I were the only witnesses," Tom smirked.

I groaned. "What on earth was I drinking? Perhaps it was food poisoning."

"Beer, wine, and whisky poisoning, more likely."

I groaned again. "I've never in my entire life been so drunk that I spewed."

"Another first for your Turtle Island memoir then," said Tom.

"What do you mean? What other firsts have there been?"

"Do you really want a list? In front of Pat?"

Pat was grinning like a Cheshire cat. "Stop it, the pair of you. Get yourself in the shower, Anna, and I'll make you something light to settle your stomach." I caught her winking at Tom. "And after you've filled the shower bucket, Tom Scarlett, you can scarper and let us get on with it."

I had to face up to what was really bugging me, sooner or later, and Pat made sure it was sooner. Poached eggs, two cups of tea, and a four-word lecture.

"Your mum needs you," she said.

TWENTY-TWO

Brisbane, Sydney, Singapore, London, Edinburgh—and finally I stepped out of the plane onto the land my mother had fallen in love with even before she fell in love with Magnus Hill. As I drove my rental car along the skinny southernmost finger of Mainland, the creatively named southern island of Shetland, my travel fatigue lifted a little. Perhaps my new love of islands had expanded my capacity to appreciate the almost treeless expanses of green and gray that stepped down to the wide blue sea. It was a lyrical day, pale blue skies and a warm sun. Not at all as I had imagined it. I was lucky, I supposed, to arrive at the beginning of August, Shetland's warmest month, although even on this day the air was many degrees cooler than Turtle Island's winter temperature when I left.

I tried not to dwell too much on Mum and her illness as I drove from Sumberg airport to the attractive fishing village of Lerwick—Shetland's capital, and the only town of any size. Now that I was there I was glad I had come. I harbored enough guilt over never having visited Mum before, and never having met her husband, without adding to my sins my reluctance to leave my own island prematurely.

Lerwick was a prosperous, well-maintained-looking town,

courtesy of the lucrative oil fields off Shetland's shores. I stopped only for a sandwich and a surprisingly good cup of coffee, knowing I had two ferries to catch before I reached Unst, the farthermost island where Magnus had his croft and kept his fishing boat. Mum had been discharged from the Lerwick hospital two days ago, stents holding open two of her arteries. The doctors had decided that a bypass operation might not be necessary, and had elected to wait and see.

It wasn't too difficult to ignore my apprehension as I watched the ancient landscape meander past. Even in August, the road was quiet, and I stopped occasionally to take photos of pretty crofts nestled into the stark landscape, almost as if they had been there as long as human history. Of course they hadn't; I did at least know—from my reading of Lonely Planet's guide to Shetland on the endless plane journey from Australia to London—that people had lived there since 3,400 BC. Then before the 9th Century AD, there were the Pictish people, whose name made them sound like something out of a fairy tale. Later came the Vikings. Apparently Unst was their stronghold.

I loved all these facts. According to Lonely Planet, Shetland was closer to Bergen in Norway than to Edinburgh, and lots of Shetlanders considered themselves more Scandinavian than Scots. From the few photos I'd seen of Magnus Hill, he wouldn't be an exception.

I swallowed my frustration as I glimpsed signs pointing to ancient settlements, field systems, carved stones, and Pictish towers. Brochs, they were called. Even the words sounded mystical. I'd had quite a thing about archaeology for a while when I was a teenager, but apart from a visit to Stonehenge with Dad when I was a kid, we'd never gone anywhere where I could see it for real. When I was quite young Dad and I would spend whole days at the British Museum, and he managed to pass on to me something of his fascination with collections of tools and bits of pottery, and the people who made them. No one else in my class at primary school was in the least interested in things like that. All it did for me later, when I was at grammar school, was brand me even more firmly as a freak. And Mum wasn't the sort to want to drive for miles to see a few standing stones in the middle of a muddy paddock. I remember being angry with her about that too, and screaming at her that Dad would have taken me to see interesting stuff but he was DEAD. I think I managed to curb my tongue before I went as far as blaming her for his death. One of the counselors I was forced to see had even had the gall to imply that deep down I wished it had been Mum who had died, not Dad. Psychobabble. I had hated it. Still did.

And now here she was, my so very English-rose mother, making this her home. I wondered if it had changed her? The grumbling apprehension deep in my gut was back, so I breathed in, a lung-filling gulp of salty air, and breathed it out again, but my guilty thoughts weren't that easy to expunge.

I should at least have come to their wedding. It didn't look too good to make my first visit to see them contingent on Mum having a heart attack. Magnus was going to have a lovely, warm feeling about me. I shook my head and turned the car radio on, twiddling the knob until some jolly Scottish music blasted out.

I could see the car ferry—much larger and more modern than I expected—coming towards me when I putted into Toft. Opening up its giant jaws, it swallowed my little car and me, and regurgitated us twenty minutes later onto the next island, Yell. To get to the northern end of this took no more than half an hour, and after another, shorter ride on a smaller car ferry,

I was at last on Unst, the northernmost inhabited island in the British Isles. By now it was early evening, although the sun was still bright. Checking the directions I'd written down, I drove north for about ten kilometers, along a carless road bordered by peat bogs and green meadows scattered with pink, yellow, and white flowers. Behind were the smooth ripples of gentle hills covered in browned heather, with spare white and gray and pale apricot houses, sometimes in clusters of two or three, and sometimes alone, looking out across their own private expanses of sea and sky. Everywhere there was water—ponds, freshwater lochs, sea inlets, and always the vast Atlantic stretching to infinity. But even that was dwarfed by the sky, still pale blue but now drawn with wispy, pinkish clouds.

Turning left at a sign to "The Westing," I bumped along a narrow road until I came to a gate with another sign, "Hill's Houl." I was there. A rough farm track led to a croft that began at one end with an oblong stone house of normal height, chimneys at each end, and attached to that three more buildings, each lower and smaller than the previous one. Low stone walls enclosed an area of grass behind the house, presumably to keep out the sheep dotting the rougher grazing outside. Two brown-and-white Shetland ponies gazed curiously at me from inside the wall before dropping their shaggy heads and resuming their grazing. Beyond the house the ground sloped down to the sea.

I parked my small car behind an old truck, and, breathing in the sea-washed breeze, picked my way through a mosaic of sheep pellets and walked around the smallest end building, which was so low that my head was level with the slate roof. Along the front of the house was a paved area surrounded by a low railing fence. I stepped over the small gate as the door in the main building swung open and my mother stepped out.

The shock of her pure white hair almost halted me, but I collected myself and stooped to hug her small body. Surely she had shrunk? She had never been a tall woman—I got that from my father—but now she seemed to reach no farther than my chest. The doorway darkened as Magnus squeezed out, and I looked over Mum's head at him, feeling scarily as if Mum were our child. I had seen photos of him, but none in recent years. I knew he was only ten years my senior, but seeing him in the flesh brought that vividly home. I suppose Mum's new frailty made their age difference starker, and I shivered in the cooling air.

Magnus reached his hand out and I shook it, surprised that he stood no taller than me. It was the door that was small, requiring him to bend his head to get through. He had a nice face and a shy smile, and my stomach settled.

"Du is welcome, lass. Dine mither widna rest wi'ou du."

His voice was low-pitched, his words slow and less lilting than the Scots I was more familiar with. He was not like my image, garnered from vague memories of those few photos I had left back in Boston. My mother either, although I had seen her a few times in the ten years since their marriage. Probably from his wedding photo, when he seemed to tower over Mum, I had visualized Magnus Hill as a Viking in modern garb, but he was of medium build, although tough-skinned and brown, with sandy, graying hair—plenty of it—and clean-shaven.

"Come inside, Anna, and Magnus will fetch your bags from the car." Mum took my hand and I stooped down and followed her into a smallish kitchen, thankfully high enough to stand up in. A delectable smell of roasting lamb made my stomach gurgle and my mouth water. The room was dim, with light streaming in two narrow beams from the small, deeply mullioned windows set into the three-foot stone walls. Magnus maneuvered my case and backpack through another door that involved bending double, and we crawled into a tiny bedroom with a beamed ceiling that soared about a foot above my head. Then after a tour of the main house—the other buildings contained the laundry, a milk and cheese outhouse, and the smallest a stall for their two Shetland ponies—we sat outside on the stone patio and watched the luminous light on the sweeping half-moon bay below, the vivid green of the low hills all around almost too bright. It was, quite simply, magical.

"We mightn't get another evening as perfect, so I wanted you to see it like this," Mum said. I could now see the mother I remembered, the artist's light making her soft peaches and cream complexion glow, and turning her white hair, still in the same chin-length bob, to the gold it used to be.

"It's wonderful. I can see why you love it," I said, following her gaze and drinking it in.

"Winter is not quite so easy, but I often spend a few weeks in late January and February in London with Jane." Jane was her older sister, an aunt who had never married, and had always seemed too sophisticated to be bothered with me.

Mum insisted her heart would stand a small glass of the wine I had brought all the way from the Australian duty-free shop, and we drank to my arrival and Mum's good health before squeezing into the kitchen where Magnus served the best plate of melt-in-the-mouth, home-grown-and-hung Shetland lamb and home-grown-and-dug tatties I had ever tasted. I noticed Mum ate almost nothing of her small helping, and after we had finished with bread still warm from the oven and Magnus's own sheep-milk cheese, she went willingly to bed.

As Magnus and I washed up, the light still glowing through the small windows although it was close to ten o'clock, Magnus told me about the croft. The main house was the new part, built around 1840, and the smaller buildings were considerably older, and were once where his ancestors lived, often in the same room as their animals. I asked him about Mum's heart attack, and he told me that, in retrospect, she had been getting breathless quite easily, when once she could walk for hours without a problem. Apparently she had been having a lot of indigestion as well, which was almost certainly angina. Her doctors wanted her to see how things went with the stents and her medications before discussing any further the possibility of a bypass. So far they were happy with her progress.

"It's guid du came," he said. "She wadna hae asked."

Next day Mum was, as she said, bone-weary with all yesterday's excitement, and spent most of the day in bed, or lying on the couch in the small sitting room. The golden weather, as she had predicted, had not held, and a chilly wind swept around the stone croft. The sea was dark gray under an eerie yellow sky, lowered by black clouds. After breakfast, Magnus left her in my care and drove off in his truck. His fishing boat was moored in Belmont, where the Unst ferry docked, and he said he had a few maintenance jobs to do on his fishing nets. While Mum slept, I explored the fields around the croft, and walked for a short distance along the bank that dropped a couple of meters to a stony beach directly in front of the croft. Farther round, a pale sandy beach followed the curves of a bay. The wind was bracing, and I huddled into the fleece I had borrowed from Magnus. Every so often a black head would pop up in the gray sea, one of the many seals that lived there. Otters were apparently resident as well, although not so easy to spot. It was a haunting sort of landscape, with its low, smooth shapes repeating again and again, and everywhere the dominating sky, today barely distinguishable from the sea.

So it wasn't until Saturday—another bonus warmish day

—that Mum and I really talked. Magnus had left at dawn on his first fishing trip since Mum's heart attack, and she suggested we drive to a cafe at Baltasound for lunch, telling me in advance that the name of the cafe was not intended for her. She was laughing as we sat down below the sign, "Final Checkout." It was a general supplies store as well, and while we waited for our soup and scones I wandered around the aisles, filling a trolley with groceries. Over cups of tea Mum asked me about Pat; in my rare correspondence I had told her about the breast cancer. I waited for the inevitable question about Tom and me, but it didn't come, and I wondered if I'd avoided any mention of him in my letters. I knew I hadn't told her that we had a relationship, if that was the polite word, but surely I had mentioned his name in passing?

She was asking me about my visit to Dry Acres Artists' Community, and, because I liked seeing her laugh, I hammed up the tale of my first meeting with George. "When he appeared at the door I thought I was seeing Dad's ghost. I practically fainted in a heap at his feet, poor fellow." I pretended to swoon but stopped when I saw Mum's worried frown. "Come on Mum, that was meant to be funny. I didn't really think Dad had come back to haunt me."

Mum smiled, but her eyes were sad. "You were so un-happy when he died, and I didn't know how to make things better for you. I'm sorry, Anna."

"Heavens, it wasn't your fault. I don't know how you put up with my moods. I know you did your best, but no one could have helped me."

"Harry was a good father, and you two had a very special bond. I'm afraid I was a very poor substitute."

The anger welled up inside me as I looked at her, so little and fragile. "He didn't deserve you—or me, for that matter.

Mary put me right on the sort of person he was." I gulped down some tea, trying to dilute the acrid reflux that burnt my throat. "Why would he lie about his parents—all that cock 'n bull about his father being a violent drunk?"

"Yes, you told me that in your letter. Harry's lying was a revelation to me too. I had always imagined his father as a monster. I suppose he thought it was easier than telling me about the girl's abortion and his mother's suicide. Then when I found I was pregnant and he had to marry me, he was stuck with his lie. Perhaps that's why he cut all his ties with his sister, so I could never find out the truth."

"He was guilt-ridden about his mother's suicide, and had to make up that story to put the blame on his father. That's what I think."

"You're probably right. He was only a boy when all that happened. It must have been terrible for him."

"You always forgave him." I looked at her, the mother I had ignored for most of my life. I was as bad as Dad. "Why did he leave you, Mum? Did he have affairs?"

"Perhaps. I didn't let myself think about that. He was away so much, and working in trouble spots with exciting young women journalists. In the end I got tired of waiting for him to come home, never sure if he would. It was me who broke it off."

"Good for you. How did he take it?"

"Like a lamb, of course." She laughed. "He couldn't hide his relief."

"I knew you were pregnant when you got married, but I never worried too much about it. It never occurred to me that you mightn't have got married otherwise. Did he love you at first, do you think?"

"He said he did, and I believed him. In fact, I'm sure he

did. We had a lot of fun for a few years. So don't go blaming yourself for being born," Mum said, looking at me sternly.

"I won't. I'm so sorry for the way I treated you; the way I've always treated you, as if Dad were so much more important. It was always you who looked after me, even before he left us."

"That's the lot of mothers, I fear. Anna, it's all water under the bridge, and you're here now."

MAGNUS BROUGHT HOME SOME OF HIS DAY'S CATCH, and herrings fresh from the Atlantic sea were in no way related to the ones I had reluctantly eaten, on rare occasions, from tins. We ate outside, and I shared a beer with Magnus and listened to his now-familiar accent as he related what I suspected was a much-embellished tale of the muddle he and his fishing partners had got themselves into when hauling in their catch. Mum was giggling, and I felt the past shimmer. How young I must have been when I heard her giggling like that with Dad.

Magnus's tale became taller, and I was soon chuckling as well, more at Mum than at Magnus.

"Enough," Mum cried, "enough," and Magus bowed low. Mum wiped her eyes and became serene again. She smiled at me. "I like your hair like that. It shows off your fine bone structure."

I caught Magnus's eye across the table.

"Aye, it's bonnie," he said, smiling his sweet smile.

Later, with Mum tucked up on the couch, and the toasty smell of a peat fire smoldering in the hearth, Magnus took up a fiddle. From my cushioned seat on the floor beside the couch, I was transported. He was no amateur, and stranger though I was to Shetland, the mournful, haunting sounds closed my eyes and filled my mind with timeless fields of heather, peat bogs, stone crofts, and the cold gray lochs. I felt a touch on my head and reached back and clasped Mum's hand as she stroked my newly short hair.

TWENTY-THREE

W e settled into a kind of routine—Magnus was away by seven o'clock or sometimes even earlier, and I took Mum breakfast in bed, leaving her to read her book for an hour or two while I did whatever housework I could find, and often took a stroll along the beach, looking, invariably without success, for otters. After lunch we went somewhere in the car—to visit one of Mum's many friends, to a remote, stony beach where colorful dinghies waited patiently for the weekend, to small museums where I read more about Unst history while Mum chatted to the staff, or for leisurely explorations of one of the numerous archaeological sites scattered around the island, Viking longhouses a specialty. When we returned, I usually prepared dinner while Mum had a rest. By seven Magnus was home and, weather permitting, we often sat outside for a quiet drink—non-alcoholic for Mum —before eating. After the dinner things were cleared away, unless it was very wet, I usually went for a long walk, sometimes taking the car to the start of a walking track farther afield. Often Mum and Magnus were in bed when I returned.

Of course I thought of Tom and Pat when I was alone, and wished they could share my pleasure in this ancient landscape. I had no way of talking with them, as there was no

Internet connection in the croft. The lack of phones and mobile networks on Turtle Island negated them as communication devices as well. I could have sent an e-mail to Tom from the Baltasound library, but I chickened out. In a sense, I was relieved that I had an excuse to resort to postcards, which I sent from the northernmost post office in the British Isles, with an ornate postal date stamp to prove it.

I hadn't booked a return ticket to Australia, thinking that if Mum had a bypass operation I might not leave until after October. In that case, it would be better if I went back to Boston. Basil had agreed to collect the campers' fees, and I had cleaned and closed up Jeff's cabin as if I would never return, reluctantly obeying the tourist brochures and leaving nothing but footprints in the wet sand. Only Tom and Pat came to wave me goodbye. I didn't want the others there. Tom knew I might not return, and didn't say much other than "One day you will."

Mum was doing well, and there seemed little likelihood that she would need a bypass. I knew I was welcome there for as long as I liked, but their croft was small, and I sometimes felt in the way. Their love for each other was enviable, and I no longer saw the age difference between them. Magnus was playing his fiddle in the annual Shetland Blues Festival at the end of August, and there had been talk that we should all go to Lerwick for it and then spend a few days seeing some of the ancient sites on Mainland. After that might be a good time for me to leave. My heart sped up at the very thought. I *could* go back to the island.

But before that, Mum had set her heart on a daytrip to the northernmost coast of Unst, to walk along the dramatic cliffs where thousands of gannets and puffins nested at this time of the year. The Muckle Flugga lighthouse on a rocky outcrop near the cliffs was at the very tip of Britain, and the hike was worth it for that reason alone. It would be a good test of Mum's stents, and our daily walks became part of a carefully graduated fitness plan.

One of our favorite places for lunch was the Northern Lights, a bistro at the far end of the island run by the doctor's wife. It sold beautiful Shetland art and crafts as well as high-class food. Sitting outside in the sun, waiting for our salads to arrive, I showed Mum the stunning earrings, each a delicate leaf with tiny veins picked out in silver, I had bought for Pat.

"Pat's very special, isn't she," she said, admiring them.

"She'll love them. It will be good to see her again." I closed the little jewelry box and zipped it safely into a pocket in my handbag.

"I used to worry about you, never marrying." Mum sounded hesitant, and I felt a niggle of irritation.

"Most of the marriages I know aren't exactly blissful—with you and Magnus the exception, of course." My laugh was forced, and Mum raised her eyebrows. I squirmed, a teenager again. "Anyway, I did have a relationship years ago, when I was a PhD student. It didn't work out, and after that I decided it wasn't worth the hassle."

"You never told me."

"No, it was too painful at the time and you were a long way away."

"And we didn't have that sort of relationship," Mum said, her eyes sad.

"As you say, water under the bridge."

"I know how lonely it can be, living alone, going to work every day and coming home to a cold, empty house."

"Well, I was married to my career. I did have a few friends. Francesca, for one."

"And now Pat."

Her voice sounded strained and I frowned. "What are you getting at, Mum?"

"I know it's none of my business. It's only because I love you."

"What, for heaven's sake? Spit it out."

"Is your relationship with Pat—are you a lesbian?"

I picked up my water glass and drank half of it. "Don't be daft, Pat's a widow, she has grown kids and grandchildren."

"You know that's not an answer."

"No, Mum. I'm not gay, I've never been gay, I've never had a relationship with a woman, and I've never had the slightest inclination to have one. Is that sufficient?"

"Don't be angry, Anna. I'm sorry I've upset you."

"You're living in the past, Mum. It's no longer a crime for women to *choose* to live alone, you know, to *choose* to have no children."

"Magnus told me I was barking up the wrong tree."

"You've been discussing this with Magnus?"

"He's known for years that I wondered about it, and the other night he told me you were as straight as him."

"He did, did he. And how did he come to that startling conclusion?" My face was hot.

"That's what I asked him. He said men just know these things."

"Huh. I doubt that very much. Just a lucky guess, I'd say." We sat in awkward silence, almost snatching the plates of salad from the waitress when they arrived. I concentrated on eating, tasting nothing, my annoyance barely abating. Pushing my empty plate to the side, I glowered at Mum's bent head. "How would you have felt if I *had* been gay?"

Mum looked up, her face soft. "I'd have understood. If that's what made you happy, I would have been happy too."

"Truly? And here's me thinking you were straightlaced." I grinned at her to make it clear I was joking, although I wasn't, entirely.

Mum reached over and touched my hand. "I didn't intend to tell you this, unless you told me you were gay. When you left for the States I was so lonely. I know we never got on when you were at home, but I still wanted you there. Jane hauled me along to her feminist group; it was still a big thing in London in the seventies. To cut a long story short, I began a relationship with one of the women in the group. We never lived together but we spent weekends together. Apart from Jane, no one in my family or outside the group ever knew."

My mouth was open. I stared at her, speechless.

"You look horrified. Is it so hard to believe?" Mum asked, and I saw her hand was shaking as she picked up her glass.

"Is that why you and Dad broke up? What about Magnus?"

"I don't think I was ever a true lesbian. I was just so very lonely. I was only thirty-one when Harry left, and apart from a couple of dates with men I had no interest in, I had no one. It wasn't even the sex. It was the touching, the holding and stroking, that I yearned for. Babies aren't the only ones who shrivel up if they're not held." She scrabbled in her handbag for a tissue and dabbed at her eyes. "Even when you were a teenager, I used to pay a masseur when I could ill afford it, just to be stroked. My relationship with Marion gave me that more than anything, and we shared a love of books and music, as well as a passion for women's rights."

"Why did you break up?"

"We drifted apart after a few years. Marion enjoyed the sex more than me, and in the end she found someone who was a better fit."

"I'm sorry."

"Don't be. We stayed friends. We're still friends. By the time we broke up, I was in my late forties."

"Did you have other relationships?"

"Not lesbian ones, but I'd learned how to have meaningful friendships, and I didn't hesitate to ask for hugs when I needed them, or to give them back. And then, at fifty-eight, I came here on holiday with Jane and met Magnus."

"Does he know?"

Mum laughed. "Of course he knows. He thinks it probably made me a more adventurous lover."

"Too much information." I grinned at her, although my stomach was still in knots.

On the drive home I was lost in my own thoughts, and perhaps she was too; she was very quiet. So I jumped when she did speak.

"Jane is of the true faith. Did you know that?"

I glanced at her, sitting there next to me as demure as a seventy-three-year-old English lady. "The true faith. Is this another of your bombshells?"

I heard her giggle as a car sped past us, and I kept my eyes on the road.

"She was always a lesbian, even as a teenager."

"I don't believe you. She was always so fussy about her makeup and fancy suits and high heels."

"I think it's time you got rid of all those stereotypes. You've been cloistered too long in that lab of yours."

"Was that why you thought I might be gay? A genetic quirk?"

"It crossed my mind, but I also worried that you were so traumatized by your father's death that you might have been psychologically damaged, somehow, and scared to let a man get close to you."

"Perhaps that did make me cautious, but it definitely didn't make me gay."

That evening when Mum yawned and said goodnight, I hugged her frail body, and as she held me and stroked my back, she seemed to expand, her arms becoming a cocoon, protecting me from myself.

I slept quickly and deeply, and after waking at six, slipped out of the croft and down to the sea. As I perched on the small bank above the narrow, stony beach, I caught, out of the corner of my eye, a movement below me. Holding my breath, I sat motionless as a sharp little head retreated into the bank then came out again. Her whiskers twitching, she tested the air, then her sleek body appeared, followed by one, two, three, miniature versions. Time stood still as I watched my first otter nudge her kits into the shallow water, circling them, diving and surfacing, keeping her babies safe while they frolicked, not a care in the world, and learned how to survive.

I'D BEEN AWAY THREE WEEKS AND AT LAST I HAD MAIL. Two letters, one from Tom and one from Pat. They must have sent them with Jack on the very next boat from the island, two weeks after I left. I felt like shouting for joy, singing, dancing. I looked at Tom's writing on the first envelope, and then opened Pat's. Her letter was just like her, warm, newsy, full of delightful little morsels about life on the island—the birds she'd seen, her first snorkel over the edge of the reef since her operation, the latest hijinks Violet's kids had got up to, the joy of seeing the first noddy terns returning to construct their untidy nests.

"Braw news, lassie?" said Magnus. It was too wet and windy to take the boat out and he was making bread, another of his many talents.

I nodded. "My friend Pat, my friend who had cancer"—I hesitated—"the one who is *not* my lover. She sounds wonderful, she's even been snorkeling again."

Magnus's roar brought Mum in from the laundry, her hands covered in soapsuds.

"What's so funny?"

"Naething lass, dinna fash yer thoum." He winked at me, and I caught Mum's smile.

I took Tom's letter down to the beach, and, my heart thumping, slit it open and extracted one small sheet, torn from his notepad. It was the only letter I'd ever received from him, but his small, neat writing was as familiar as my own from the many turtle data sheets I had summarized, his often littered with notes.

Dear Anna,

It's strange not to be able to talk to you, and to know you won't get this for weeks, unless another boat comes by and it leaves the island before Jack's next visit. I hope your mum is okay and that her operation is safely over. I'm sure you would have found a way to e-mail if anything had gone wrong. I've always wanted to visit Shetland. Write and tell me all about it. Take lots of photos in case that's as close as I ever get.

It felt awkward saying goodbye and not knowing if I'd ever see you again. If you can, please come back, even if it is after October. You know you can stay with me, or if you don't want to, Pat will have you any time. You haven't really left the island until we have the proper island farewell to make absolutely sure that you'll return someday.

There's not much to tell you, as you only left a few days ago. I think I'll go over to Lost Cay for a couple of nights, and think about you.

Love, Tom.

TWENTY-FOUR

I wanted to give Mum a present. Unst had beautiful crafts—jewelry, intricately patterned Shetland jerseys and hats, beautiful photographic books of the islands, fascinating history and archaeology books. I was already loaded up with gifts for Fran, and for everyone on the island. Then I found a beautiful photograph album with handmade blue and green paper interleaved with transparent sheets, its leather cover tooled with Shetlandic designs. On my laptop I had hundreds of photos of Turtle Island, and quite a few of Boston. In my compulsive way I had, years ago, scanned in the few photos I kept from my childhood and university days. So late into the twilight Unst nights I sifted through them, finally coming up with a selection that began with the only photo I had of me as a tiny baby, the day Mum left hospital with me in her arms, Dad grinning proudly. I selected the most amusing school photos, with me looking sullen between shiny smiling girls, and a few from my holidays with Dad. Then there was one of Fran and me dressed in pristine new lab coats, standing with arms around each other in the grounds of Harvard; some nice shots of Boston, in the snow, in the fall, and in the summer; my official PhD photo, me gowned and capped; and photos of me with Rachel in the lab, and with various incarnations of research assistants, usually taken at our end-of-year lunch.

Other than my baby photo, Mum appeared in only two others. I had a copy of her wedding photo, black and white, a registry office affair, Dad in a suit and Mum looking very beautiful in a cartwheel hat and pale dress that wrapped softly around her perfect figure. In her arms she held an enormous bouquet, perhaps hiding the bump that was me. The other photo was taken, I dimly recalled, by Aunt Jane. We were on holiday at Brighton, perhaps two years after Dad died. I naturally hated every minute of it. But Jane had managed to capture us in an unguarded moment. We were both, Mum and I, eating monstrously large ice creams, Brighton Pier behind us, the sun shining off our hair, Mum's so blond and mine so dark, and we were laughing.

I scrunched up a damp tissue and fired it into the wicker basket by the door. Nostalgia was so pleasurable. Not something I was accustomed to allowing myself.

Sorting out the best photos from Turtle Island was more of a mission. One of the island from Jack's boat to signal my arrival; my cabin, with huddles of plump shearwaters on the path by the deck; a laying turtle caught in my flash, Tom crouching beside it with his headlight on; the campground when it was full of summer students; my first photo of Kirsty and Hamish when he was one day old; Hamish and me a few days after that terrifying night when I thought he might die, Hamish looking as yummy as a clam in chowder and me looking exhausted; Pat in her wetsuit, a broad grin on her brown face; the gang at Violet and Bill's for one of their barbecues; turtle tracks meandering up the idyllic beach; the turquoise lagoon; the whole gang again with our newly shaved heads. So many to choose from. I added a photo of Mary and George, and one of the gate with the sign "Dry Acres Artists' Community." I found a few of me, long hair, short hair, no hair, pale skin, brown skin, taken with my camera by Pat or Tom, and I included these. It was, after all, for Mum. And finally, because it was for Mum, I added one taken by Pat, of Tom and me.

I had discovered a printing place in a shed at the airfield near Baltasound, and with my precious collection safely transferred to a memory stick, I delivered it there one day after doing the grocery shopping, while Mum had her morning lie-in. When I collected the photos two hours later, the printer grinned at me and asked if we could swap islands.

Early on, Magnus had suggested I spend a day on his boat, but time was rapidly running out and I had yet to take up his offer. In truth, I was nervous. My fear of the sea was long gone, but the North Atlantic was another matter.

"Go, Anna," Mum said. "It's an experience. Pick a lovely day and you'll be fine."

An experience it was. I knew Magnus was a fisherman, of course, and I'd seen plenty of documentaries about fishing boats and wild seas and nets and massive catches of fish, but the real thing was mind-blowing. Tom would have loved it; it was like an exaggerated turtle rodeo. Even on this still day it was choppy, but to my relief I didn't get sick. Simply watching Magnus and the other three fisherman hauling in the nets full of slithering herrings and stashing them in giant containers of ice, and then doing it all over again, was exhausting, but exhilarating too. The smell of the salt and fish, the wind through my hair, the burn of the sun on my face, the doorstop sandwiches and buckets of hot flask tea we consumed for lunch, the burr of the men's conversation, most of it like a foreign language to my ears—I could see why Mum missed it so. Magnus told me he was determined to get her back on the boat before the end of the season.

The day before our trip to Muckle Flugga, Mum and I

stayed at home, hoping that a rest day would conserve her energy for her longest walk since her heart attack. She was in good spirits and insisted on making me a special lunch, a lamb salad and oatcakes fresh from the oven. It was the perfect time to give her my present. I hadn't looked at it since I placed the photos in sequence on the pretty blue and green pages, each photo with an inscription carefully written in my neatest writing on the transparent overlays. Here and there I had inserted a line of poetry, or a remembered line from a favorite song. On the first page I had placed her and Dad's wedding photo, and my baby picture. Mum turned the pages, looking for long moments at every photo, sometimes wiping away a tear when it landed shining on the paper, until she came to the final page. There I had placed a photo of her and Magnus, sitting in the evening light outside the croft, and another of the two of us, with the sea behind us. Then she turned back one page, and looked again at the only picture I had of Tom and me. Tom was looking at me and I at him. We were holding hands. That's all I had written, *Tom and me.*

"I'm glad," is all Mum said as she gently closed the album.

IT WAS A BRAW BRICHT DAY, AS MAGNUS COMMENTED, when we packed Mum's egg and bacon pie and Magnus's slabs of flapjack and flask of whisky-spiked coffee, and set off for Hermaness National Nature Reserve at the top of Unst, home to Shetland's largest gannet colony. It took us an hour to walk from the car park to the cliff edge, Mum breathing easily and striding along like a fifty-year-old. It was from these dramatic cliffs that the rocky outcrop called Muckle Flugga with its iconic lighthouse could be seen, appearing so close that a brave giant could leap the swirling gap. We picked our way along the cliff face, peering down fissures to the boiling sea thundering far below, Mum and I with hearts in our throats as Magnus stepped delicately along slippery, shit-coated ledges to examine a wildflower he had spotted twenty feet down the cliff face.

The acrid smell of guano transported me back to Turtle Island as I gazed at the countless thousands of screaming gannets crammed onto every stack and into every crack in the glistening rock. They turned the sky white, lemon heads shining in the sun as they soared on their slender wings nearly two meters across from one blue-black tip to the other, diving and dancing like skaters on a crowded Boston lake. Aggressive, dive-bombing great skuas added to the ear-shattering noise, and Magnus pointed out other seabirds almost lost in the gathering—fulmars, guillemots, and gulls. Many of the twenty-five thousand puffins that returned to the same mate and the same nest site every summer had already fledged their chicks and left, but there were still hundreds of late breeders nesting precariously in nooks and crannies on the sheer rock faces. Never had I been so charmed by a bird as they entertained us with their clown-like masks and quaint waddling gaits while we ate our lunch in the sun. Oh, magnificent day!

We made our way back across the grassy cliff tops, skirting water holes caught in boggy patches and admiring the fluffy heads of bog cotton bobbing in the sun. Magnus lagged behind, his binoculars often clamped to his eyes as he stood motionless, some new bird caught in his sights.

"Tell me about Tom," Mum said.

So I did, almost everything, avoiding *too much information*, of course. I told her about Morrie, and Tom's father, and Tom's reluctance to be tested for the gene. I told her that he didn't want me to stay. I even told her he was ten years younger than me.

"Can you imagine life without him?" she asked, stopping and forcing me to look at her.

"I don't want to, but what choice do I have?"

"Tell him. Make sure he knows how deeply you love him."

"But what if he doesn't love me? He's never said it." My heart was knocking on my ribs.

Mum grasped my arms firmly. "This is not a research grant you're losing or a career you're giving up on, it's your chance to be whole. Don't let pride, or embarrassment, or that low self-esteem you used to have stand in the way."

"It's not fair to put him in that situation. He's only forty, Mum, with his life ahead of him. What good will it do him to be tied to someone as old as me?" The words slid out of my mouth before I could stop them.

Mum laughed and looked back at Magnus, crouching down over a patch of blue flowers. "Try another excuse."

"Sorry. You two have shown me it can work, but Magnus doesn't have Huntington's hanging over him."

"All I ask, Anna, is that you tell him what you want and how strongly you feel. You can't make his decisions for him and you shouldn't. If it's not to be, at least you'll not live the rest of your life wondering if more honesty on your part might have made the difference."

I HAD BOOKED MY FLIGHTS BACK TO AUSTRALIA, AT AN exorbitant cost, in the old-fashioned way—through a travel agent on the other end of the phone. Mum had called Aunt Jane and asked if I could stay for the two nights I was spending in London before my flight. I was looking forward to it, now I knew Jane's love story. She was living with her partner of twenty years, a girl she had met in high school. After ten years of an on-off relationship, they had lost touch, but met again at a feminist convention in Paris many years later. Both had recently lost their lovers, and in their mid-fifties had fallen in love all over again. My memories of Aunt Jane, the haughty sophisticate, were overdue for updating.

Before we left for Lerwick, I posted a letter to Tom, although it was unlikely to reach him before I did. I didn't say much, just that I was coming back, and that I loved him. Then I put my future away and focused on my last week on Shetland, in the delightful company of my mother and her Magnus. Magnus was a walking encyclopedia on the history of Shetland, and his quiet way of telling the old and not-so-old stories was compelling.

More stories, in song and dance, got the feet tapping and the whisky flowing at the Blues Festival, where Magnus and his band were clearly longtime favorites. I discovered that the fiddle wasn't his only instrument as he took up the banjo and guitar at some of the jam sessions we went to every night. Mum didn't come to them all, but her stamina was impressive nevertheless. On our last night, in a crowded snug above a cozy bar, Magnus beckoned Mum into the center of the circle, and after a single note on the fiddle, they sang, unaccompanied, a haunting love song. The words were Gaelic, but I didn't need to understand them to know what they meant. And I hadn't even known she could sing.

ON A BLUSTERY DAY, INKY STORM CLOUDS HANGING LOW over a slate sea, after four wonderful days exploring Mainland, I flew away from Shetland, turning back just before I entered the aircraft to wave to my gang on this other island. They were standing close, Magnus's arm in place around the woman he

loved. I couldn't see Mum's tears but I knew they were there—
I could feel them on my own cheeks. They waved back and I
breathed in one last lungful of Shetlandic air, certain now that
I would return.

My flight arrived the day before Jack's regular fortnightly trip to Turtle Island, and he greeted me with a hug when the taxi dropped me, my luggage, and three boxes of food on the wharf.

"Where did you spring from?" Jack grinned. "Reckoned you'd have a hard time staying away."

I hugged him again and high-fived Nick, who appeared from the boat shed.

"It's so good to be home." I wanted to dance with the very joy of it. The sun was hot and the sky was blue and the breeze was balmy.

"Pat will be over the moon to see you. She's been moping about like a chook with no feathers," Jack said.

"Or a bird with no hair," Nick added.

"You're both terrible." The laugh spluttered out of me. "Bloody Aussies, you're all the same."

"Hairless, the lot of us. I see yours has grown a bit. I'll get the shears." Nick made a V with his hands and clapped them together above my head.

"Get off. I like it like this." I looked around. "Am I the only passenger, or is my watch fast?"

"You're it, by the look of it," Jack said. "Hey Nick, perhaps we should cancel the trip. We won't make much dosh if Anna's the only taker." He winked at me. "How would you like two weeks' holiday here in Gladstone, and we'll put you on the next boat?"

"Stop teasing. What about all these food boxes?" The wharf was stacked high with them.

"Oh, well, I suppose we'd better go. Get yourself on board, woman, and put the kettle on."

My bubble of happiness was punctured about halfway to the island when Jack joined me on the deck and handed me a sandwich. "Did you hear about Tom?"

"No, what?" I stopped breathing.

"He had to go back to Sydney. His father's real sick. Tom wanted to get to him before it was too late."

"Oh, no. Poor Tom. When will he be back? When did he leave?"

"He came over to the mainland with us two weeks ago. That's all I know."

My hard-won resolve to make Tom understand how much I loved him and somehow convince him we could be happy together curled up inside me. I stood at the railing, the wind blowing through me. How could I even be thinking of my own needs while Tom was watching his father die? No wonder he didn't want me to stay with him. He knew me better than I knew myself.

I realized Pat wouldn't have received my postcard telling her when I was coming back, but as we docked I spotted her familiar shape walking along the beach. Leaving my bags and boxes for Nick to deliver to my cabin, I ran towards her, skidding to a stop as she threw open her arms, her smile wide.

"Anna, I don't believe it. Why didn't you tell me?"

I clung to her like a child, feeling the flatness where her breast used to be, my tears pooling in my eyes. She pulled back and looked at me.

"It's not that bad to be back, is it?"

I blinked hard. "It's wonderful. I've missed you so much." I touched her new gray curls.

"So these are tears of joy, then."

"Jack told me about Tom; that his father's dying."

Pat nodded, her smile gone. "We haven't heard anything, so I don't know when he'll be back. If his father does die, it might be a while. His mother will need him there to help with all that stuff that has to be done."

"Should I go to Sydney, do you think?"

"Would he want you there?" Pat's voice was gentle.

"I don't know. Probably not. Watching Huntington's patients die is not something families find easy to share."

"I'm sure he'll let us know soon how things are. He promised to e-mail Basil if he had any news." Pat looped her arm through mine as we walked back towards the boat.

"Did you know his father had Huntington's?' I asked, suddenly aware that I might have broken a confidence.

"He told me just before he left. I didn't know before. What a terrible thing it is."

After I unpacked and checked the campground, which looked as if it hadn't seen any campers for a while, I wandered over to Basil's. I found him on his deck engrossed in a newspaper, his fortnightly indulgence on boat arrival days.

"Hi Anna. Nick said you were back. How's your mother?"

"She's fine, thanks. She didn't have to have an operation after all, so we had a lovely holiday together."

"That's good news. You'll be happy to be back though, I bet. The road home is always the best one."

I smiled at him. "Yes, it does feel like home. But I'm worried about Tom. Has he e-mailed you?"

"Not yet, although I haven't checked today. Come on in, and we'll have a look now. Make us some coffee while I fire up the computer."

It seemed to take forever, and the coffee was perking when I heard him call from the room next door.

"There is one here from him. Sad news, I'm afraid."

I was already beside him reading Tom's message.

Hi Basil, Dad died yesterday, and the funeral is on Monday at 2 p.m. I'm not sure when I'll be back but not for a couple of weeks at least. Can you tell Pat and Bill please? It was a relief in the end. He had a rough time and so did Mum. She's exhausted and I'm afraid the funeral will probably be quite a big one as my folks have lived here a long time. I'll stay for a bit to make sure Mum's all right. Say gidday to everyone, Tom.

Tom's father had been dying within kilometers of me as I waited for hours at Sydney airport for my plane to Gladstone.

"Poor blighter," I heard Basil saying. "His dad's been sick for a long time, but it's still hard."

I looked at the e-mail address. It began "GwenScarlett@" so I supposed it was his mother's. "We should write a reply."

"I'll keep it simple, in case his mum looks at it," said Basil, banging with one finger at the keyboard.

Hi Tom, Sorry to hear about your father. Everyone here is thinking of you and your family. I hope the funeral goes well. Anna came back today and sends her love.
Best wishes, Basil and Anna.

He looked up at me. "Is that okay?"

"Yes, it's fine. I wish I could talk to him though. Do you know his mother's phone number?"

"Nope. I'll ask him. You could phone him then through Skype." He added a PS to his e-mail and clicked send.

Hopefully by tonight Tom would have e-mailed back with a phone number and I could call him. I had no idea where his mother lived or where the funeral was to be. Neither Pat nor Bill had any contact details for him either, although Bill was pretty sure their family home was in North Sydney.

By five o'clock I had made up my mind to go to the funeral. I was still suffering from jet lag and it took some sorting out, but using Tom's Internet connection I managed to book a flight from Gladstone on Sunday—tomorrow—leaving at half past two. I had to go via Brisbane and wouldn't get into Sydney until seven thirty in the evening. I booked a hotel in Crows Nest, in North Sydney, hoping it would be somewhere near where the funeral was to be. Once there, I would just have to phone every Scarlett in the phone book until I found Tom, or perhaps there would be a funeral notice in the Sydney newspaper. Tom hadn't replied to Basil's e-mail and I had little hope that he would. He would be far too distracted.

Poor Jack had planned to stay over on the island on Sunday night and go back Monday, but he didn't hesitate when I told him I needed him to leave at the crack of dawn the next day to make sure we got to Gladstone in time for my flight. "The boat trip's on me," he said. "You can take all our good wishes with you. Tom's a good man."

IT ALL WORKED OUT, AND BY SUNDAY NIGHT I WAS SITTING in my hotel room, rifling through the Sydney papers. Luckily the woman on the desk had a copy of the Saturday *Sydney Morning Herald*, because that's where I found it.

> *Scarlett, Thomas Lloyd. On September 11th. Loved husband of Gwen, son of Isobel, father of Tom and Hilary, and granddad of Beth and Zac. A service on Monday, September 14th at 2 p.m. will be held at St Peter's Presbyterian Church, Blues Point Road, North Sydney, followed by a private graveside service at Waverley Cemetery. No flowers please. Donations in memory to Huntington's Disease Association.*

I had e-mailed Tom from Turtle Island to say I was coming, giving him the name and phone number of my hotel, but the phone in my room didn't ring. I pushed away my disappointment, knowing that checking his e-mail would be the last thing on his mind. As far as he knew I was still in Shetland. I looked up Scarlett in the phone directory but thought better of ringing every Scarlett in North Sydney and asking if a Tom—no, not the Tom who just died—was there.

It hadn't occurred to me that the funeral service would be in an actual church. Tom was a dedicated atheist. It was stuffy in my room, and I cracked the window open and looked out at the cars and people below, plenty of them even on a Sunday night. The air was still warm at nine o'clock, and all I had packed as options to wear to the funeral were the black trousers and blue shirt I had worn when I first arrived on Turtle Island, and never since, not even on chilly nights in Shetland, and a sleeveless summer dress, dark blue with dramatic white flowers that I had bought in an exclusive London boutique, with Tom in mind. Even with the short-sleeved blue jacket that was part of the look, there was no way I could wear it to this funeral. And I would suffer heat stroke in the ugly trousers.

I could see plenty of shops out my window, so it was to be an early start for me tomorrow. I'd have to find something suitably somber hidden amongst the bright new summer fashions. My nerves were already beating me up and it wasn't even tomorrow yet. Why oh why had I come?

IN THE MORNING MY NAUSEA WAS WORSE AS I SLIPPED ON my blue sleeveless dress, and after a coffee and nothing else, went shopping. My self-esteem always hit rock bottom in fashion shops. Telling myself that I made more money and had more university degrees than any saleswoman made no difference. But I sallied forth, credit card trembling in my handbag, past caring about cost. It was someone else who thought twice before spending more than $50 on any single item of clothing.

Perhaps Aussie saleswomen were not as snooty as the Boston and London variety, or perhaps I struck it lucky on this quiet Monday morning. The older woman—about my age, probably—who asked if she could help as I flipped desperately through racks of sexy dresses sounded like Pat.

"That's a beautiful old church," she said when I told her I needed a complete outfit to wear to a funeral there in less than four hours. By the time she had zipped my credit card through her machine, I knew exactly what Pretty Woman felt like. Not that she'd had to dress for the funeral of a man she'd never met and whose grieving family had never heard of her.

Back in the hotel I forced down a sandwich and gulped another cup of coffee before showering and dressing, this time for real, in my funereal outfit. I couldn't imagine when I'd ever wear it again. By one o'clock I was as ready as I would ever be, and I took one last look in the long mirror on the wardrobe door. My dress was dull black with a small, pearly gray pattern. It had an elegantly draped skirt—cut on the bias, according to my saleswoman—that swirled about my knees when I spun around, and a fitted top with three-quarter-length tight sleeves decorated with pearl-gray buttons. A soft V neckline showed off my entwined dolphins, resurrected for the occasion. The silver dolphin earrings I had discovered in Shetland dangled from my ears, having been forced with some difficulty and a few spots of blood through the almost closed holes that had been pierced in my earlobes in my first year at university. They did look rather good with my new hair, and I silently thanked Aunt Jane for insisting I have it shaped and styled by her London hairdresser. It had grown back thick and glossy in the three months since the shaving, but I hadn't thought it possible to cut such short hair and have any left. Fortunately I was proven wrong, and its four-centimeter length now swept to one side, exposing my high forehead and barely feathering the tops of my ears. I thought I might not bother growing it ever again.

My sheer black pantyhose felt strange, but not as strange as my new black shoes with their five-centimeter heels—not that high as high goes, but higher than any heels I'd ever worn. So far they felt surprisingly comfortable, but I suspected I'd be hobbling before the day was out. I smiled at myself to make sure I had no lipstick on my teeth, picked up my new Italian leather black and gray clutch bag, took a deep breath and then another one, and walked unsteadily to the lift.

When the taxi drew up outside the church I almost told the driver to keep going—to take me anywhere but there. Groups of well-dressed people were disappearing through the church door and others stood about outside, conversing seriously. I clambered out of the taxi, tasting the sour air rising from my stomach where the tiny bubble of confidence that had formed as I gazed in the mirror was rapidly deflating. Holding my head very still, I walked carefully through the crowds of Scarlett friends, these people who had a right to be here, imagining them whispering as I passed, *Who is she? What does she think she's doing here?* I nodded to the young man at the door, who smiled solemnly and handed me a program. For a moment I wondered whether I'd got the wrong church, or the wrong time, and this was an organ recital or some other churchy thing. But then I glanced at the folded page and saw Tom's face, older and not quite the same, smiling at me. *Thomas Lloyd Scarlett, 1944–2009. In Memory* was written below it. He was only fifteen years older than me.

The church was already nearly full, a sea of dark clothes, the organ playing in that quiet, lamb of God way that comes before an almighty crescendo. I was about to weave my way into an empty space I could see halfway along one of the back pews when a second young man appeared in front of me and led me down the aisle to a pew only four rows from the front. Everyone in the pew obediently moved along and I sat down quickly on the blue cushion, smiling my thanks to the man I had displaced from his prime aisle seat. I would have gladly changed places with him. He nodded at me but thankfully didn't speak, and I looked at Tom's father's picture and folded it back and read the order of service. Three eulogies, Tom's name against one of them, and "The Irish Blessing" to be sung by the Blues Point A Cappella Male Singers. I was already on the edge of tears. My experience of funerals was limited to two non-sectarian services in chapels attached to crematoriums, both for parents of work colleagues. They had been draining enough and I didn't even know my work colleagues very well. I read the short biography of Tom Scarlett senior: A competitive yachtsman in his youth, a boat designer, and the founder and past CEO of one of Australia's largest boat-building companies. A music lover, a fisherman, a man who spent his Saturdays coaching young sailors, a son, a husband, a father, a grandfather. An entire part of Tom junior's life that I knew nothing about.

The three front pews on the other side of the aisle were empty, waiting for the family, and at the front of the church the coffin sat, a single wreath of golden flowers and delicate greenery its only decoration. It was a beautiful old church with a high, beamed, wooden ceiling. The intense Australian light mellowed as it filtered through the stained glass in the arched windows, painting the pale stone walls with splashes of rainbow.

I started as the impressive pipe organ at the front of the church changed key and from a side door hidden from my view a silver-haired man in a dog collar appeared. My stomach settled down—no cassocks and robes here in this spartan Scottish kirk.

The dark-haired woman who led her family through the side door looked serene, and I had no trouble recognizing her from the photo in Tom's bedroom, taken close to thirty years earlier. I supposed I'd been thinking she'd look elderly and gray. The other family members were a blur—I saw only Tom, tall and solemn, so handsome and strange in his dark suit and blue tie, his hair brushed almost smooth. I did notice one other: dearest Morrie, his wheelchair pushed by a young boy.

The minister's welcome, a prayer, "The Lord's My Shepherd," some more words from the minister about the man lying in the coffin. An invitation to everyone to go back to the family home for refreshments after the service. I swallowed. How would I get to that? My eyes kept straying to the back of Tom's head, sitting in the middle of the front pew between his mother and an elderly lady who must be his grandmother. Tom's sister bravely stood up to give the first eulogy, her two children with her, and talked movingly about her dad before bending and kissing the wreath on his coffin.

The pain that gripped my heart brought my hand to my chest and I took in some deep breaths, not daring to move. The pain disappeared and I tried to swallow, but my throat was blocked with tears. I'd never had the chance to tell Dad how much I loved him, and to say goodbye. He'd simply disappeared, and no one had been allowed to show him they cared about him, and that his silly faults didn't matter. *Goodbye Dad. I love you*, I whispered in my heart. *I'll always love you.*

Tom's sister was saying the same words to her father, and then she stepped back and her daughter, no older than eight or nine, a yellow butterfly amongst the black, read a poem for her granddad that had everyone scrabbling for a tissue. And now Tom was walking to the front. He stood for a moment, his hand on his father's coffin, his struggle to speak more potent than words. The stillness in the church was immense, and I wanted to look down, to shield myself from his grief. But I held steady, silently sending my strength to him, loving him more than I thought was possible. He looked up and, after a wobbly start, soon had everyone laughing as he recounted amusing stories about his father that clearly reverberated with many of the people there. He talked about his grandmother and his mother, and their dedication to their families; he thanked the hospice nursing staff; and then, looking down again at the coffin, he thanked his dad for loving him.

"Dad was a bit of a mixture, as most of you know. In many ways, he was a true-blue Aussie, but he never let us forget our heritage. His dad came from Edinburgh and his mum from Belfast. Long before he died he made sure we knew what music he wanted at his funeral. 'None of that "Waltzing Matilda"' he said. 'Send me off with an Irish blessing and the swirl of the bagpipes.'"

Eight men sitting in front of me had risen and moved around to stand on the other side of the coffin. *"May the road rise to meet you, May the wind be ever at your back . . ."* Their harmonies sent shivers up my spine, and I looked at Tom standing there so alone. *"May pure be the thoughts that surround you, May true be the hearts that love you."* I saw the pain in his eyes before he looked down at the coffin. He stood silent for a long minute in the hushed church, and when he finally looked up, his eyes were clear. He blinked as if the world had suddenly returned, and he glanced around at all the people there, sharing his goodbye. Then, as his gaze moved to my side of the church, I saw his eyes widen, and I smiled at him through my tears.

A final prayer, the benediction, and then the mournful sound of a sole bagpipe. The congregation turned as one to see ten or more kilted Scotsmen striding down the aisle to stand behind the coffin. As the single pipe was joined by all the others and "Amazing Grace" filled the church, Tom and five other men moved over to the coffin, lifted it to their shoulders, and walked slowly down the aisle, followed by the family. As Morrie wheeled past he saw me and, twisting his head to one side, gave me a huge smile. Chased by the bagpipes, we all walked outside into the bright sun and watched as the hearse moved away. Before I could feel awkward, Morrie was beside me, and I bent down and hugged him, my words of greeting lodged soundlessly in my throat.

"Anna."

I turned around and was in his arms. He hugged me tight and then stood back, actually grinning. "Look at her, Morrie. She could almost pass for a Sydney chick."

I blushed scarlet, I am quite sure, and glanced around to see who was watching. Nobody was, and Morrie's flailing arm smote me on my side.

"Sorry," he croaked. His eyes were twinkling. "You l-l-look l-l-lovely."

"How did you get here? Why didn't you tell me you were back?" Tom asked.

"I got back to the island on Saturday, and heard about your father. I'm so sorry, Tom."

"Poor Dad. If he could have gone sooner, he would have." He touched my face. "I can't believe you're here."

"Is it okay?" My heart was pounding.

"It's okay, Anna. More than okay." He grinned again. "I suppose I'll have to introduce you to Mum and Hilary now. No telling tales out of school."

Now my heart was leapfrogging. "Nothing to tell," I said, and heard Morrie's sudden deep laugh.

THE FAMILY HOME WAS A GRAND OLD LADY NOT FAR FROM the church, with views across a reserve to the sea. Tom introduced me to Gwen, his mother, and to his grandmother and Hilary and her husband, and after that I couldn't take in any more names. "My friend from Turtle Island," he called me.

Tables covered in savories and sandwiches and cakes rested under giant old trees. The atmosphere was almost festive. Inside the large entrance hall there was a display of photos of Tom Senior, and when everyone had eaten, after a toast to his memory and another to his family, the stories flowed as fast as the wine. The soft grass made it necessary to slip my high heels off, and the grass felt so good under my feet, even through my silk hose. At five o'clock, clearly guided by some secret sign invisible to me, everybody said their good-byes en masse and walked out the gate to their cars and taxis.

"Can I phone for a taxi?" I whispered to Tom when I managed to get him alone for a minute.

"We've got the burial now," he said. "You're welcome to come if you like."

"It's for family. Thank you, but I should go." I was feeling more and more flustered. Hilary was herding her children into the house to get their faces washed, Morrie was somewhere inside, and I felt like I shouldn't still be there.

"I'd like you to come. You're my family from the island." His eyes darkened as he held my gaze, and I reached up and touched his face, so strained, so sad, so like the father who only a day ago I hadn't known.

"If you're sure your family won't mind a stranger there," I whispered.

He kissed me quickly. "Of course they won't mind. You've come all this way for me."

TWENTY-SIX

I stood behind the family as they said their final goodbyes, each throwing a handful of earth onto the coffin lid as families have done for generations. In spite of the never-ending graves stretching in every direction, Waverley Cemetery was a good place to lie, looking over the sea.

After dropping his grandmother and mother back at the house, Tom took me back to my hotel, promising to pick me up around five the next evening. Gwen had insisted that I come and have a quiet dinner with them, so they could get to know me better. Hilary had chimed in, saying that her lot would be leaving the day after that, so it was her only chance to tell me what an annoying brother Tom had been.

I spent the day in a dream, wandering around Crow's Nest, sitting in cafes, tired and sad and hopeful. The evening with Tom's family was very pleasant, and I was made to feel welcome. Encouraged by Tom, I told them about Unst and the puffins and my otters.

"What's an otter?" Zac, Hilary's five-year-old, asked.

"It's sort of like a platypus," eight-year-old Beth informed him.

I tried not to smile at Zac's withering look of disbelief. "Is it, Uncle Tom?" he asked.

"We-e-ell, sort of, I suppose," said Uncle Tom. "Like a platypus without a beak or a pouch."

Zac caught my smile and I blushed.

"Uncle Tom knows everything about animals and sea creatures," he told me sternly.

By nine o'clock everyone looked exhausted and Hilary shooed her mother and grandmother off to bed.

"Come on, Anna, I'll take you back to your hotel," Tom said.

Hilary hugged me. "Look after our Tom on that island of his. Thanks for coming. It meant a lot to us all."

Outside the hotel we sat in the car, the silence feeling to me like goodbye.

"Do you want to come in?" I asked, not daring to look at him. "For a cup of tea."

"Thanks, but I don't think so. You need your bed, and so do I."

"When do you think you'll be home?" My voice rose to a squeak. "To the island."

"I don't know. Two or three weeks, perhaps. There's a lot to do here. I want to make sure Mum's all right."

"It was a beautiful funeral. You're so lucky to have a family like that."

He didn't speak and I turned and looked at him. He was gazing straight ahead, out the window, but I knew he was crying. I reached over and took his hand and he squeezed mine back, not letting it go.

I LOVED THE SMELL OF MY CABIN. IT HIT ME AS SOON AS I unlocked the big glass doors and slid them wide. I knew I would never forget it as long as I lived. Everything on the island was just the same, yet so different. The days were long because I was waiting for Tom to return and short because I wanted to hold on to every moment, in case this was my last first day of October, my last second day of October, my last day there. One minute I felt a little glimmer of hope—Tom was happy that I came to his dad's funeral, surely that must mean something—and the next, certain that nothing had changed for him. One minute I was confident I'd be able to convince him that my love was deep enough for both of us, and the next I was shaking with the very thought of even telling him.

I looked at my e-mail daily, or even three times a day, to see if he'd sent me a message. And he did, quite often, but just short updates on his mum. I was losing hope that he'd be back before Jeff returned in the last weekend in October. Pat could see my turmoil and understood without my saying a word.

"You'll stay with me," she said, "until Tom comes home."

"What if he never comes home?"

She laughed. "What if turtles could fly?"

TEN DAYS BEFORE JEFF'S RETURN AND MY PLANNED departure, I took the long way around the beach to Tom's house. I hadn't had an e-mail from him for days. And there he was, sitting on the sand, gazing out over the lagoon, as if he'd never left. Joy, anger, hurt, pain, relief—all of it and more—vied for space in my poor head.

"How did you get here?" were the first words out of my mouth, as if that mattered. Tom knew it didn't matter and didn't answer.

"Are you all right?" I tried.

He nodded. "Just getting myself balanced again."

"You're not all right." I sat down and tried to hold him, but he shook his head, and I pushed myself away a little in the sand.

"I know I'm hurting you, but I need to be alone for a bit," he said after a while.

"I'm meant to leave here in ten days. Do you want me to?" My stomach was somersaulting.

"I do want to talk, but not yet."

"Will you tell me when you—when you are ready to talk?"

He nodded and I stumbled back to my cabin, my eyes too blurred to see the half moon rising over the reef.

A MISERABLE WEEK LATER, TOM APPEARED AT MY CABIN.

"Hi," I said.

"Hi."

"Do you want a drink? Have you eaten? I could make you something."

"Let's go for a walk," he said.

It was dark, with only stars to light the way. We walked in silence until at last Tom stopped at Shark Bay. We sat on the sand looking out at the ink-filled lagoon.

"I want to tell you how Dad died." His voice cracked.

My heart slowed a little. This is not what I had been expecting.

"Mum had to feed him three times every day with a teaspoon. Each feed took about an hour, and he spent most of that time choking."

"Why didn't they insert a feeding tube into his stomach?" I whispered.

"They wanted to but then he might have lived for weeks— months, even. We decided as a family that we wouldn't agree to that, and we couldn't let him starve to death—it's illegal, anyway. So Mum had to feed him. The nurses didn't have the time."

My heart was aching for him as I sensed him struggling to go on.

"Mum was so tired that sometimes she would start crying at the dinner table when she got home. But she refused to let me help. The day he died, I was with her. I begged her to let me feed him a little. I tried to make her believe that I wanted to, to show him how much I loved him."

Tom turned his head and looked at me, and in the starlight his face looked haunted. "She finally said yes, and I sat there by his bed trying to force that yellow baby food into his sore mouth, holding his head up so he wouldn't choke."

I wanted to close my ears and not hear any more.

"But he did choke, and this time we couldn't stop him. Mum rang the bell and the nurses came running in and took over, but he went blue and then he was still."

"Oh, Tom," was all I could say. "Tom."

"Thank god it was me who was feeding him when he choked to death. I only wish Mum hadn't been there, watching." His gaze returned to the sea, and after a while I put my arms around him and held him so tight he couldn't push me away. He started to shake, and we sat there, crying.

A long time later, it seemed, we managed to separate. My eyes were dry and sore and my insides felt as if they'd been scraped out with a file. Tom took my hand and stroked each of my fingers. "Why so many tears, Anna?"

I knew what he meant. He could see inside me. My tears started again, coming from some bottomless pit. "I never said goodbye to my dad. I never had the chance to tell him I loved him. He had no funeral, no memorial service even."

"I know, love, I know," Tom's voice murmured as he cradled me and rocked me, until at last I had nothing left.

"And now I know he lied about his parents, and Tom, it hurts so much."

"He never lied to *you*. He was a teenager who made a mistake, that's all. He was ashamed, that's why he blurted out that lie to your mother. Poor guy, he was scared she would leave him too if he told the truth. Then he would lose his baby —you—as well."

"You would never do something like that."

"Oh Anna, how innocent you are. Give your dad some slack. Getting a naive girl pregnant when abortion was illegal. It was one understandable mistake and then he had to live with his mother's suicide on his conscience. Isn't that enough?"

I nodded. I was incapable of speech.

"Seems like your dad and me have a lot in common."

I found my voice. "What do you mean; did you get a girl pregnant?"

Tom laughed. "No, I had a much more powerful reason to keep my genes from straying."

"Oh, your vasectomy."

"Believe me, long before I was permitted to have that, I was the safe sex poster boy."

I felt stupidly relieved. "How are you like Dad then?"

"We're both passionate about the sea, and we both love you more than life itself."

Did he say that? I felt dizzy. I closed my eyes and felt the warm breeze on my face and breathed in the salt air. "You love me?" I whispered.

Tom took my hand again. "I shouldn't have said that. I love you, you must know that, but it won't work, us staying together. Anna, love, I'm sorry."

I could hear the desolation in his voice and I closed my eyes again. *Don't take it back, please don't take it back.* I don't know if I pleaded out loud or if it was just in my head.

"That's why I wanted to tell you about Dad's death, so you'd understand."

"Understand what?" I heard my voice far away.

"I know you've probably seen or at least heard about deaths like Dad's, but this is my dad, this is me. I need you to understand why I can't ever let you go through what Mum has had to go through."

"But you probably don't even have the gene," I almost shouted.

"Anna, I got tested before Dad died. I had all the counseling and I got tested. I got the results just before I came back here."

"Oh no, please no."

"I know. I've had time to get used to it. I always thought I had it anyway, but I guess I had some hope. It was harder than I thought."

"Why did you change your mind? You said you would never get tested," I croaked.

"For you. For us. I wanted us to be together, and I decided it was worth the coin toss."

"If you had tested negative, you would have let me stay?"

"I would have asked you to marry me," he said. "Perhaps you've had a lucky escape." A smile traced his lips and I threw myself at him, knocking him flat.

"We still can. Please, Tom. You probably have years before you get it. Don't do this to me." I wanted to pound my fists on his chest. "There'll be a cure for Huntington's symptoms by the time you get any, I'm sure of it."

"I hope so."

He eased me off him and I rolled over onto the sand and lay there, frustration and helplessness marshaling in my aching head.

"Now that I know you," Tom said, his finger smoothing the crease between my eyes, "I believe a cure *will* happen one day. Before, all that research didn't seem real. Go back to Boston, Anna, and take up the cause again. It might not be in time for me, but if it helps Beth or Zac . . ."

"Oh, no, Hilary has it too." I heard my wail as the agony of what I'd done, pushing Tom to get tested, hit me in the gut.

"Easy, Anna. Hilary hasn't been tested. She's even more determined now not to flip the coin."

"She can't have it; not her too. That would be so unfair."

"There's no harm in a bit of magical thinking, even if you're a researcher." Tom grinned at me. Then his smile faded. "If Hilary's lucky, there will be someone else's Beth or Zac out there to save."

He pulled himself into a sitting position, and sat there, still as only he could be still. Then I saw what he'd already seen, the head of a turtle at the edge of the water. I watched him, watching the sea he loved so much, and as if he felt my gaze, he turned his head and smiled down at me, still lying on the sand. "It's time, Anna, time for you to go back to the real world. I love you, and that's why nothing will change my mind."

MY LAST THREE DAYS WENT PAST IN A DAZE. I TOLD PAT, and asked her to explain to everyone why I didn't want a farewell party. Tom and I talked some more, but not about us. I didn't try again to change him. The day I left I asked him not to come to the wharf and say goodbye. He was upset, and

Pat too. "It's what we do for our own," she said. "Then we know they'll come back."

That's why I didn't want him there.

I couldn't stop the others, and I tried to be strong and hugged each of them—Basil, Violet, Chloe, and little Danny. "And another hug from Bill," Violet said. "He went off with Tom."

Pat held me tight and promised to visit me in Boston. I knew she would. Then I walked up the gangplank and waved as Jack and Nick, without their usual banter and shouting, backed out, and turned and pointed towards Gladstone and Boston and away forever from Turtle Island.

I heard the screaming motor before I saw them, the two dark figures on the dinghy doing their crazy circles around the lagoon. Then I saw Tom dive in and disappear for minutes before he surfaced, a giant turtle in his arms. Bill was struggling to get the rope around the turtle's flippers so he could secure it while it was measured. Jack was standing next to me and I pointed towards the dinghy. "They can't manage with only two men."

"Shall we go over and see, girl?" Jack said, already waving at Nick in the wheelhouse. Our boat made a wide turn and puttered towards the dinghy. Bill had got the turtle fastened and was measuring it by the time we came close, and Nick cut the engine. Tom turned in the water, and I saw his grin flash. He swam over to us and pulled himself up on the ladder on the side of our boat. Not right up, but just far enough so our lips could meet when I bent down.

"Goodbye my turtle whisperer," I whispered.

"Goodbye my sweet Anna," he said.

EPILOGUE

‒‒‒‒‒‒‒‒‒‒‒‒

Today is my seventy-fifth birthday. Turtle Island is blessedly little changed from that day in 2009 when I celebrated my fiftieth birthday. The same can't be said for the rest of the world, but that's another story.

Tom lives in Pat's house now. She sold it to him when she left, fifteen years ago, on the understanding that she could stay with him any time. We often coordinated our visits over the years, although I usually stayed much longer than she. Pat isn't here for my birthday; she died two years ago, at the grand old age of eighty-eight. Her house has changed little except for ramps replacing the steps onto the deck, widened doorways, and a sit-down shower instead of a bath. Tom has a satellite dish on the roof that connects him, via fast speed broadband, to me when I am in Boston, and to the rest of the world.

Many of my old island friends are here for this grand occasion. The cabins once owned by Violet and Bill, and now run by their daughter and her partner, are full. Violet and Bill are here, of course, delighted to spend time with their new grandson, the only baby to be born on the island since Hamish. Jack delivered me to the island two days ago, and is staying for my party. He often comes over with his son, who now skippers the boat. Diane and Ben, still passionate about diving, posted a lovely letter written on their boat somewhere in the Bahamas, and even George, still living at Dry Acres Artists' Community and rather forgetful these days, sent me a card. Basil will be missing. He died peacefully in his cyclone-proof house a few years ago.

And of course Kirsty and Hamish are here. Hamish is twenty-five and a beautiful young man. His career choice was difficult—marine biology or medicine? In the end he chose medicine, but now that he is a qualified doctor he has decided to go further. He begins a PhD in genetic engineering in Boston later this year. I'll expect regular visits from him when he can wrench himself away from MIT. This morning when he gave me a birthday kiss before leaving for a dive with the incumbent turtle tagger, he reminded me of my father, perhaps because my happiest and saddest memories of Dad are of him in a wetsuit. There is no genetic reason why Hamish should resemble Dad, of course, but as the grandson of my heart I think he has rearranged my memories of my father in some mysterious way.

I can see Tom now, rolling along the beach, his face aglow with the pleasure of his regular morning stroll. His wheelchair resembles a 4WD with its wide wheels, designed for sand and beach-rock hopping. It also clips securely to the rear of his amphibious boat and allows him, even when alone, to putter out over the reef edge when the tide is high. Once there, he falls backwards over the side of the boat and is again in his element, floating over the wonders below, his contorted movements vanquished and his twisted body young and perfect again.

Tom feels he has been lucky. His Huntington's symptoms didn't become a problem until he was in his early fifties, and by then there were medications that dramatically reduced the psychiatric symptoms without side effects. I tell myself that without the basic research I and so many other researchers spent so much of our time on, these cutting-edge drugs might not have been developed.

I used to blame myself for manipulating Tom into having the genetic test all those years ago, torturing myself with the thought that if he hadn't, he would have had many more years of hope. But he insisted that it was his decision alone, and that it proved to be the best option.

"Living in hope soon becomes a burden," he told me. "Once I knew, every day without the disease was a gift."

Hilary has continued to resist being tested, and still shows no symptoms. Before Beth and Zac had children of their own, they each underwent testing—with joyful results. Chances are higher now that Hilary is therefore free too.

Last night Tom and I strolled on the beach at high tide, me still walking unaided and strong, and Tom in his wheelchair. Lit by a full moon we watched, spellbound, as a turtle lumbered up the sand to lay her eggs. I was not expecting to see nesting turtles this late in the season, but Tom recognized her as Eve, the very first turtle I saw laying so long ago. She is likely the same age as me, but rather more fertile.

My work for the past twenty-five years has been as a medical practitioner in a community medical center where I have patients from babies to the very old. But my interest in working with Huntington's families has led to the opening of a specialist clinic staffed by therapists, genetic counselors, and social workers, as well as doctors, a sort of one-stop shop for families who harbor genetic conditions. I take my turn there two afternoons each week, offering a genetic counseling and testing service.

I try to keep up with the latest discoveries in Huntington's research, and it has been wonderful to be a part of the movement to eradicate the Huntington's gene from the human race. Even the Catholic Church has succumbed to the pressure of Huntington's Action groups, reluctantly permitting genetic testing and IVF for those of their flock who potentially carry the gene. Contraception is still frowned upon, but the Pope can't see through bedroom walls. Within another generation, in most countries, Huntington's will be a disease of the past. The genetic engineering research that Hamish wants to become part of has made enormous strides as a result of the pioneering work on Huntington's disease, and is already making a difference to many disorders.

All this has been too late to save Tom, but I've learned to live with that. On my twice-yearly visits to Turtle Island, I warm myself with his contentment, and that has long been more than enough.

Francesca was over here for breakfast earlier. She'll be staying for a few days before setting off on a group 4WD tour up Cape York to the tip of Australia. Fran has already outlived the Professor by fifteen years, and although she forgave him, and was convinced he had given up his philandering, I always felt angry on her behalf. My hard-earned ability to stand back and let those I cared about live according to their own wishes stretched me to the limit when it came to Fran. At least I managed to keep my feelings to myself. Since her husband's death, Fran has blossomed, and in the end has lived the life she always deserved. My mother also continues to be an inspiration to me, even though she is long gone, Magnus following her within a year. Until her death I spent many holidays on Shetland, although they came to Turtle Island only twice.

I sometimes wonder if I would have been happier if I had

had my way and inveigled Tom into letting me live with him. When I am here I am often certain this is true, but then remember that Tom didn't choose it. As my father's daughter, I could have applied for Australian citizenship and joined a medical practice in Brisbane or Sydney. But it would have been cheating. The alternative, in the end, was the better choice for me as well as for Tom.

This evening we will have my party. It is to be in the turtle tagger's house, which is exactly the same as it used to be, even down to the same couches. Everyone on the island is invited, including any campers in Jeff's campground. Jeff will certainly be there. I'll sit on the deck, my old hand holding Tom's, and enjoy the young people dancing and flirting. We'll drink a toast to Morrie's memory, and remember our last day with him—the day he swallowed the pills that legally allowed him to slip peacefully out of this world.

Together we will share a joint, also legal now for medicinal purposes, and the only medication that calms Tom's body. He believes it has held his cognitive decline at bay as well, and perhaps he is right. I no longer think double blind scientific drug trials are the Holy Grail. I know that he self-tests his cognitive abilities monthly using a specially designed computer program, and that when his scores decline to a point he has already had programmed into his computer he will not procrastinate. Tom always knew his mind. I have offered to help him but my turtle whisperer gently declined my offer. My last act of love will be to stand back when he takes his final ride out over the reef edge and falls backwards into his beloved sea.

AUTHOR'S NOTES

After reading this novel you may be interested in finding out more about two of the central topics raised: the conservation of marine turtles and Huntington's disease. I can only cover a few details about each, of course, but this may stimulate you to seek out more detailed information, easy to find on the Internet, and perhaps add your donation to any one of the many charitable bodies dedicated to one or other of these important causes.

MARINE TURTLE CONSERVATION

Although the green turtle (*Chelonia mydas*) and loggerhead turtle (*Caretta caretta*) featured in this novel nested on Australian beaches, these species, as well as the hawkesbill turtle (*Eretmochelys imbricata*), the olive ridley turtle (*Lepidochelys olivacea*), and the giant leatherback turtle (*Dermochelys coriacea*) occur worldwide throughout the tropical and temperate seas. The flatback turtle (*Natator depressus*) is restricted to the tropical areas of the continental shelf of Australia, southern Irian Jaya, and southern Papua New Guinea. Marine turtles throughout the world, including in Australia and the USA, are in urgent need of protection. All are endangered, with the hawkesbill and leatherback being critically endangered.

Marine turtles come from an ancient lineage of terrestrial reptiles, and as they adapted to life in the ocean they developed paddle-like limbs. They have an acute sense of smell but not of taste, well-developed eyes with color vision, and hearing that is restricted to very low frequencies. Like terrestrial reptiles, they must surface to breathe, and they lay their eggs on land. Green turtles are herbivores and graze on sea grasses, algae, and seaweed, and the other species of turtle eat soft sea animals like sponges, shrimp, squid, jellyfish, and crabs. Copulation occurs in the sea. Every two or three years the female turtles return to the beach they were born on, or a nearby beach, to nest multiple times in one season, laying large clutches (60–80 plus) of soft white round eggs the size of ping-pong balls. When the hatchlings emerge, those that safely reach the ocean are often not seen again in the sea until they are about dinner-plate size. Their feeding grounds may be a long way from their breeding beach, and indeed is often in the waters of a different country. When they are mature at 20 or 30 years, they migrate vast distances to return to the beach where they were born to lay their own eggs. For successful incubation the eggs must be buried in ventilated, low salinity, high humidity nest sites that are not subjected to flooding or erosion and have a temperature range of 25–33°C. Both the sex of the hatchlings and the length of incubation is determined by the nest temperature. Once the eggs are laid, they are on their own, and the tiny baby turtles have to make their own way down the beach to the sea and into the vast ocean without any assistance from their parents.

These ancient behaviors make turtles vulnerable to numerous man-made dangers: increased mortality through marine debris, oil pollution, and boat strikes; habitat loss; predation of eggs by feral animals; noise and light pollution at nesting sites; vehicles and houses on nesting beaches; and tourist disturbance during nesting. Although most countries now protect marine turtles, in some countries, including Australia, an exception is made for their harvest by indigenous peoples, and if this is not controlled, this too can have an effect. The illegal trade in turtle shell and turtle meat is also a major problem. Of course the natural predators of the turtle also continue to threaten the species: bird and feral animal attacks on the hatchlings as they make their way to the sea, and shark attacks of the adults once at sea.

Watching a mother turtle preparing her nest and laying her eggs is a wonderful experience, as is observing a nestful of baby turtles explode out of the sand and toddle down to the lighter sea, hopefully avoiding being picked off by seabirds. If you do get a chance to visit a turtle nesting beach, take care not to disturb the nesting mother—avoid shining lights or making a noise, and sit well behind her so she is unable to see you. Never buy turtle shell trinkets, and of course never eat turtle meat or turtle soup. These illegal activities should be reported. Join campaigns against marine and beach pollution, and if you can, donate to an appropriate research body or conservation society in your country, or a country you are visiting.

HUNTINGTON'S DISEASE

Huntington's disease (HD) is at the center of one of the most remarkable stories of discovery in medical history. In 1872 George Huntington, a North American general practitioner, published the first unambiguous description of the unrelenting neurodegenerative disorder in *The Medical and Surgical Reporter*. The title of his article was simply "On Chorea," referring to the strange involuntary contorted movements made by people with HD. His description of this type of chorea as a specific hereditary disorder became quickly and widely accepted. Careful pedigrees of generations of HD families around the world have since confirmed his theory by documenting that 50 percent of the children of a parent with HD will develop HD if they live long enough. That is, HD is an *autosomal dominant hereditary disorder.*

Simply put, HD is caused when one gene (or allele) of a usually healthy gene pair we all carry is abnormally elongated. This HD gene mutation is dominant, so that anyone who carries it will develop HD. Each child has a 50 percent chance of inheriting the mutated allele from a parent who has it, even if the parent has not yet developed any HD symptoms. On the bright side, the child also has a 50 percent chance of inheriting the HD parent's healthy allele, in which case the child will never develop HD and will never pass it on. Until it is known for certain whether or not a descendant of a person with HD has inherited the HD mutation, that individual is said to be "at risk." When Tom's father was diagnosed with HD, Tom's risk for developing HD became 50 percent, and if he had children they would immediately be at risk as well, but their risk would be 25 percent. If Tom was diagnosed as HD positive by the predictive genetic test (or if he developed symptoms) any children he had would now have a 50 percent risk of having the disease. If Tom's predictive test had shown that he did not carry the HD gene, his risk and any future child's risk would drop to zero.

HD symptoms usually become apparent between the ages of 35 and 45, although there may be subtle signs of the disease long before this. In rare cases, the symptoms do not become apparent until much later, even into a person's seventies. Chorea is the most common and prominent motor symptom, and is usually amongst the earliest symptoms to develop, due to damage to the basal ganglia, a deep structure in the brain involved in motor movement. These random and abrupt movements usually progress over the course of the disease, from restlessness with only a mild, intermittent exaggeration of expression and gesture; to fidgeting movements of the hands; to an unstable, writhing, dance-like gait, or a continuous flow of disabling, violent, "crazy-looking" movements. Sustained muscle contractions resulting in twisting, repetitive movements, and abnormal postures are also common. Tremor can also occur in HD, although this is more often associated with Parkinson's disease (PD), another movement disorder, but one that is not usually genetically determined. Other motor abnormalities that HD and PD have in common are rigidity and a slowness of movement that can result in freezing, a terrible symptom where the HD patient is unable to move. Gait abnormalities are obvious in patients who have had HD for some years, with a wide-based, staggering gait—often mistaken for drunkenness —being a common feature. Fortunately, choreic movements largely cease during sleep, although in the latter stages of HD the patient may be sleepy during the day and wakeful at night.

Eye movement abnormalities occur early in the disease in most patients and gradually worsen, resulting in an increasing problem with focusing the eyes. Slurred speech is common, and early in the disease speech rate and rhythm are often abnormal, worsening over time until speech becomes unintelligible. Some patients become mute even before their motor disability is very severe. Eating difficulties include inappropriate selection of food, inappropriate rate of eating, retention of food in the mouth after swallowing, and regurgitation. Choking and asphyxia are also common and distressing symptoms.

As HD progresses, other parts of the brain are affected, including the outermost neuronal layer of the brain—the cortex—and especially the frontal cortex, resulting in patients experiencing cognitive symptoms and ever-worsening "executive" impairments, including difficulties in abstract thinking and planning ahead, and problems shifting thoughts from one topic to another. In the latter stages of HD, serious loss of weight and muscle bulk occur in spite of an adequate diet and feeding. This is not simply the result of constant excessive movement but appears to be an integral aspect of HD.

Many patients with HD experience psychiatric symptoms. Depression is common, especially in the early stage of HD, when the patient is fully aware of their condition and their grim and unalterable prognosis. Suicide rates are almost four times higher among HD sufferers than in the healthy population. Many other psychiatric and behavioral problems are also common—the vast majority of HD sufferers regularly show signs of low mood, agitation, irritability, apathy, anxiety, an inability to inhibit inappropriate behaviors, and euphoria. Delusions and hallucinations are problems for a small number of HD patients. Other symptoms that cause concern for families, and which probably often arise from the psychiatric symptoms already mentioned, include moodiness, aggression, violent behaviors, hypersexuality, paranoid suspicions, lying, stealing, a loss of interest in personal appearance, marked self-neglect, and mutism. As the patient becomes more demented and loses insight, apathy may increase and depression decrease.

In the final stage, patients are severely physically disabled and demented, and thus totally dependent on others. About 20 percent of HD patients become incontinent near the end. Death usually results from a combination of weight loss, immobility, a tendency to aspirate food, and an increased vulnerability to pneumonia, cardiovascular disease, and other diseases.

There is currently no cure for HD and no way to delay its progression, and the only way to stop it affecting generation after generation of an HD family is by ensuring that no children are born with the gene. Thus couples where one partner is at risk for HD are increasingly opting for assisted fertilization options. For example, the genetic makeup of the fertilized eggs can be determined and an embryo without the HD gene reimplanted in the mother. Other alternatives, including adoption, using a non-HD sperm or egg donor, or choosing not to have children, are also increasingly used. All these decisions require genetic counseling, and in some countries, cultures, and religions none of these alternatives are permitted, acceptable, or available, often resulting in couples risking the birth of a child with the HD gene.

Studies have shown that 90 percent of people at risk for the HD gene decide, as Tom initially did, NOT to have the predictive test. Clearly, for most people, the 50 percent chance that you will discover that you have the gene is worse than not knowing and retaining the hope that you will not have it. In most countries, while it is permitted to test an embryo for the HD gene, once a child is born parents cannot choose to have him or her tested; children must be old enough to decide for themselves, usually in their late teenage years or older.

In common with a number of other medical conditions, the stimulus for setting up research and support institutions for HD initially came from individuals who had themselves been personally affected by the disease. The Hereditary Disease Foundation, which promotes research into HD, was initiated by Dr. Milton Wexler after his wife died from HD and is continued by his daughter, Dr. Nancy Wexler. The foundation has played a central role in the remarkable study that began in 1979 of a large HD population living by the shores of Lake

Maracaibo in Venezuela. This group is the best example of how quickly a dominantly inherited genetic disorder can take over a small, isolated community. Painstaking research has revealed that one ancestor with HD who lived in the early 1800s has so far left more than 18,000 descendants, 14,000 of whom are still alive today and many of whom have HD or are at risk for it. This detailed and unique pedigree was a crucial factor in locating, in 1983, the approximate location of the gene involved in HD. In 1993 after further painstaking work by many research groups in the US and UK, a group lead by Harvard Medical School researcher, James Gusella, isolated the precise causal gene and identified the mutation of the gene that causes the disease. At this point an expanded group, called the Huntington's Disease Collaborative Research Group, published its findings. This group was a collaboration of six US and British research teams, and although Gusella's team isolated the gene, the credit was rightly given to the entire collaboration, as the research that preceded the gene's precise identification was an essential aspect of the discovery. This truly collaborative effort is a superb example of how medical and other scientific research should be conducted—a cooperative endeavor motivated by the determination to find the truth and make a difference rather than by competition and the desire for personal aggrandizement.

Marjorie Guthrie, the wife of the iconic American folk-singer Woody Guthrie, who developed HD symptoms around 1952 and died in 1967, when he was only 55, founded the Committee to Combat Huntington's Disease, which led to the formation of the Huntington's Disease Society of America. The aim of this society is to promote education, research, and services for families of HD sufferers. Your donation to any of these bodies, or other HD research or family support associations in other countries, would be money well spent.

Much of the above information about HD has been excerpted from a chapter in my book, *Trouble In Mind: Stories from a Neuropsychologist's Casebook*. It relates the true and moving story of an amazing family and how they coped with HD (it has an uplifting ending!). The chapter is named for one of Woody Guthrie's songs, in his and Marjorie Guthrie's honor: "Hard, Ain't It Hard: A Family's Fight with Huntington's Disease."

ACKNOWLEDGMENTS

Many people over the years have taught me how to write, if not this book specifically, my other books. Too many folk, in fact, to name. But for help with this novel I especially want to thank Philippa Donovan of Smart Quill Editorial, UK, whose insightful editing made it better and gave me hope that perhaps one day someone else might read and enjoy it. I also thank my many friends and family for either asking me how my novel was coming along or refraining from doing so when I said, before they had a chance to speak, "Don't ask!" Thank you to the caring teams at She Writes Press and SparkPoint Studio in the United States, with a special high-five to Brooke Warner, Cait Levin, Krissa Lagos, and Stacey Aaronson for their wise and experienced piloting through the vagaries of the publishing world, and to Julie Metz for the evocative cover. Thank you to She Writes Press authors for their help with titles, proofing, and sharing of experience, especially Laura Diamond, Tammy Hetrick, Céline Keating, Diana Paul, and Jodi Wright. To Caitlin Hamilton Summie, my superb publicist, thank you for believing in my book and telling others about it, and thank you dear friends of my Street Team for doing the same. But most importantly, I thank John, my long-suffering husband, who never wavered in his support of my lovely obsession.

READING GROUP QUESTIONS
and
TOPICS FOR DISCUSSION

1. In Chapter 1, 49-year-old Boston neuroscientist Anna Fergusson describes herself as "introverted," " a washed-up old spinster," and "an ivory tower nerd, clueless about people." This fits a popular stereotype of older, unmarried women scientists. By the end of Chapter 1, what was your "deeper" impression of Anna? Did you see any other more positive personality characteristics in her that made her decision to rent a cabin for a year on a tropical island on the far side of the world believable?

2. Losing a major research grant is equivalent to being made redundant from a long-term job—especially difficult for middle-aged people. Have you (or a family member) ever been in a similar situation? How did it make you feel? Do you think young people today have a different attitude to changing jobs than baby boomers, and if so, what can baby boomers learn from them?

3. Have you ever been to a tropical island? Looking back, what evokes the most powerful memories for you of that experience? Can you imagine living on such a small island for an entire year? Some people see themselves as primarily "city" or "country" people. Do you think Anna would have viewed herself as a "city" person at the beginning of the novel, with rural or wild places for holidays only? What are you: a "city" or "country" person?

4. Whether you are a "city" or "country" person, or somewhere in between, do you sometimes find solace being alone in a "wild" place? Do you think that this need is an intrinsic aspect of human nature, or is it learned—for example, from good wilderness experiences in childhood?

5. Ever since *The Horse Whisperer* by Nicholas Evans was published in 1995—selling over 15 million copies, making it one of the best-selling novels of all time—the label "whisperer" has been attached to all sorts of things: dogs, babies, books, ghosts, and Alzheimer's disease sufferers, among others. There are hundreds of books with "Whisperer" in the title on Amazon. What did Tom's tongue-in-cheek nickname, "The Turtle Whisperer," convey to you when it was first mentioned? Did the metaphor with Anna as the reclusive turtle, hiding in her shell and being whispered out by Tom, become clear to you at some point in the novel?

6. Wild places and wildlife—particularly turtles—and the wonder and joy these bring to Anna play a pivotal role in her transformation. She almost seems to identify with turtles—their reclusive nature, their mothering instincts, and perhaps the fact that they are central in Tom's life. Have you ever had a strong emotional connection with an animal—perhaps a pet? What do you think of the notion that lonely people are more likely to build such deep bonds (even if only one-way!) with animals?

7. When it comes to sex and intimate relationships, double standards are still present. Even today, older

woman–younger man intimate relationships raise some eyebrows. Certainly Anna, with her low self-esteem, didn't hold out much hope that Tom would find her desirable. How did Tom convey to Anna that in his eyes she was attractive and the difference in their ages was of no account? If Anna had not seen for herself the love between her mother and her younger husband, do you think she would have had the confidence to take the courageous step of almost begging Tom to let her stay with him? If you are middle-aged or older, do you ever feel invisible, and do you think this is primarily an experience women, and not men, have?

8. As we discover Anna's backstory, it becomes clear that she's always favored her father over her mother. Later in the novel we meet her mother, and it is difficult to believe that she was ever the uncaring or distracted mother Anna remembers from her childhood. Where parents are separated and one parent (usually the mother) is the primary caregiver, and the other parent just takes the child out for treats, do you think it understandable that the child sees the "treat" parent as her or his "hero"? How might this situation be avoided?

9. Anna comments that she is "clueless about people" and perhaps believes that that is why she has difficulty making friends, both as a child and an adult. Why do you think the residents of Turtle Island befriend Anna so readily? Is this an example of the city/country situation, where people in cities prefer to be anonymous but in small communities this isn't possible—or is it simply that perhaps Australians are more friendly than

Americans? How often do you extend the hand of friendship to new people in your area?

10. Pat becomes an important part of Anna's life. What is it about Pat that draws Anna to her?

11. Neither Tom nor Anna likes Tom's boss, Collette, very much. In Tom's case, do you think he would have been more comfortable if his boss had been a man, or do you think personality was more the issue? In a work situation, does gender ever matter to you, or is this always secondary to personality, management style, etc.? (Be honest!)

12. Anna originally trained as a doctor, but discovered she was "hopeless at anything that involves actual patient contact" and thus retrained as a lab-based scientist. On Turtle Island she is challenged by a number of medical issues: Hamish's birth; Pat's breast cancer; her own menopausal symptoms; Morrie's Huntington's disease symptoms; and, most dramatically, the possibility that Tom has the Huntington's disease gene. Do you think Anna's responses to those situations are influenced by her medical training, or are her responses simply those any one of us might have in similar circumstances? If you had to deliver a baby, do you think you would know what to do and be able to follow through?

13. When Pat returns to the island after her first round of chemotherapy, she is moved when she is greeted at the wharf by all her friends who have shaved their

heads in support. Would you shave your head if you thought it would help a friend with cancer feel more supported? Why do you think symbols like this can bring forth such strong emotions?

14. During the birth scene, did you think something would go wrong? Were you surprised when it all went smoothly? How real did it feel to you? Whose "head" were you in while you were reading the scene—Anna's, Kirsty's, or perhaps poor Ben's? Generally when reading a novel, are you in the head space of the character whose point of view is prominent (Anna, in this case), or do you find yourself experiencing the situation from the point of view of one of the other characters, perhaps a character you empathize with strongly?

15. When Anna first meets Morrie, given that people like Morrie are the very participants she has been researching for years, she is ashamed of her initial feelings of repulsion and fear. Do you think her decision as the head of the lab to have her research assistants work on a one-to-one basis with the Huntington's disease patients and their families so she could avoid personal contact with them suggests that she has been exploiting them for the sake of her research? Anna's reaction is perhaps extreme, but it is not uncommon to feel fear or other negative or inappropriate feelings when we first meet someone very different from ourselves—especially people who are severely mentally or physically disabled. What strategies can you think of to help yourself or your children feel at ease with all kinds of people, and to "see" the person inside?

6

16. Anna's specialty area is Huntington's disease. When she finally discovers why Tom won't commit to a long-term relationship, she can't understand his decision not to be tested. After all, he has a 50 percent chance of not having the gene, and then they could be together forever. There are many difficult ethical decisions to be made when deciding to have this test, and clearly Tom has made his decision. Do you think Anna would have had a different response if she had not been an HD specialist? (You may find it helpful to read my "Author's Notes" on HD to get an idea about what Anna knew about HD as an expert, and what Tom had experienced as he watched his father deteriorate.) Have you ever been in a situation where someone you love makes a health decision you disagree with? Imagine a scenario where your partner refuses to have treatment for a heart condition that may extend his or her life, or decides to have a vasectomy or a tubal ligation because he or she doesn't want children even though you desperately do. Do you think there are some health decisions that should be jointly made? If partners can't agree, do you think you might see your partner's decision as a sign that he or she doesn't love you enough?

17. In the first 49 years of her life Anna loses much that she loves: her father; the man she was having an affair with; the baby she was carrying; her career; and even her mother, in the sense that she feels they have no connection. On Turtle Island she feels that she is losing baby Hamish, she almost loses Pat, she loses her trust in her father, and she loses her dream of staying

with Tom on Turtle Island. Yet her life becomes richer as the Island people become her family, and she reconnects with her mother and forgives her father. When she at last accepts that Tom must make his own decision, she learns the hard lesson that love is about letting go. What do you think about this? Can you let go?

18. One of the authors who endorsed this novel commented that *A Drop In The Ocean* is "a story about belonging—and the ripples that can flow from the family we choose to the family that chooses us." When Anna met her father's sister and her son, she liked them, but they did not feel like family; her Island friends had become that for her. How did her "chosen" family help her to bond with her mother and forgive her father? What is it for you that makes a family?

19. Tom's father's funeral is a turning point for Anna. Funerals often seem to have this effect on us—our tears may not be just in empathy with the grieving family but also for people in our own lives whom we have lost. Did this scene evoke any emotions in you?

20. How did you feel at the end of the story (before the Epilogue) when Anna had to leave Turtle Island and Tom?

21. Was the Epilogue important for you? If there had been no Epilogue, how do you think you would have wanted Anna's future life to unfold?

"Ogden's renowned skills as an observer of important neuro-psychological phenomena, combined with a novelist's descriptive touch, has produced a casebook that will fascinate at the same time as it educates. A superb achievement!"

—MICHAEL KOPELMAN, PhD, Professor of Neuropsychiatry, King's College, London

"Ogden brilliantly illustrates the role of clinician as detective, delving into the worlds of neurological patients to reveal the mysteries and vulnerabilities of the human brain. She combines the expertise of a neuroscientist, the insight of a psychologist, and the eye of a novelist."

—MICHAEL CORBALLIS, PhD, Professor Emerita of Psychology, Auckland University, author of *Pieces of Mind*, and *From Hand to Mouth: The Origins of Language*

"Ogden reaches into deep levels associated with personal diagnosis and treatment whilst covering a very wide range of emotional and social consequences. Readers will be spellbound."

—BARBARA A. WILSON, PhD, ScD, OBE, Oliver Zangwill Centre for Neuropsychological Rehabilitation, UK, editor of *Neuropsychological Rehabilitation*

"One of the world's premier neuropsychologists shares her caring experiences and evaluations of patients who exhibited a rich variety of neurobehavioral disorders. Reading these stories is like having actual clinical experiences."

—KENNETH M. HEILMAN, MD, Professor of Neurology, University if Florida College of Medicine, author of *Clinical Neuropsychology*

"Appealing to the general reader as well as experts is rarely achieved, yet Ogden manages it with supreme confidence and great skill. She combines her natural talents as a storyteller and gifted writer with her considerable experience as a highly-regarded neuropsychologist."

—*Taylor & Francis Online*

"Losing your mind, that quintessential 'me,' even partially, through trauma, disease or disorder, frightens most people. Ogden's stories about patients she has worked with who have suffered just that—losing part of their mind—are written with feeling, equal to Oliver Sacks at his best."

—KEVIN ORRMAN-ROSSITER for *Australian Bookseller & Publisher*

"The product of three decades of hands-on clinical experience, Ogden's insightful, entertaining, and informative cases will captivate the general reader and inspire students of neuropsychology and cognitive neuroscience in their quest to understand the links between the brain and behavior."

—SUZANNE CORKIN, PhD, Professor of Behavorial Neuroscience, Massachusetts Institute of Technology, author of *Permanent Present Tense: The Man with No Memory and What He Taught the World*

"Ogden is an engaging writer with the skill to move as well as inform. Her narratives illuminate the lives and troubled minds of a well-chosen variety of cases from 'HM', the most intensively researched patient in the history of neuropsychology, to 'ordinary' people with 'ordinary' neurological conditions. The message, ultimately, is that when it comes to the workings of our fragile brains, nothing is ordinary."

—PAUL BROCS, PhD, best-selling author of *Into The Silent Land: Travels in Neuropsychology*

"Through her writing style and expertise in clinical neuropsychology, Ogden empathetically conveys the emotional impact of neurological injury to patient, friends, and family together with detailed descriptions of the facts of the case from a scientific perspective. This book shows us the uniqueness of each patient, and reminds us that all of our most interesting cases are real people."

—*Journal of the International Neuropsychological Society*

ABOUT THE AUTHOR

photo credit: Dominic Chaplin

Jenni Ogden grew up in a country town in the South Island of New Zealand, in a home bursting with books and music. Armed with NZ and Australian university degrees in zoology and psychology and now with four children, Jenni took up a postdoctoral fellowship at Massachusetts Institute of Technology and worked with H.M., the most famous amnesiac in history. Returning to an academic position at Auckland University, she immersed herself in clinical psychology and neuropsychology, writing about her patients' moving stories in two books, *Fractured Minds: A Case-Study Approach to Clinical Neuropsychology* (OUP, New York, 1996, 2005) and *Trouble In Mind: Stories from a Neuropsychologist's Casebook* (OUP, New York, 2012; Scribe, Australia, 2013). Jenni and her husband now live off-grid on a spectacular island off the coast of NZ, with winters spent traveling and at their second home in tropical Far North Queensland.

Jenni has had a love affair with the Great Barrier Reef

since her twenties, when she spent summers on a coral cay rather like Turtle Island, tagging sea turtles. Her novels, not surprisingly, often have psychological and medical subthemes, and her settings draw on her love of exotic and far-flung locations—frequently remote islands.

When she is not writing or traveling, Jenni can be found on the beach—always with a book—or spending time with her family, now expanded to include five grandchildren. Visit her at www.jenniogden.com and sign up for her monthly e-newsletter, and read her blog at *Psychology Today.*

Duck Pond Epiphany by Tracey Barnes Priestley. $16.95,
978-1-938314-24-7. When a mother of four delivers her last
child to college, she has to decide what to do next—and her
life takes a surprising turn.

Play for Me by Céline Keating. $16.95, 978-1-63152-972-6.
Middle-aged Lily impulsively joins a touring folk-rock band,
leaving her job and marriage behind in an attempt to find a
second chance at life, passion, and art.

Stella Rose by Tammy Flanders Hetrick. $16.95,
978-1-63152-921-4. When her dying best friend asks her to
take care of her sixteen-year-old daughter, Abby says yes—but
as she grapples with raising a grieving teenager, she realizes
she didn't know her best friend as well as she thought she did.

A Cup of Redemption by Carole Bumpus. $16.95,
978-1-938314-90-2. Three women, each with their own secrets
and shames, seek to make peace with their pasts and carve out
new identities for themselves.

Things Unsaid by Diana Y. Paul. $16.95, 978-1-63152-812-5. A
family saga of three generations fighting over money and
obligation—and a tale of survival, resilience, and recovery.

Wishful Thinking by Kamy Wicoff. $16.95, 978-1-63152-976-4.
A divorced mother of two gets an app on her phone that lets
her be in more than one place at the same time, and quickly
goes from zero to hero in her personal and professional life—
but at what cost?